lost in time

Ich widme dieses Buch allen Künstlern, die mit ihren fabelhaften Ideen und Graffiti diese Fotos möglich gemacht haben.

I dedicate this book to all the artists, who with their fabulous ideas and graffiti have made possible these photographs.

marc theis lost in time

Mit einem Essay von Boris von Brauchitsch.
With an essay by Boris von Brauchitsch.

PEPERONI BOOKS

contents

6 – 7
Vorwort von Marc Theis | Preface by Marc Theis

8 – 123
Fotografien | Photographs

124 – 131
Essay von Boris von Brauchitsch

132 – 138
Essay by Boris von Brauchitsch

140 – 141
Biografie | Biography

142 – 143
Danksagung | Acknowledgements

144
Impressum | Imprint

vorwort

Ein spontaner und sehr überzeugender Anruf meines guten Freundes Christian Schlegel, an einem sonnigen Frühlingsmorgen im Jahr 2004, war der Auslöser: „Marc, du musst unbedingt sofort hierher kommen. Stehe an der Einfahrt zu dem ehemaligen Conti-Gelände in Limmer. Du glaubst nicht, was ich hier sehe. Das ist der Wahnsinn, das solltest du fotografieren!" Ich fuhr hin, war genauso beeindruckt wie Christian und wusste erst gar nicht, wo ich anfangen sollte zu fotografieren.

Es folgte zuerst ein grandioser Fototag innerhalb dieser einmaligen Kulisse mit der weltbekannten Rockband aus Hannover, den Scorpions.

Nach einem längeren Gespräch mit dem zuständigen Leiter der Wasserstadt Limmer bekam ich die Fotoerlaubnis und einen Schlüssel und konnte ab sofort jederzeit dorthin. Ich war dann mit meinem Assistenten Jan Krause vom Herbst 2004 bis zum Frühling 2005 an einem guten Dutzend Tagen, stets mit Bauhelm, auf Entdeckertour auf dem riesigen, fast gespenstischen Gelände unterwegs.

Auf der Suche nach neuen Spuren durchforsteten wir mit unserem gesamten Equipment samt superschwerem Stativ sämtliche Räume inkl. der Keller und Dachböden der über 30 Hallen. Nur bei schlechtem Wetter schlichen wir umher – es musste immer bewölkt sein, die Sonne durfte nicht scheinen. Es war fast wie in einem Krimi: ungewöhnliche Geräusche überall und immer die Sorge, hinter der nächsten Ecke könnte doch noch eine Leiche auftauchen, was Gott sei Dank nicht geschah. Die Faszination, welche die seit 1995 leerstehenden Räume auf mich ausstrahlten, kann man wie eine Zeitreise in eine andere Welt beschreiben, zurück in die Zeit, in der viele Menschen auf einem riesigen Industriegelände Tag für Tag der gleichen anstrengenden Arbeit nachgingen – es war einfach unglaublich für uns.

Das Entdecken der speziellen Motive, die das Verlassene mit dem Verfall und den besonderen, teilweise künstlerischen und „verbotenen" Spray- und Graffiti-Arbeiten verbinden, wurde zur Sucht. Nie begegneten wir einem Menschen, außer den Bauarbeitern, die mit dem Abriss beschäftigt waren. Die Graffiti-Sprayer aber waren, wie Geister, immer anwesend.

Aus mehr als 500 Aufnahmen wurden die Motive für diesen Band über die, nicht nur innerhalb der Zeit, verschwundenen Bilder ausgewählt. Alle Hallen wurden mittlerweile abgerissen.

Marc Theis

preface

A spontaneous and very convincing call from my good friend Christian Schlegel on a sunny spring morning in the year 2004 was the trigger,"Marc, you have to get here immediately. I am standing at the entrance to the former Conti-area in Limmer. You do not believe what I am seeing here. This is awesome, you should photograph that!" I went there, was as fascinated as Christian and first did not know where I should begin photographing.

What followed was a magnificent photo shoot within the unique scenery with the world-famous rock band from Hannover, The Scorpions.

After a longer conversation with the responsible manager of Wasserstadt Limmer, I got the photo permit and a key and from that moment on I could go there any time. My assistant Jan Krause accompanied me on the discovery trip on that huge, nearly ghostly area about a dozen days from autumn 2004 till spring 2005, always wearing a hard hat.

In search of new traces we trawled all rooms of the more than 30 halls, including the cellars and attics, with all our equipment and along with the super heavy tripod. We lurked around only in bad weather, it had to be cloudy, the sun was not allowed to shine. It was almost like a crime movie: bizarre noises everywhere and always the worry that a corpse could still appear around the next corner, which fortunately did not happen. One can describe the fascination, which these rooms, left empty since 1995, had on me with a time travel to another world, back to a time, when many people performed their same exhausting job on this huge industrial site day after day – it was simply unbelievable for us.

The discovery of the specific image-motifs, which combine the abandoned with the decay and the special, partly artistic and "prohibited" spray- and graffiti-works, became an addiction. We never met any people, except the construction workers who were occupied with the demolition of the buildings. But like ghosts the graffiti sprayers were always present.

From over 500 photographs we chose the motifs for this illustrated book about images that vanished not only due to the course of time. All halls have been demolished by now.

Marc Theis

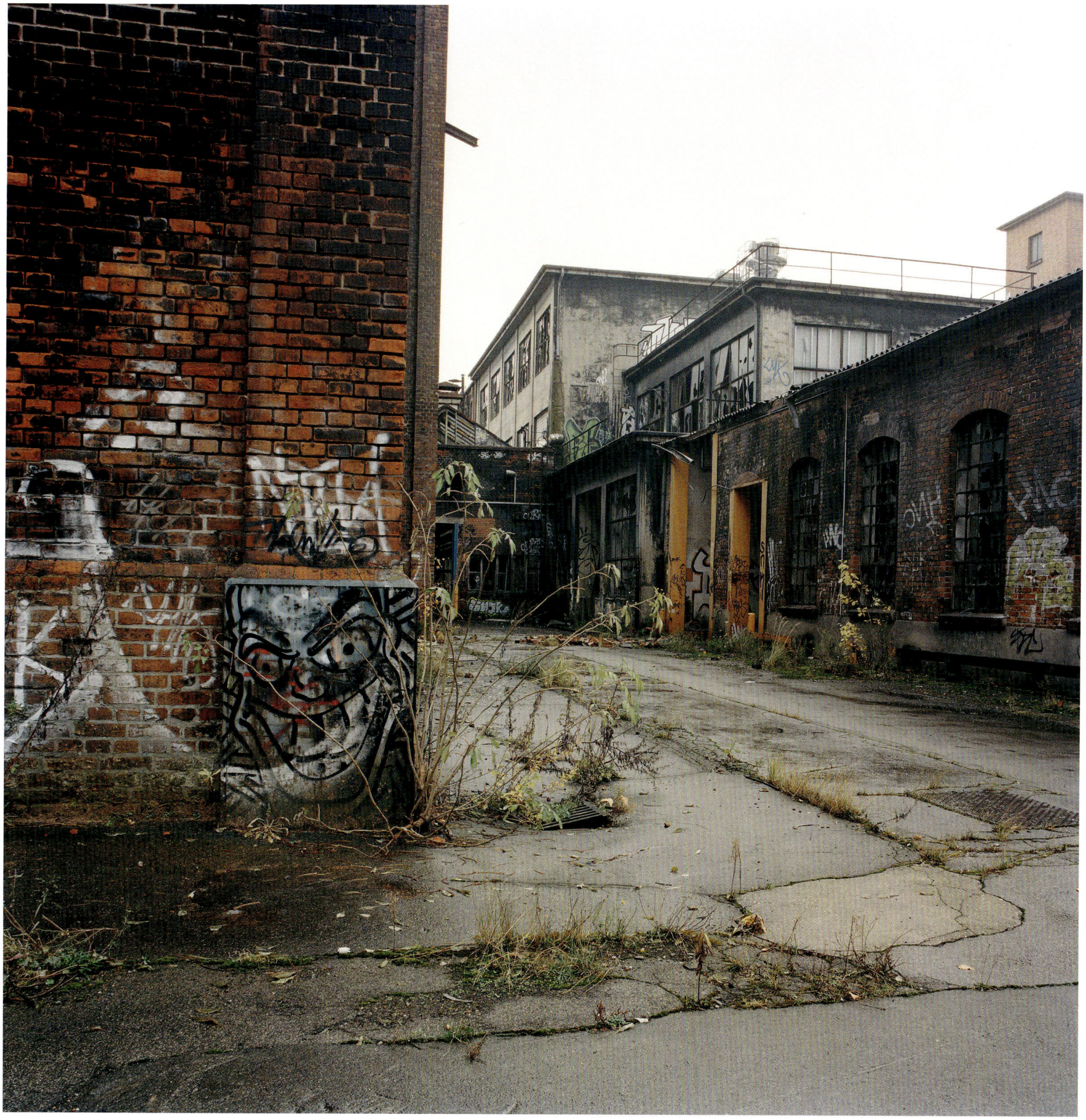

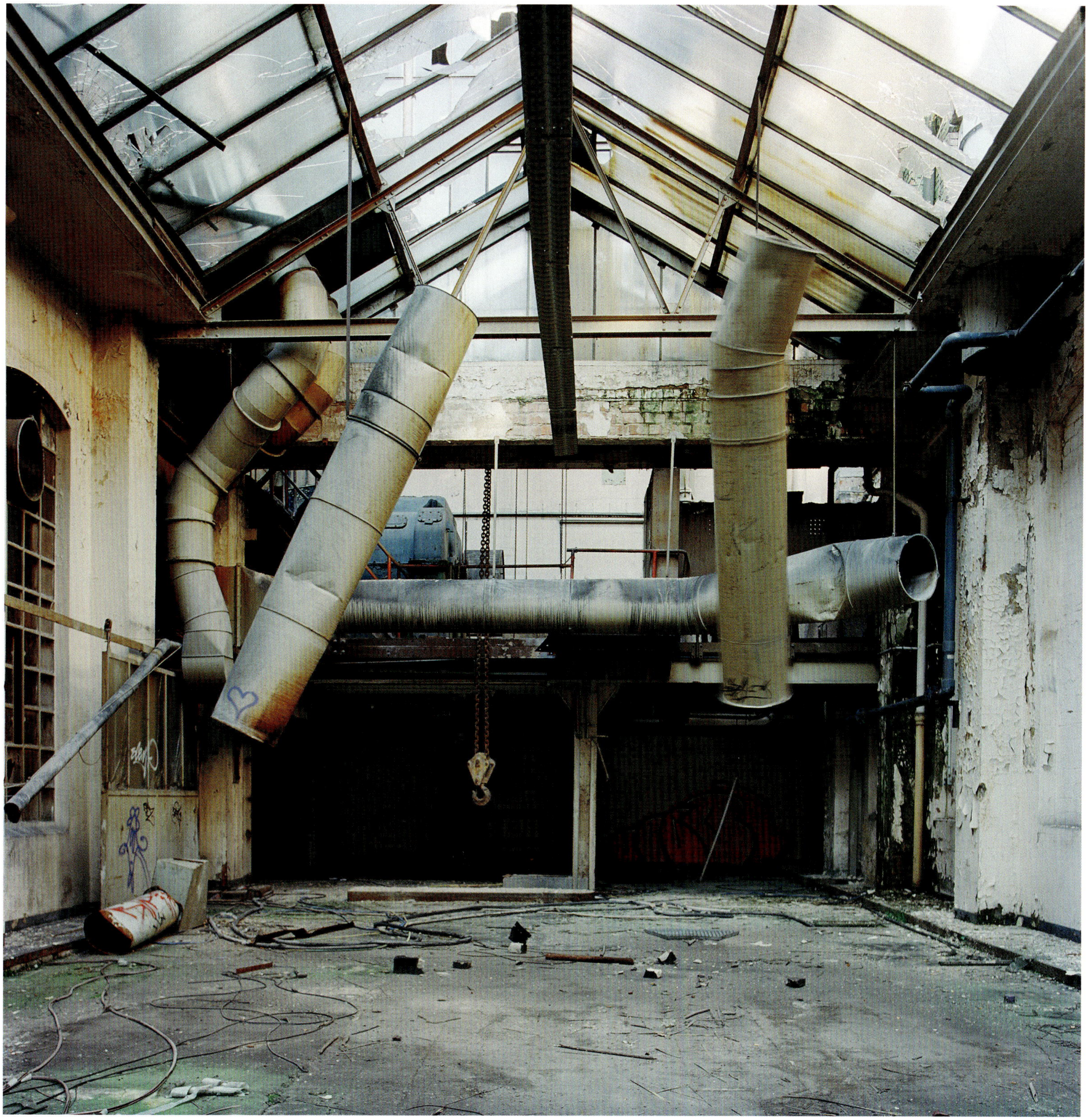

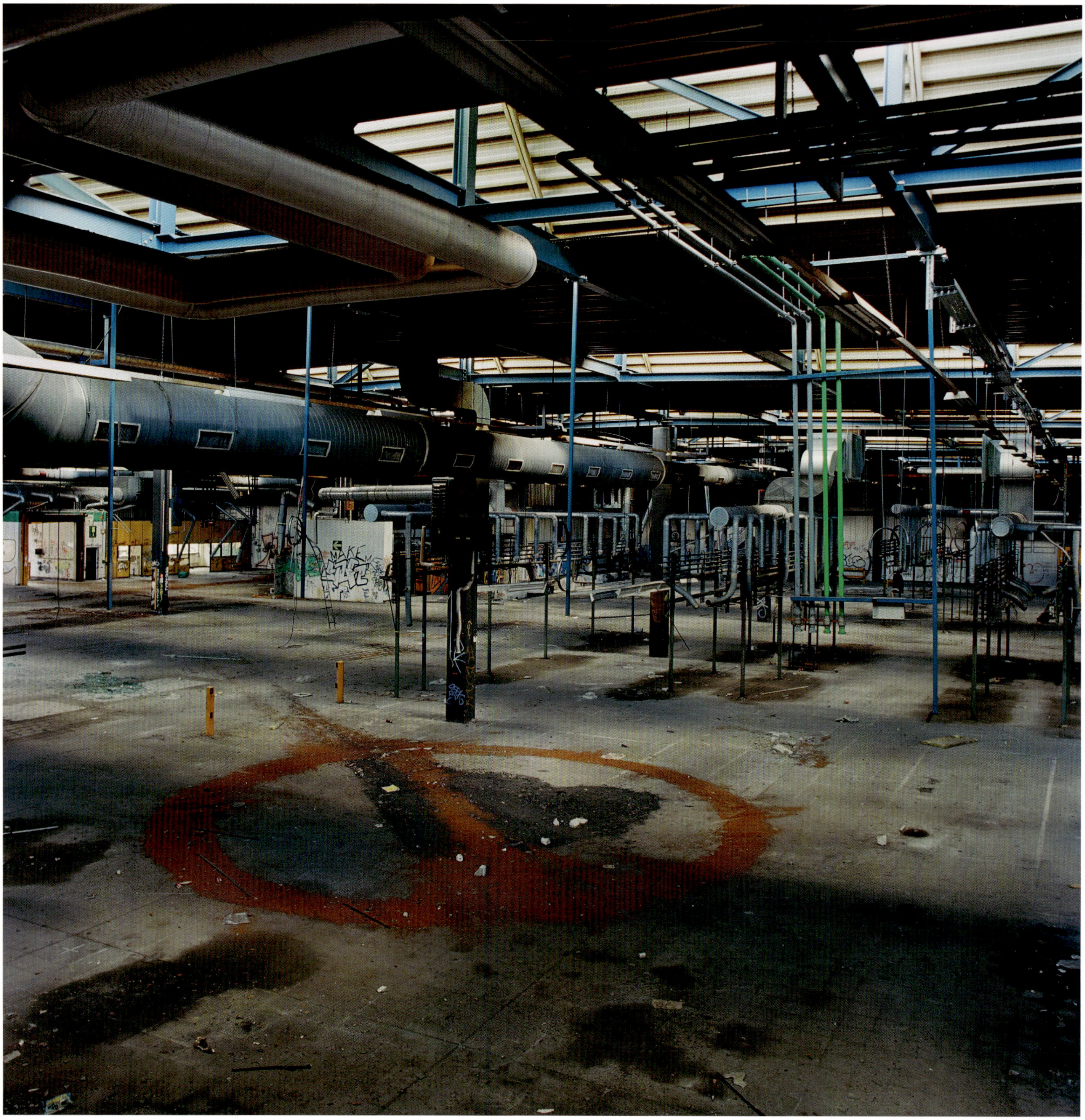

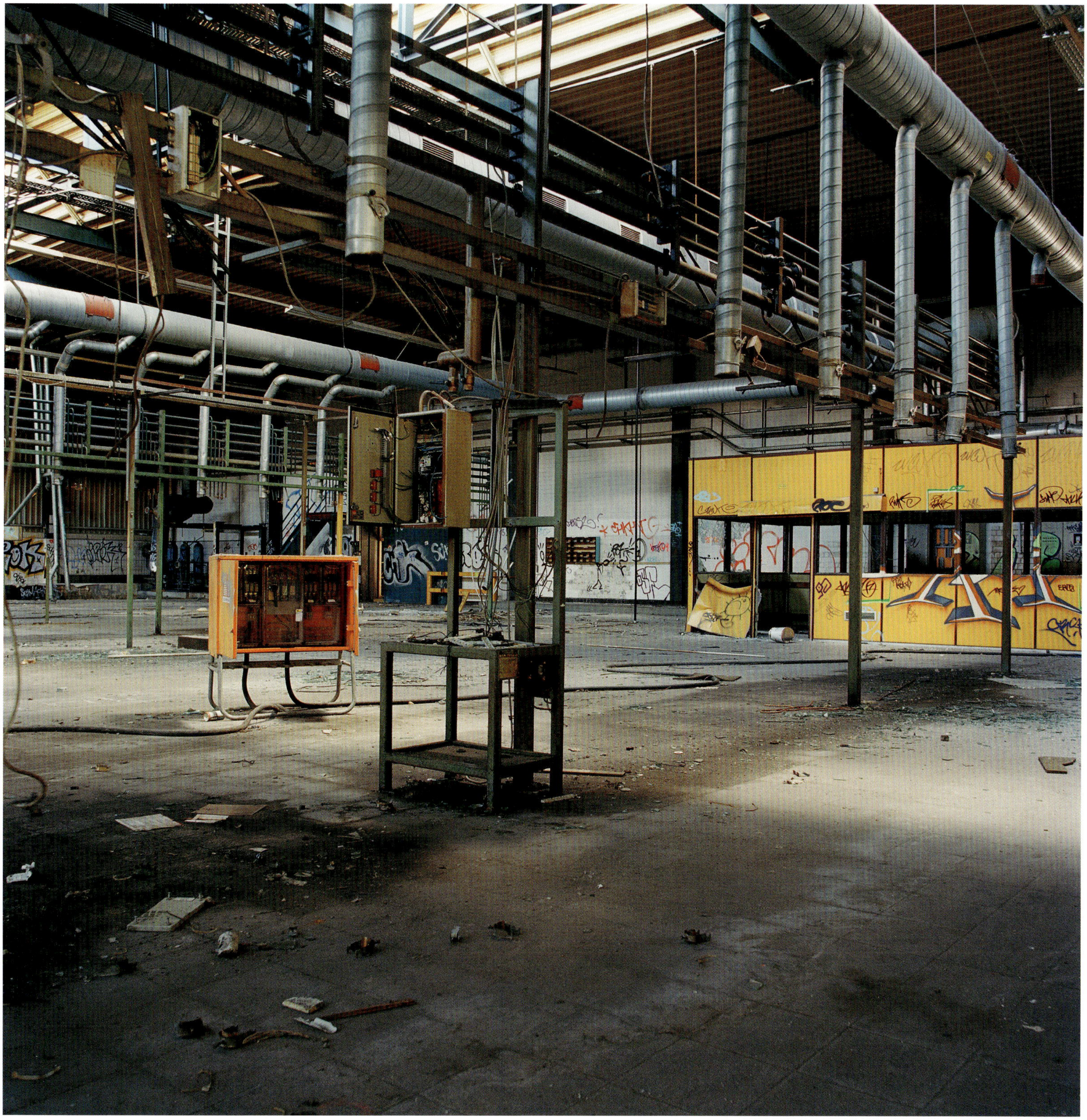

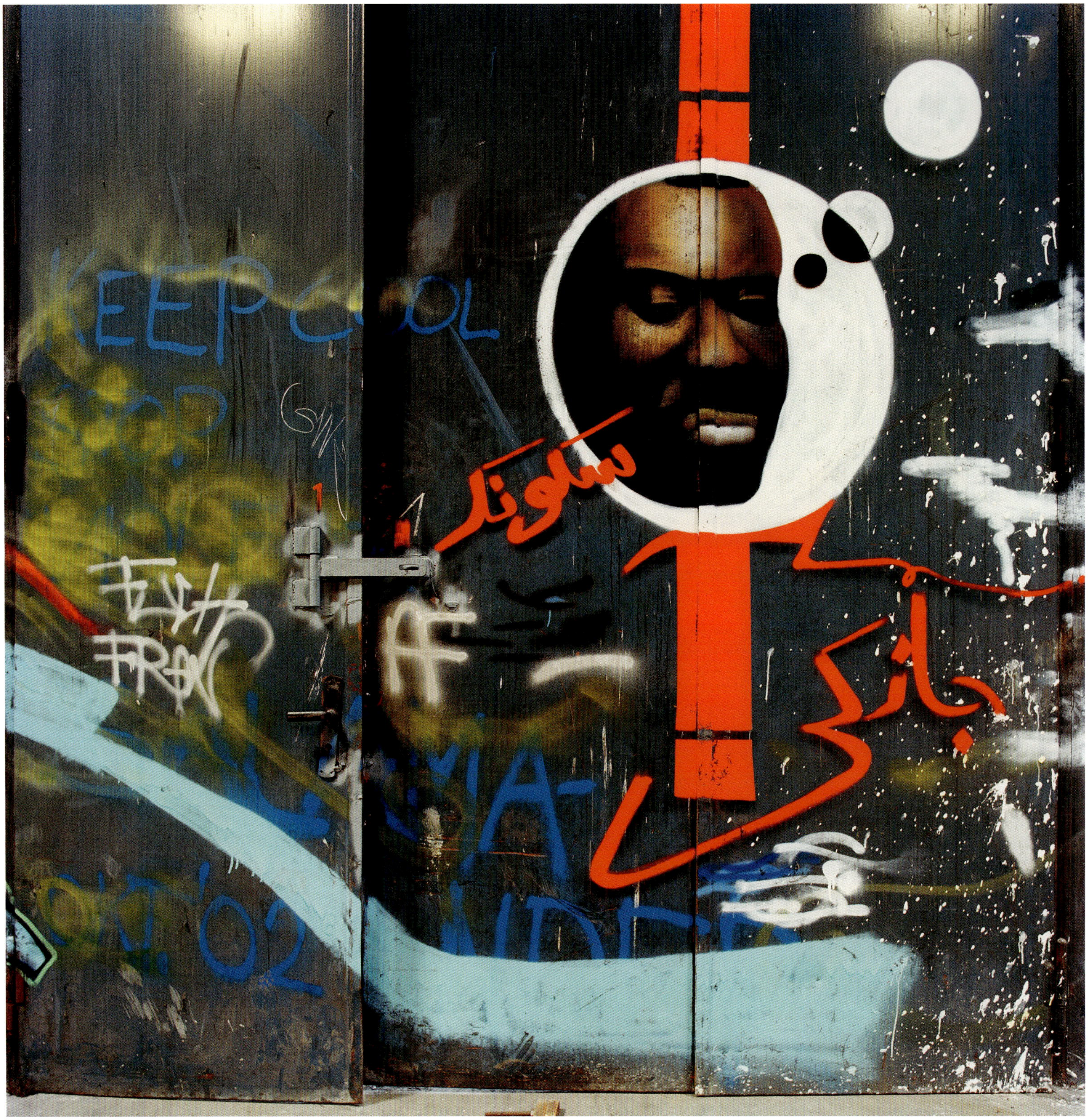
KEEP COOL

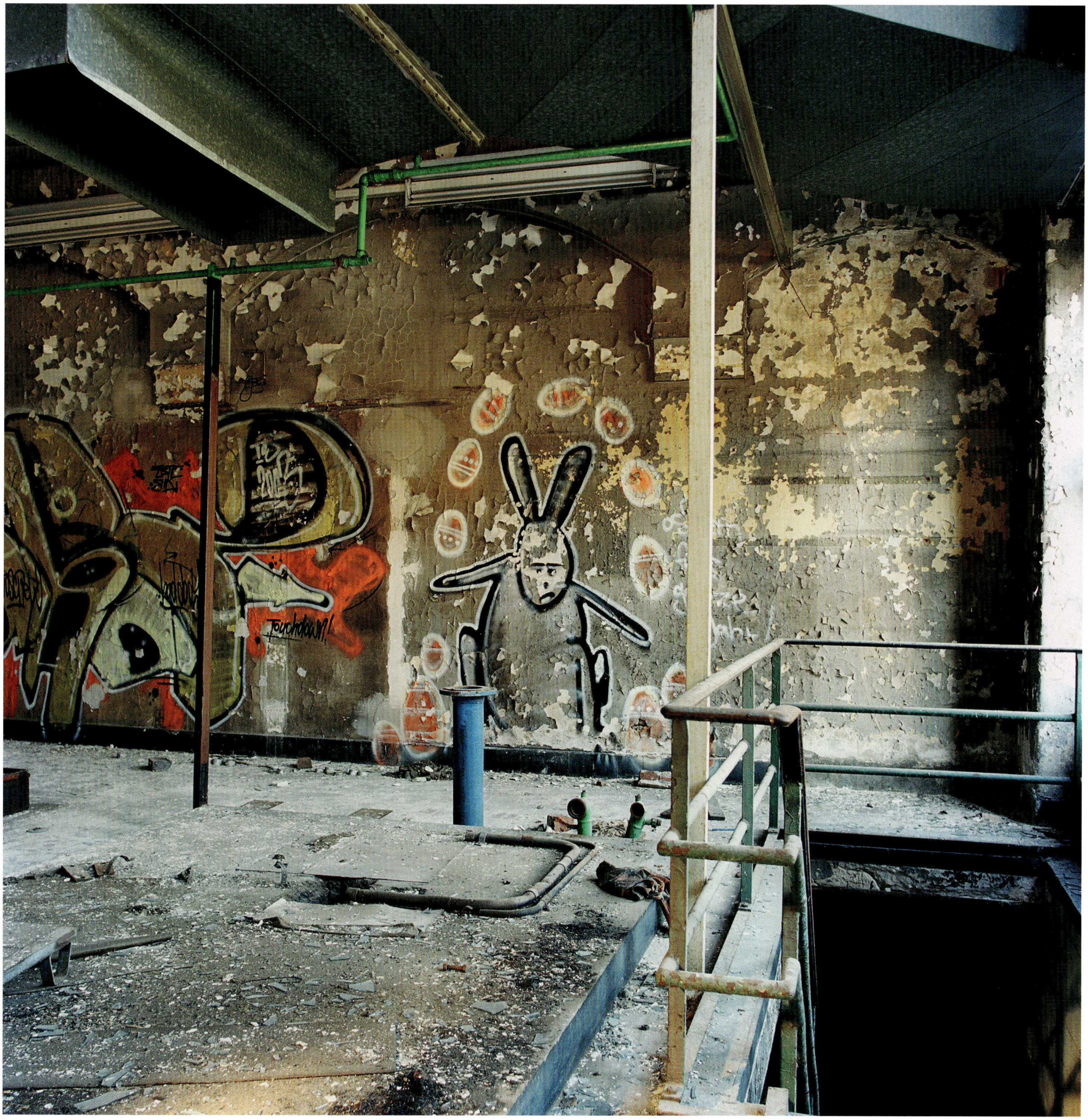
touchdown!

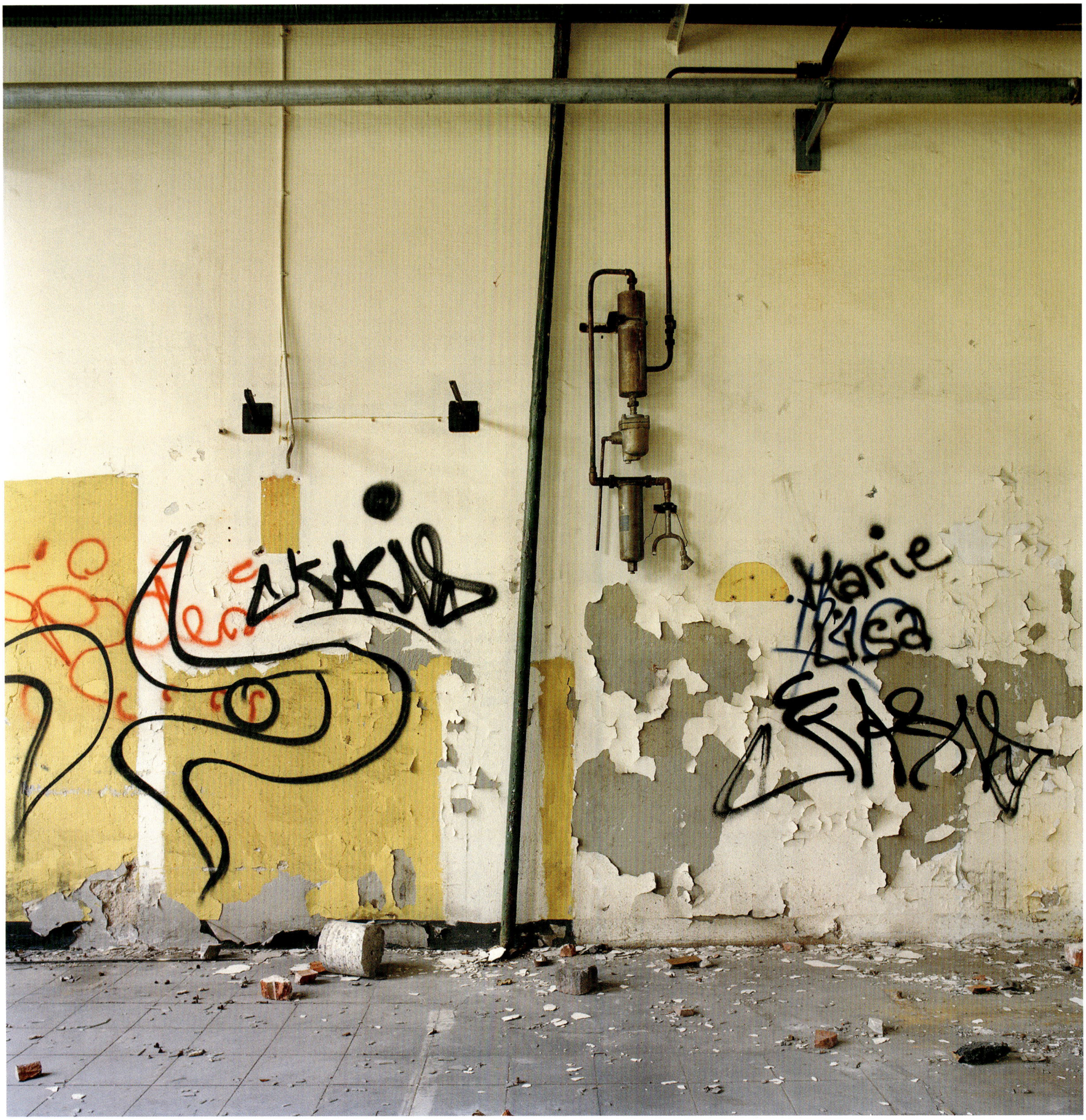

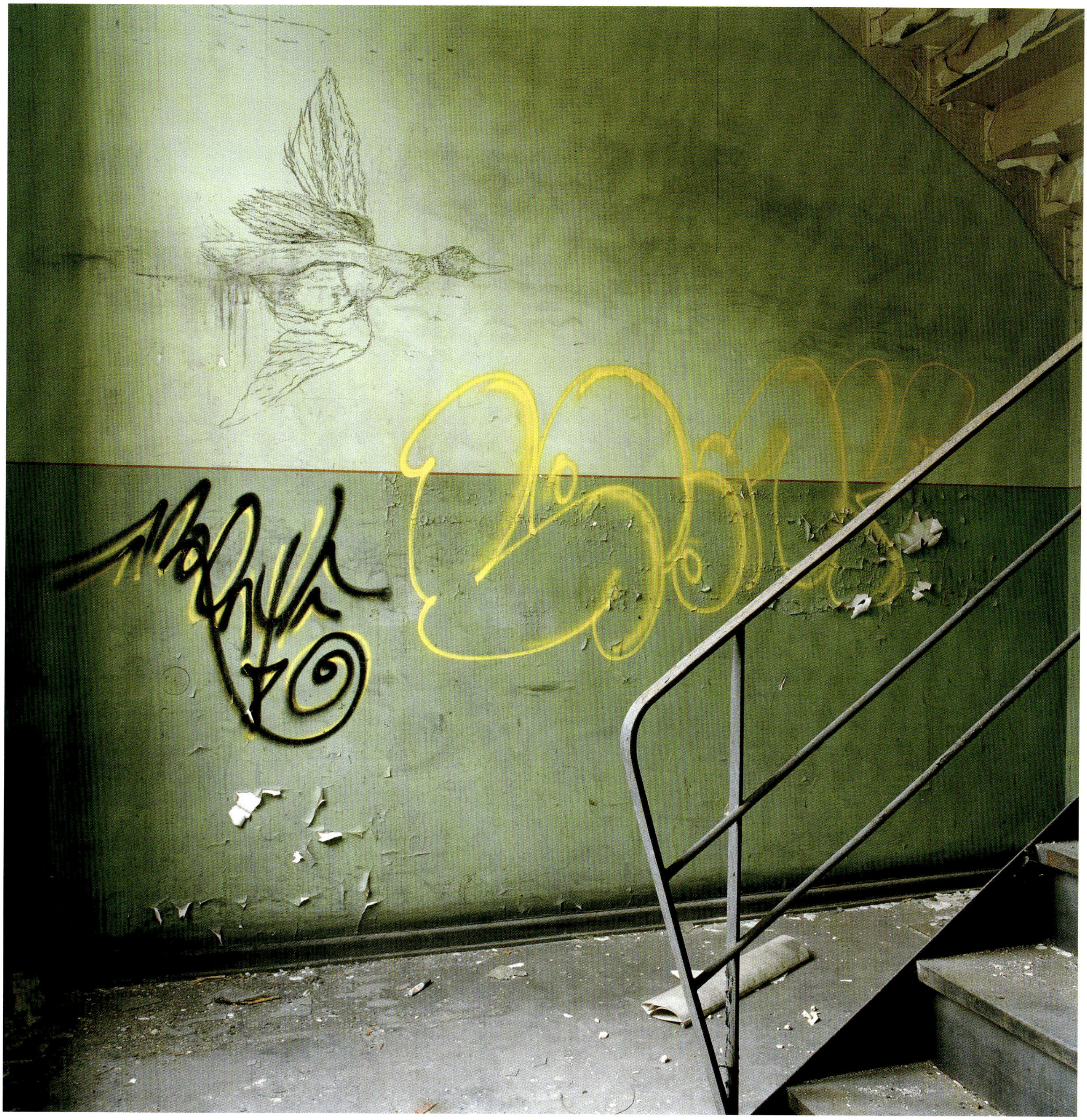

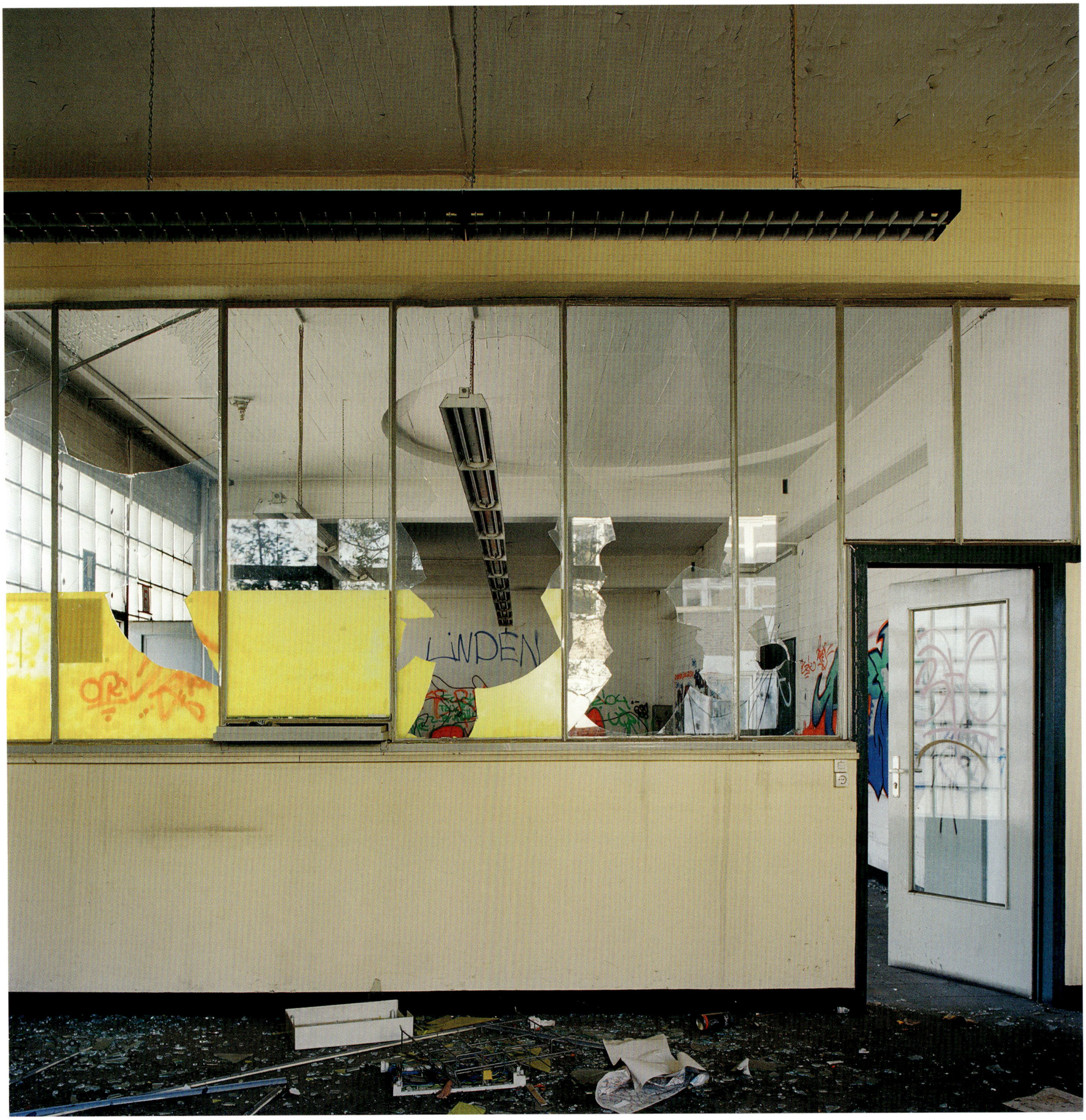
LINDEN

GERO
BRAIK
MEKS
WANK
YASH
POKER
CIDO
SLEAK
KOBOLT
BIO
UFO
NOEL
JEKL
GUES
SURCH
STICK
AZED
SN
BLÖT...

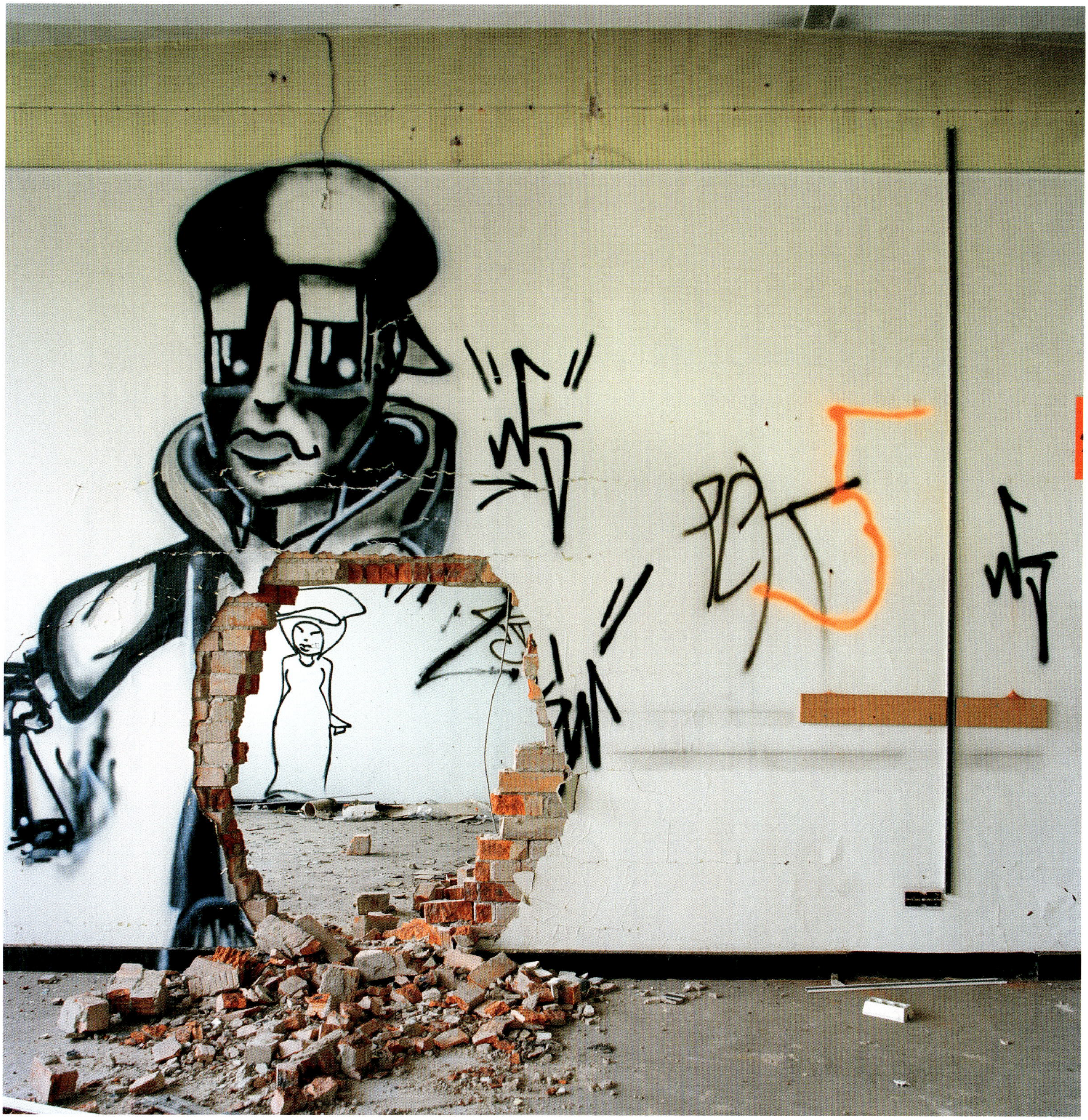

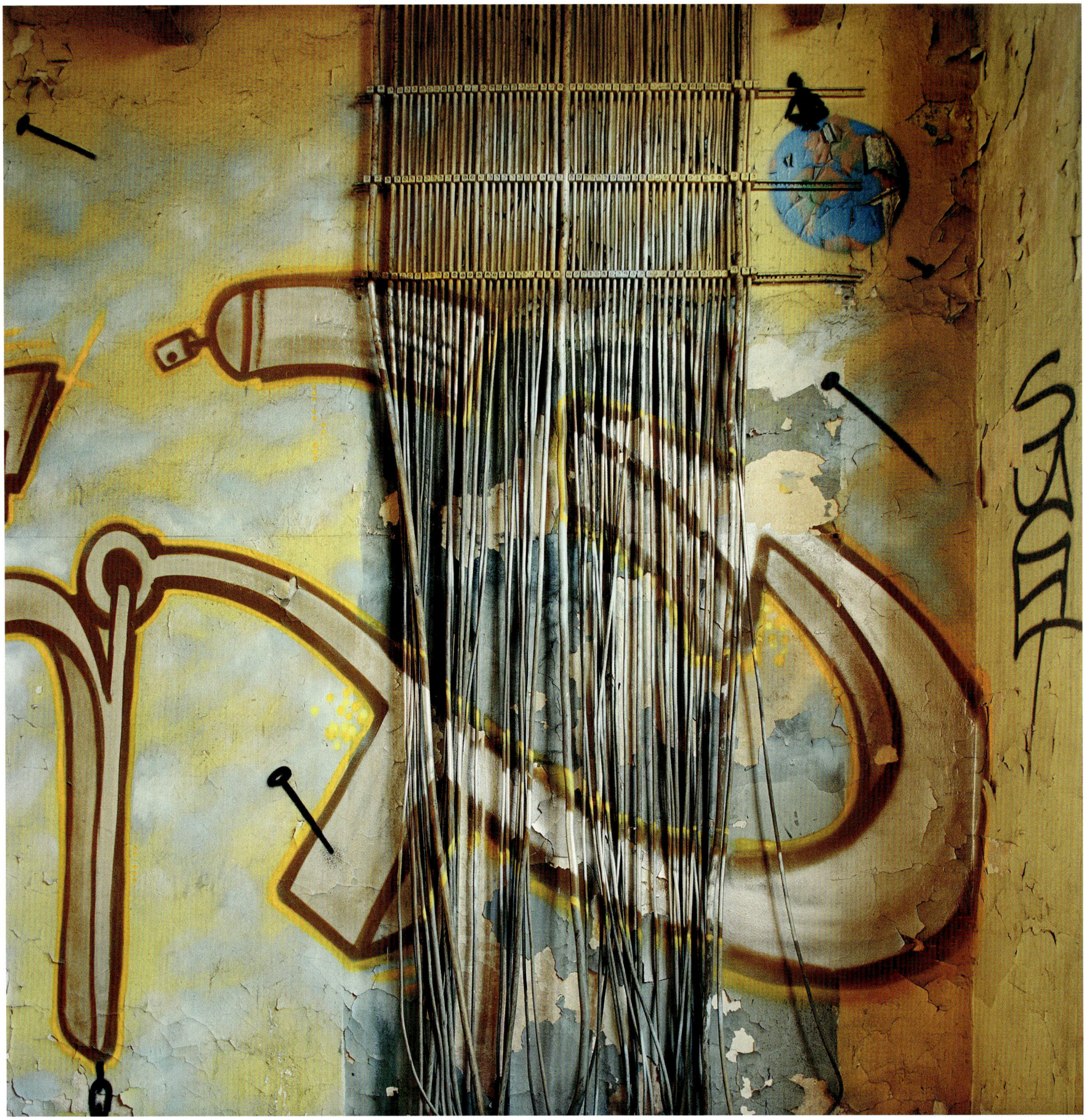

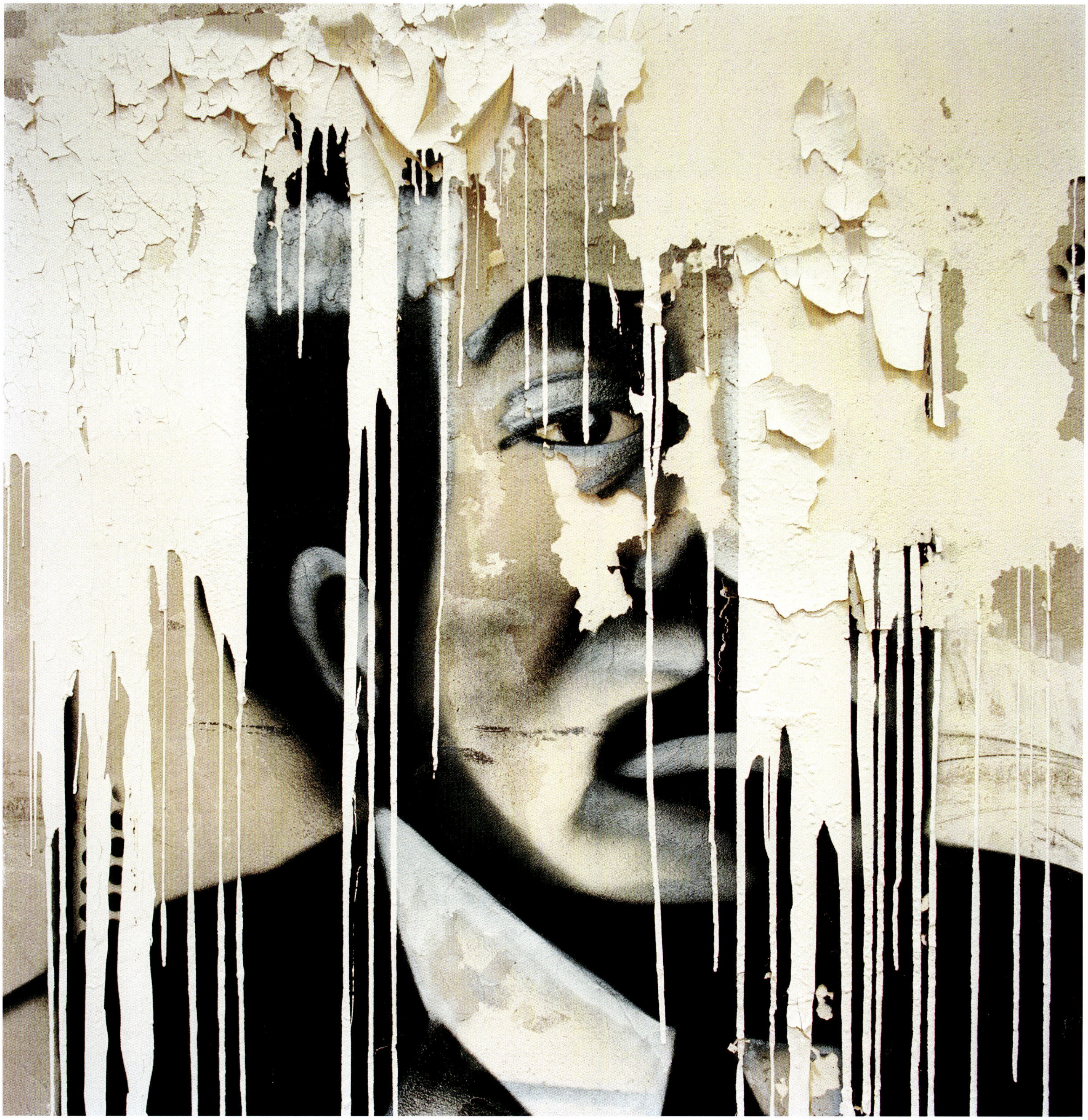

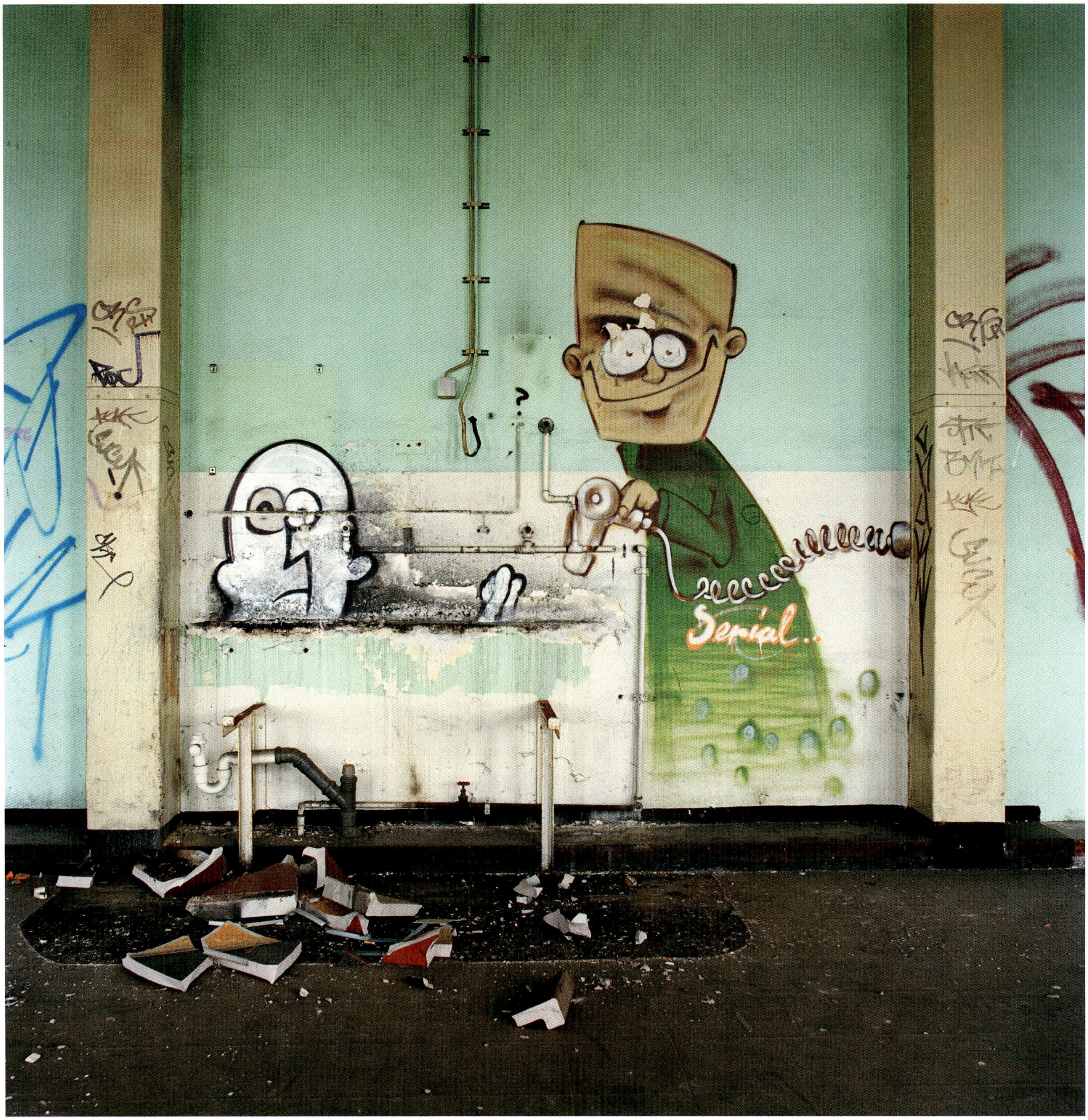
Serial..

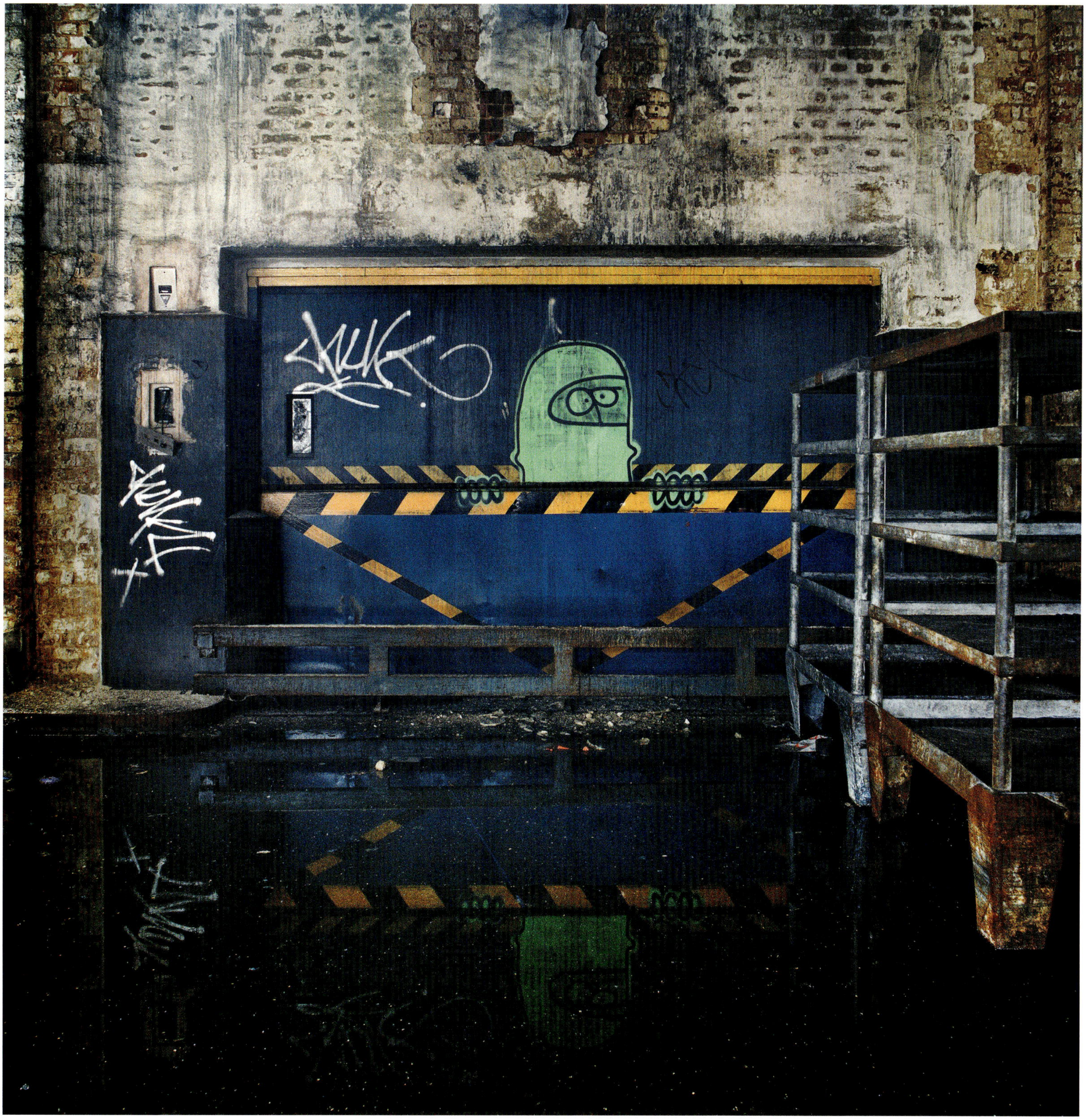

Feuer u. Unfall Tel. 6333 Abt. 16800
Entstörung: mechn. Tel.
» elektr. » 233
Betriebsleiter: Tel.
Meister:
Bekanntmachungen!

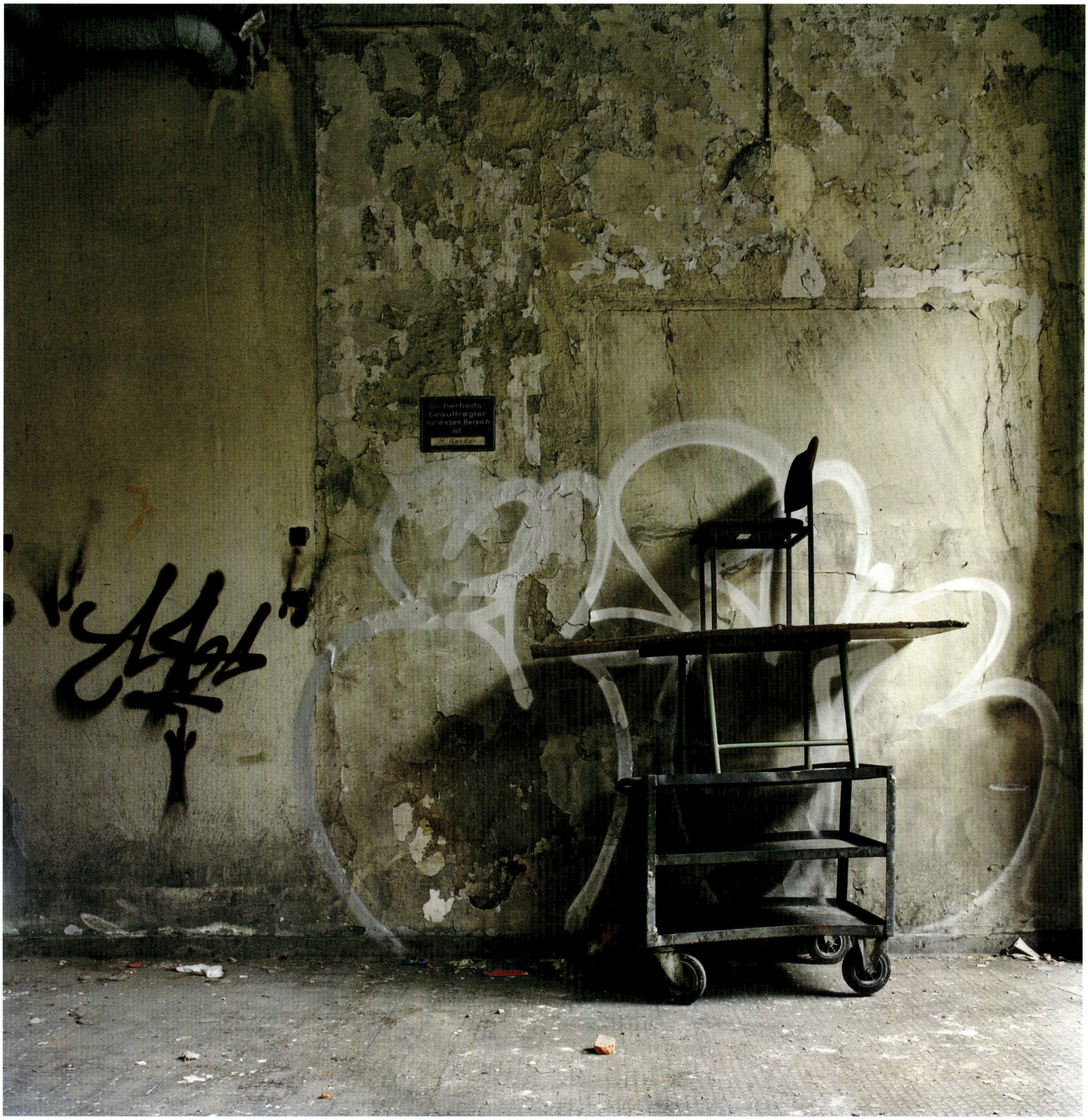
Sicherheits-
beauftragter
für diesen Bereich
ist

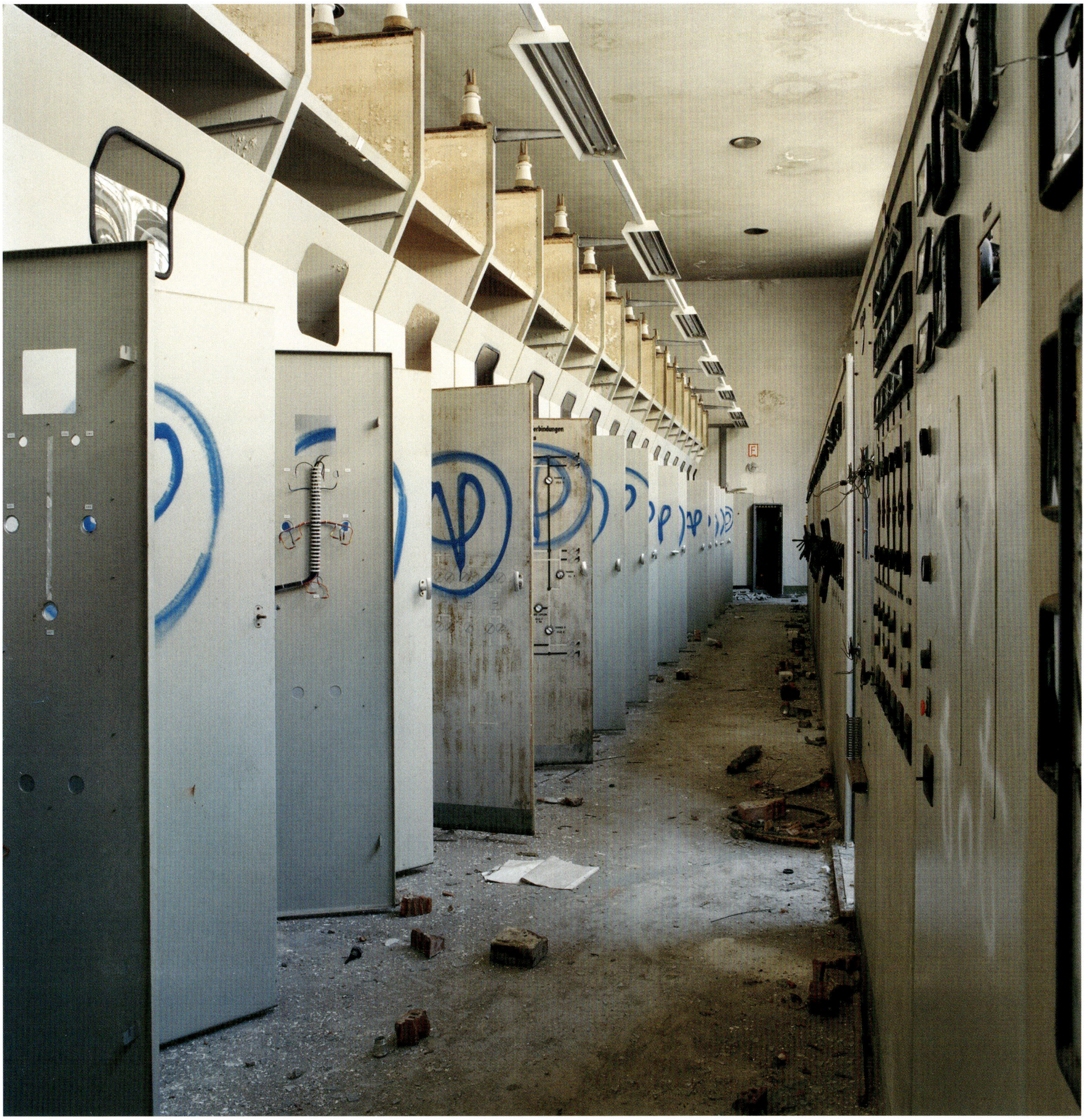

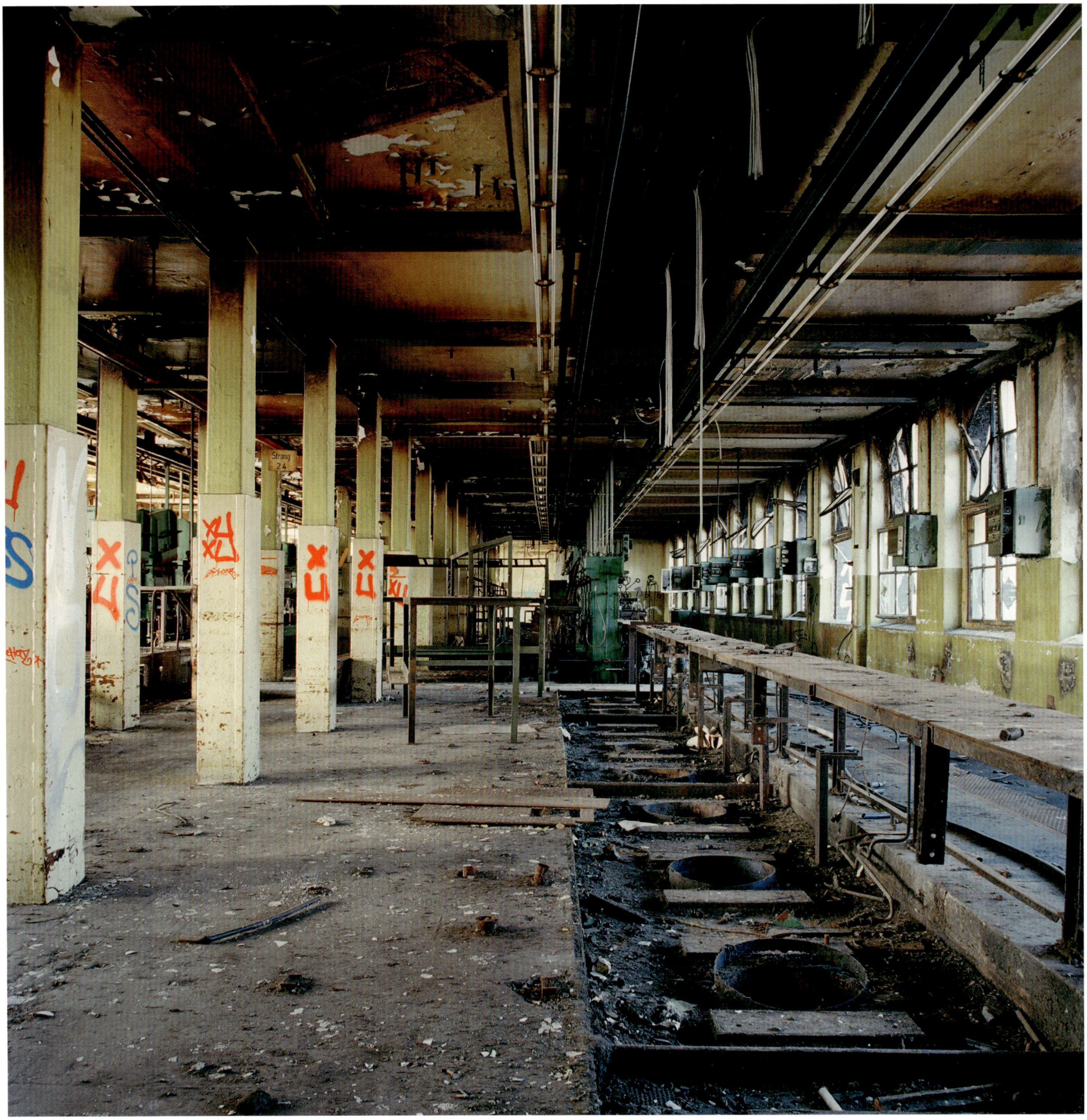

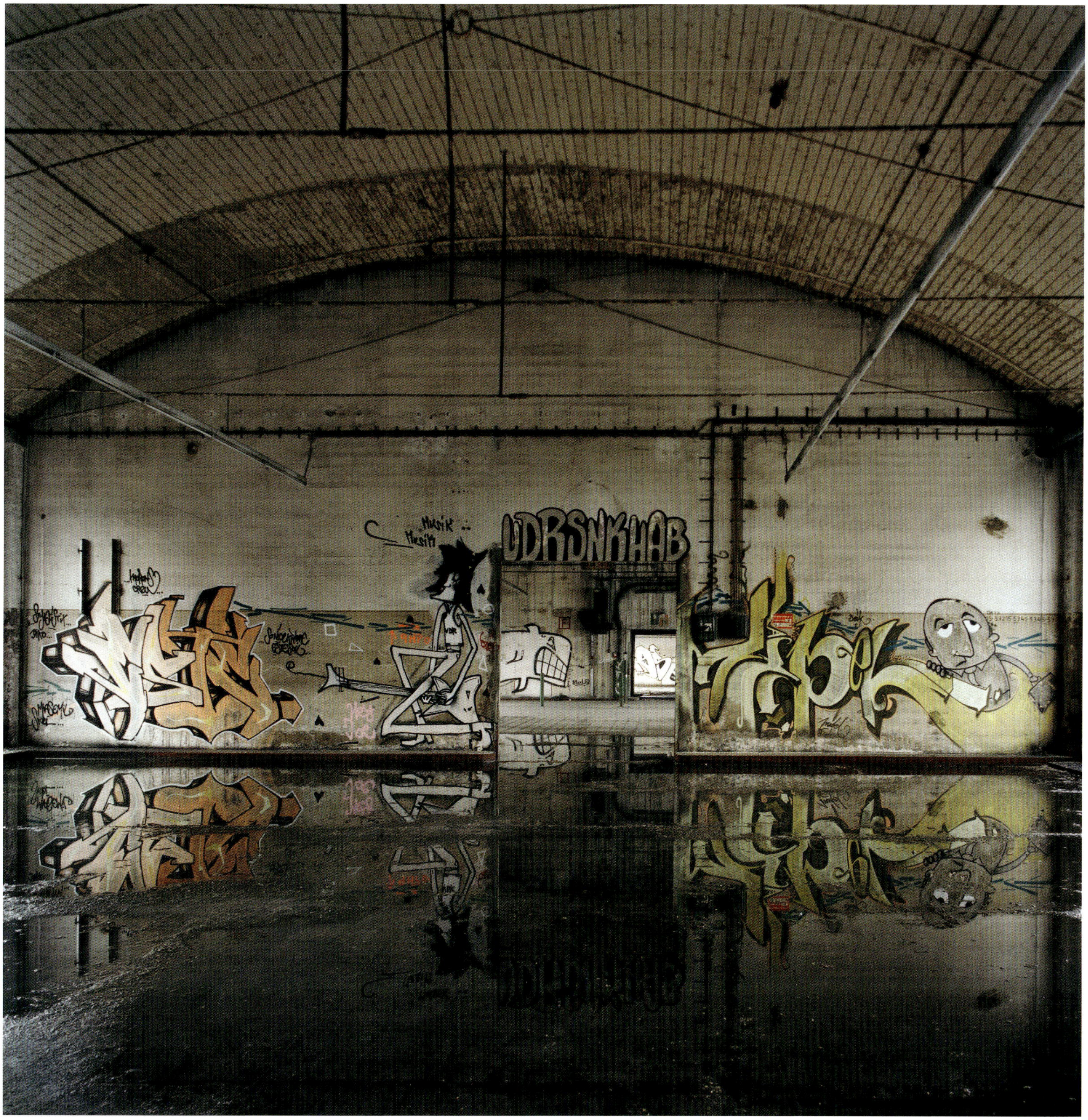
UDRSNKHAB

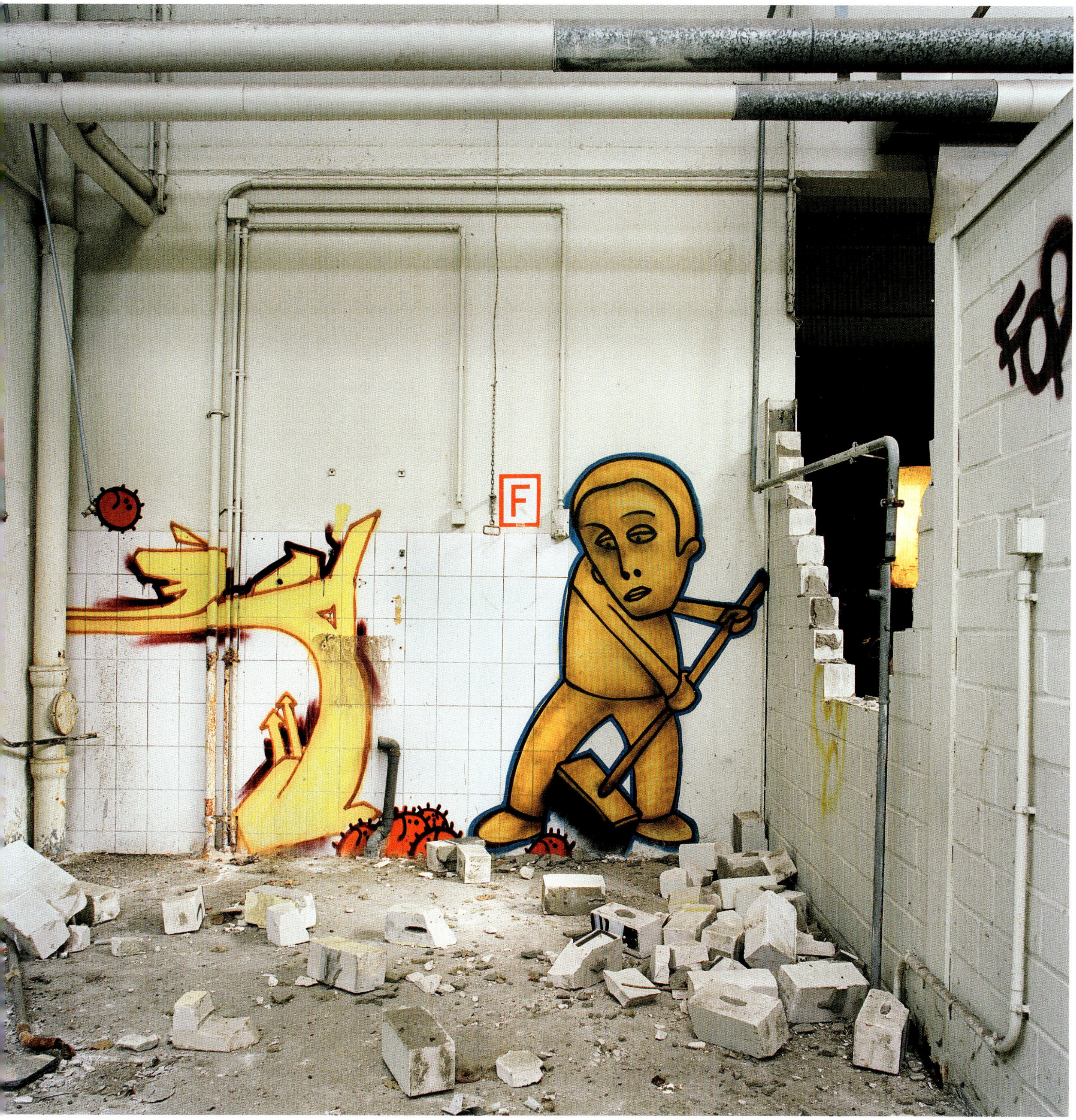
F

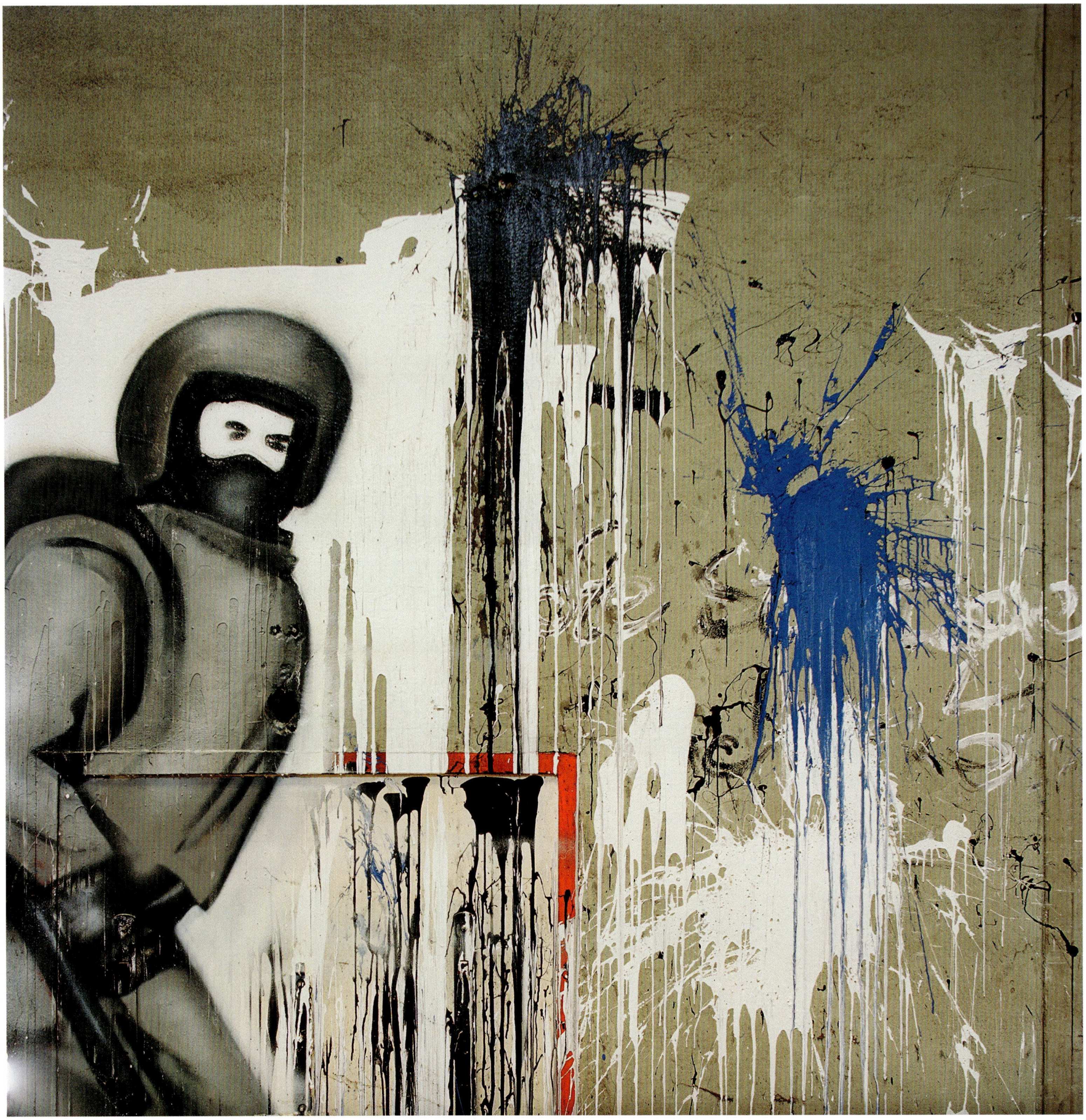

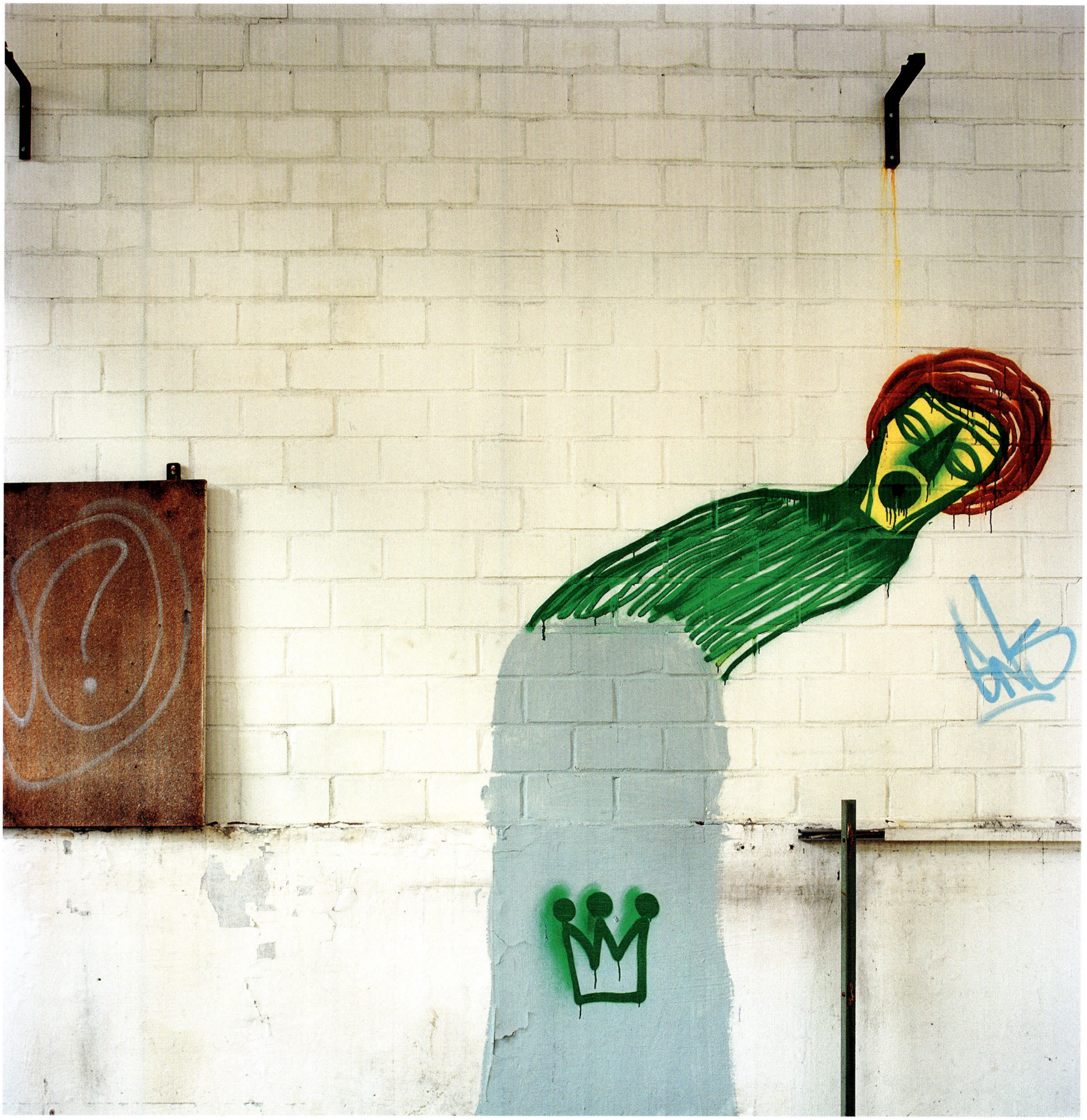

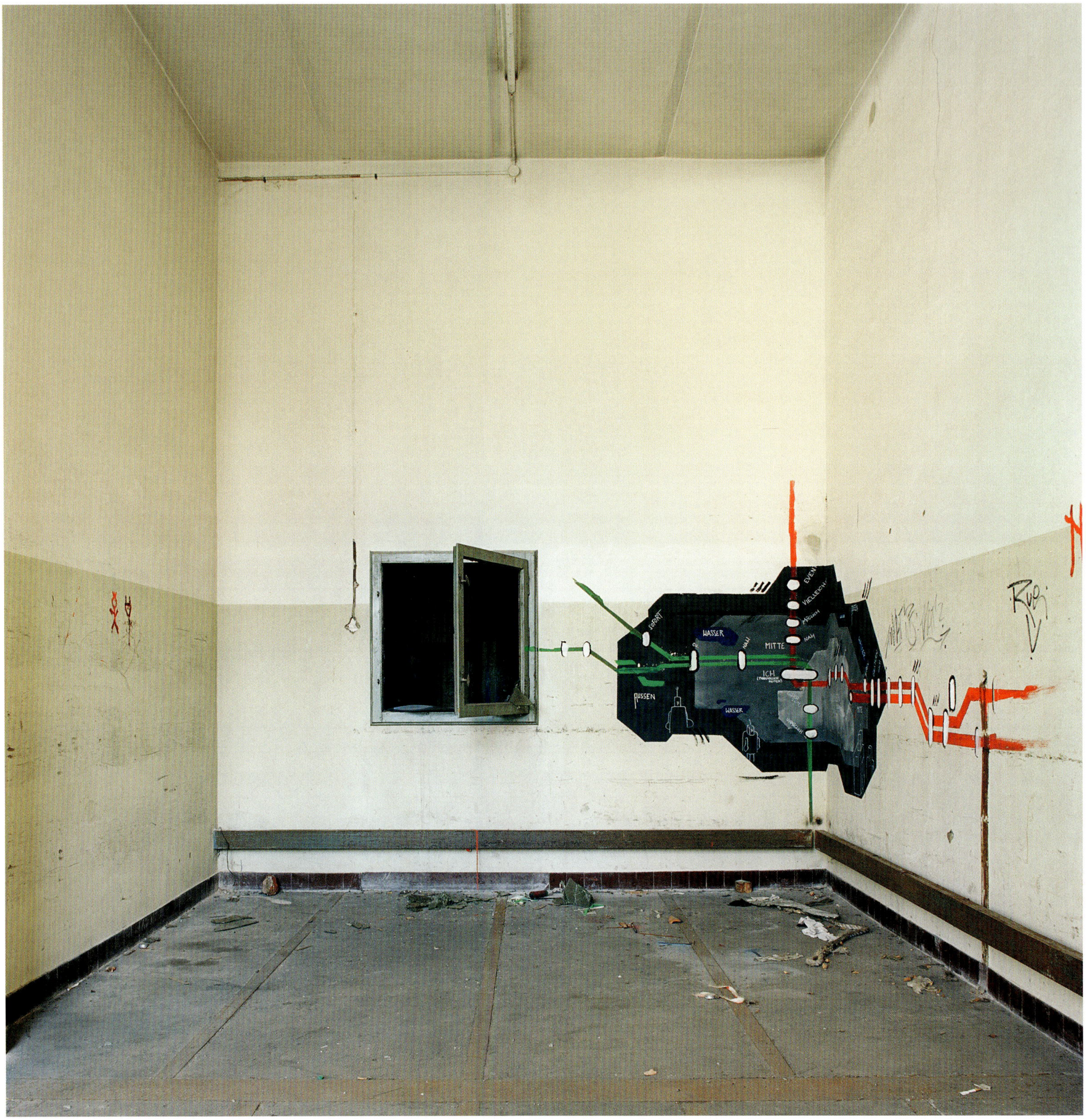

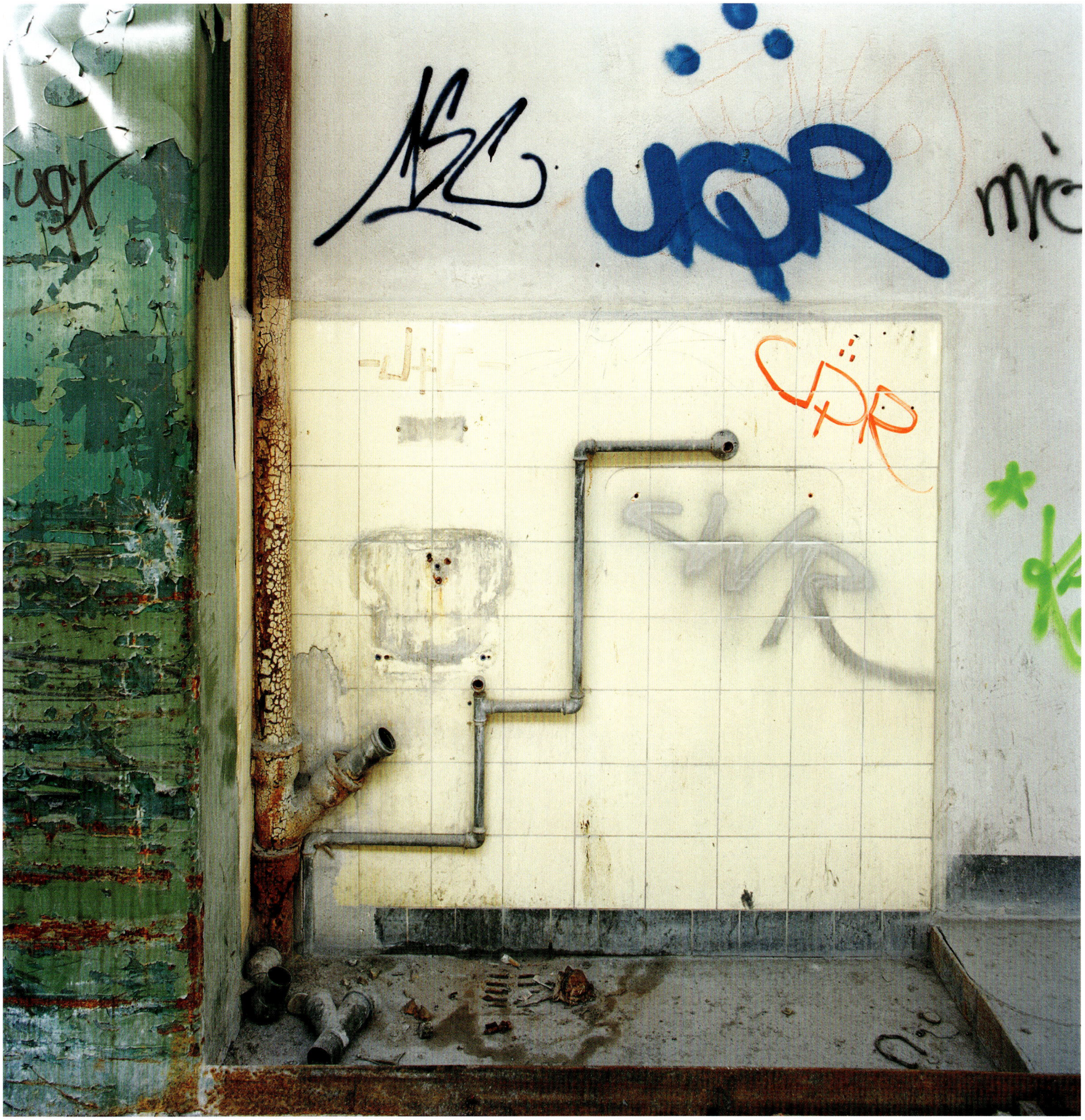

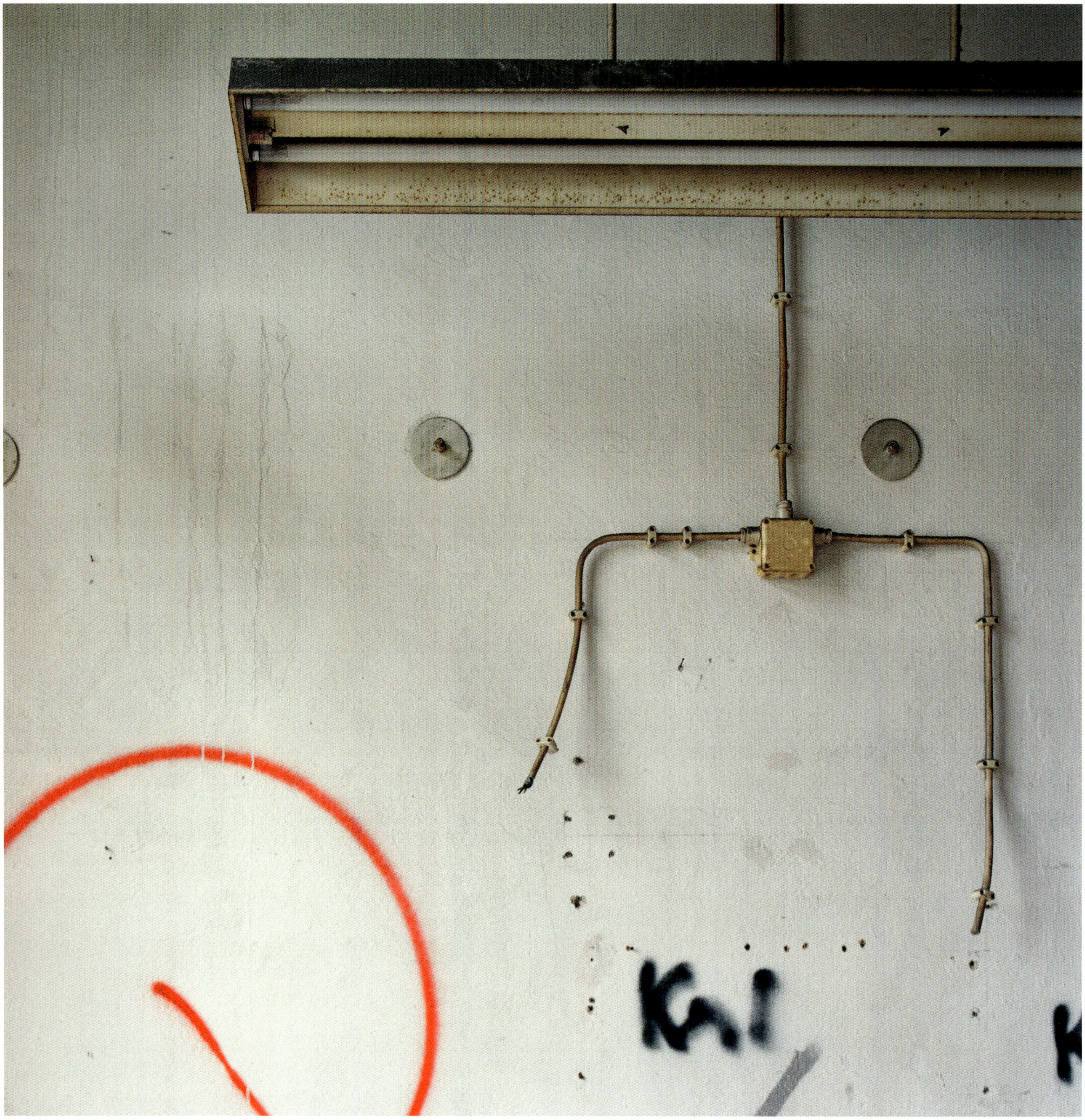

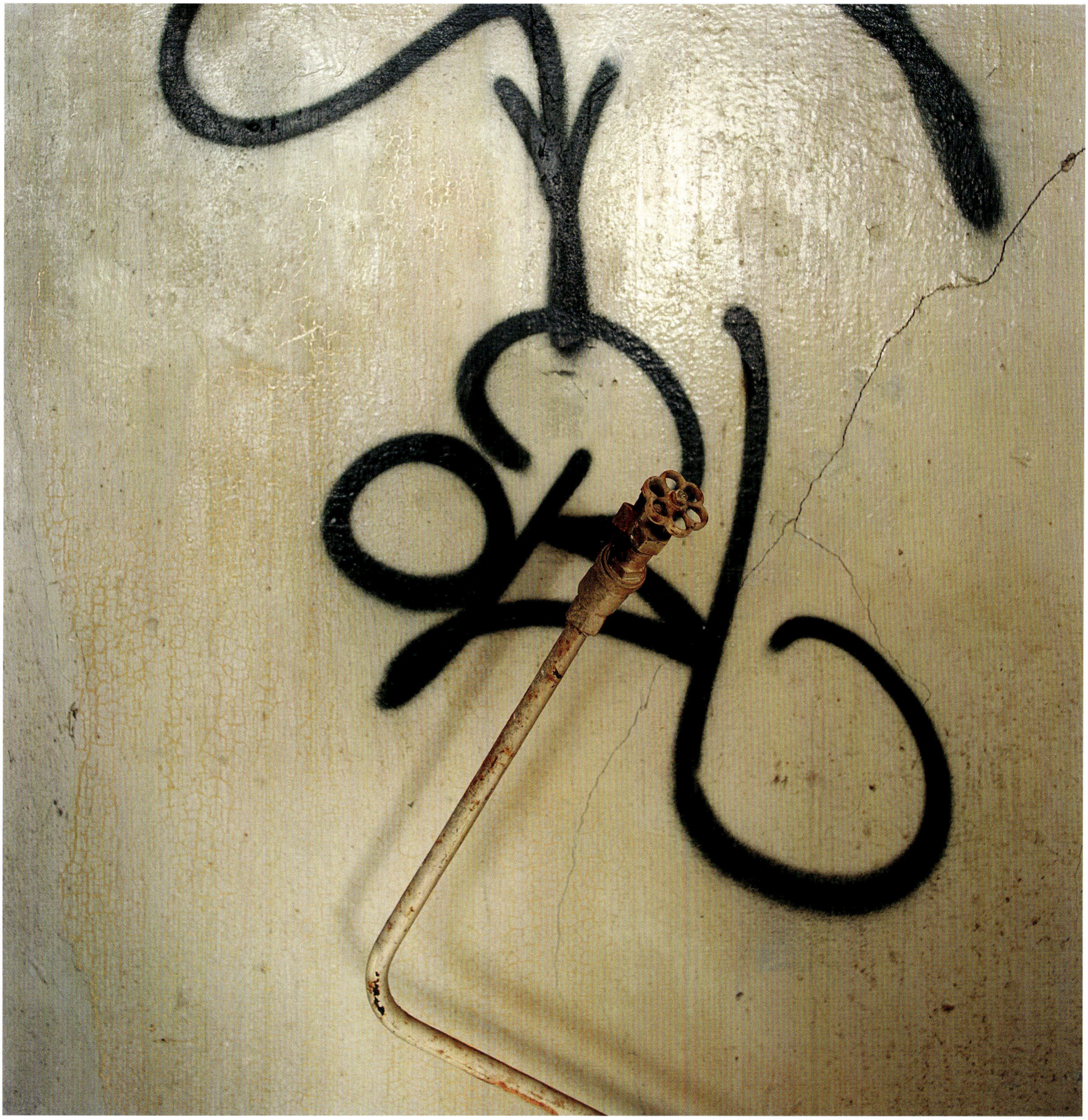

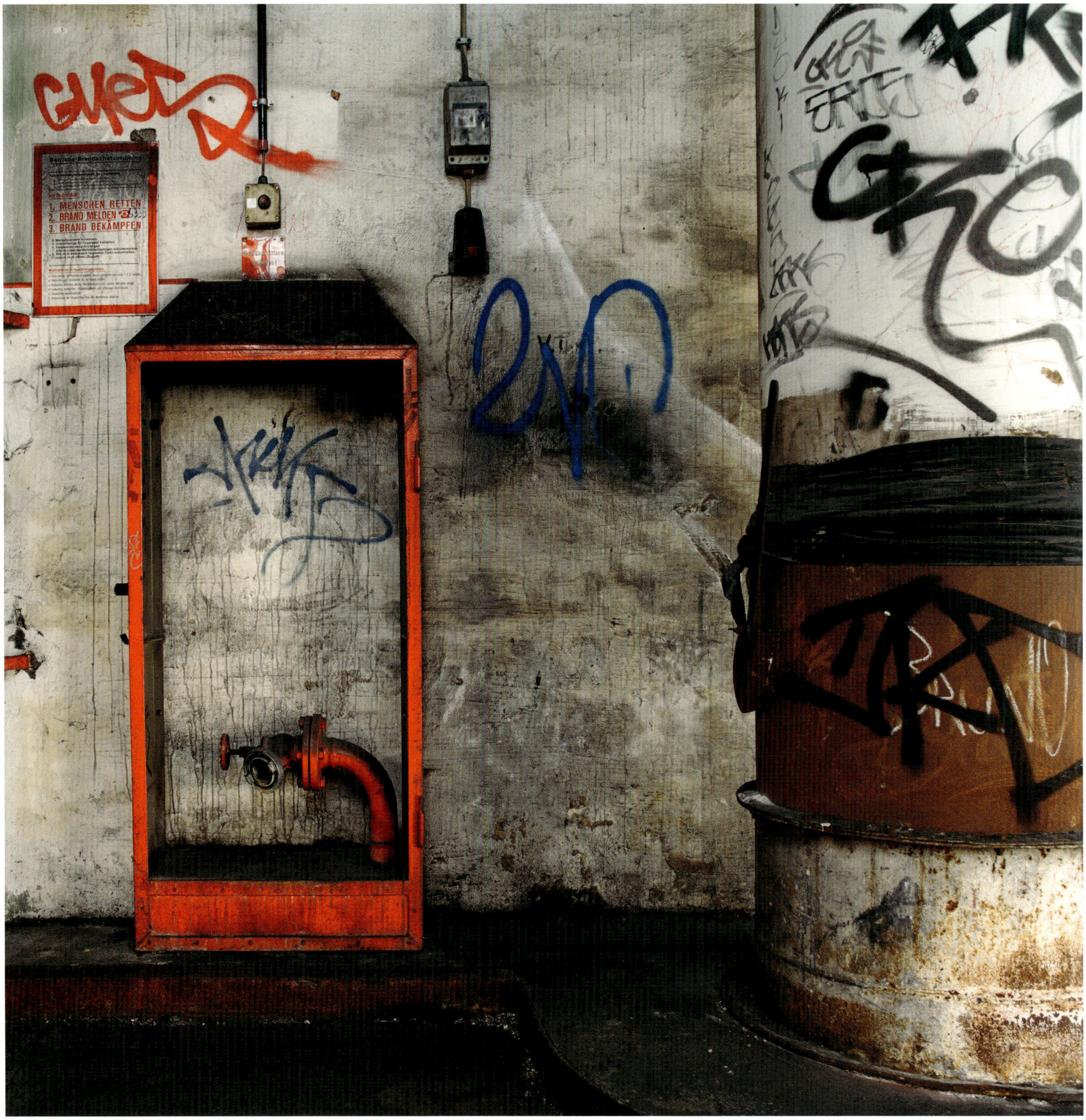
1. MENSCHEN RETTEN
2. BRAND MELDEN
3. BRAND BEKÄMPFEN

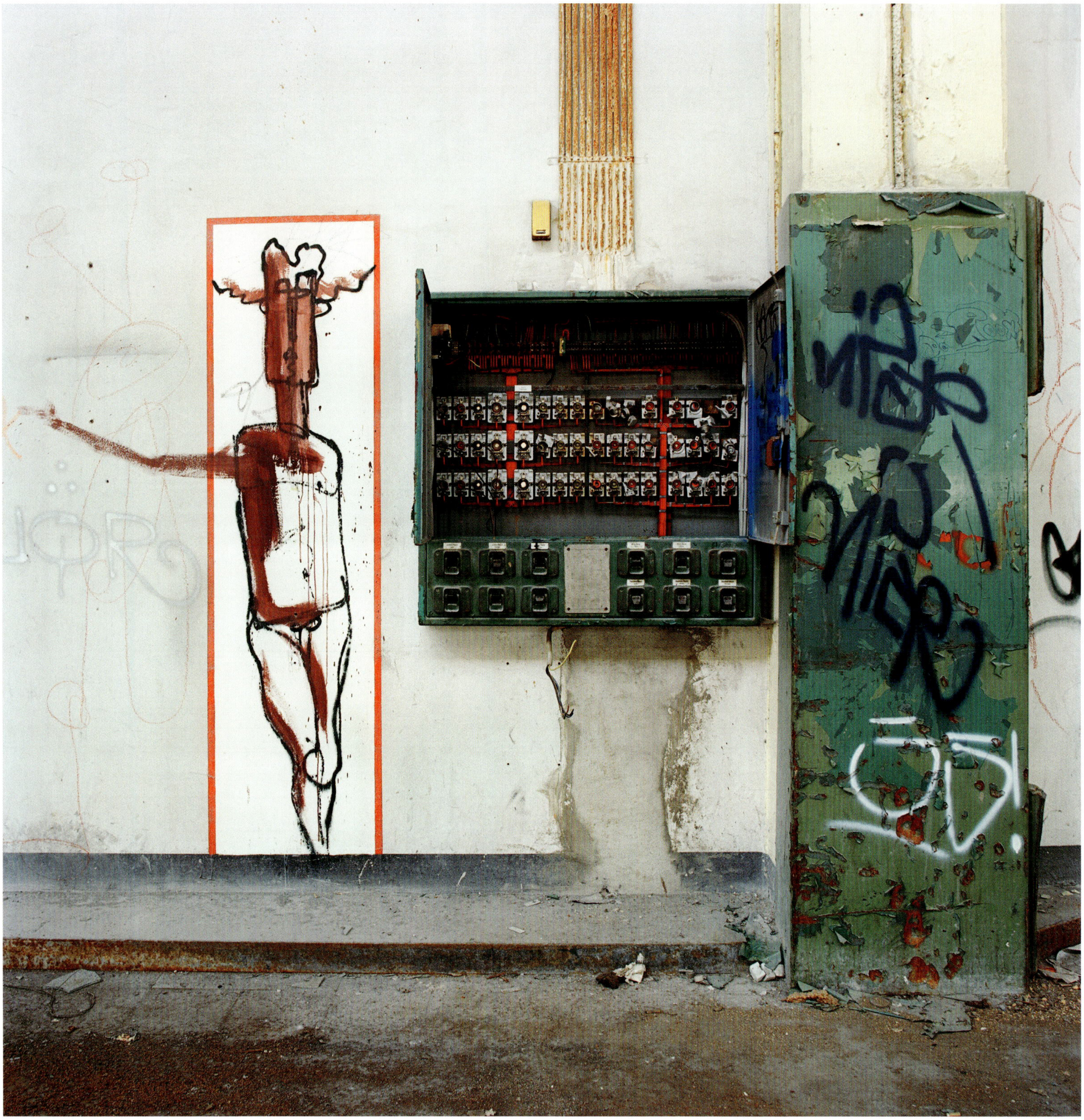

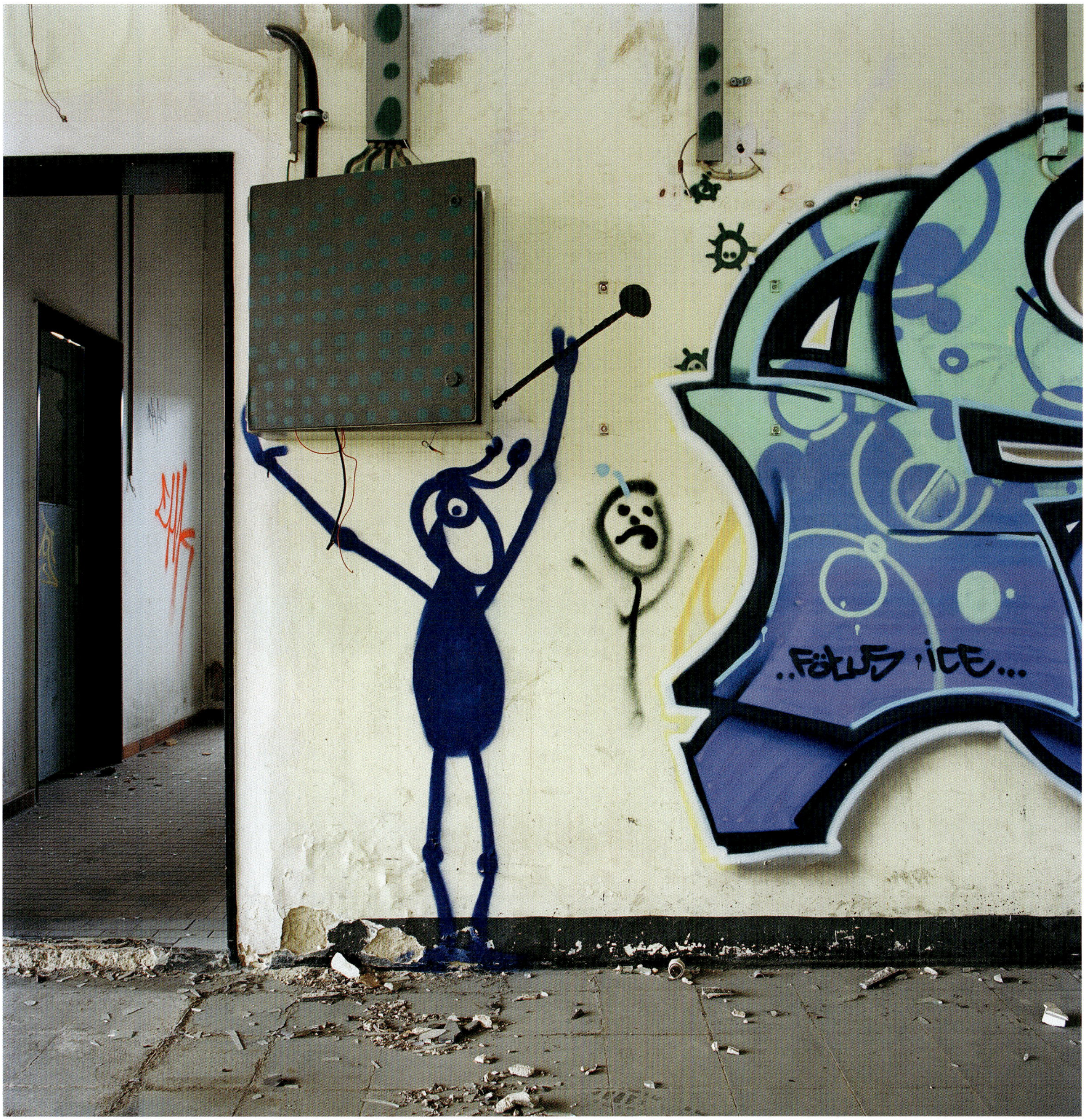
..FÖLUS ICE...

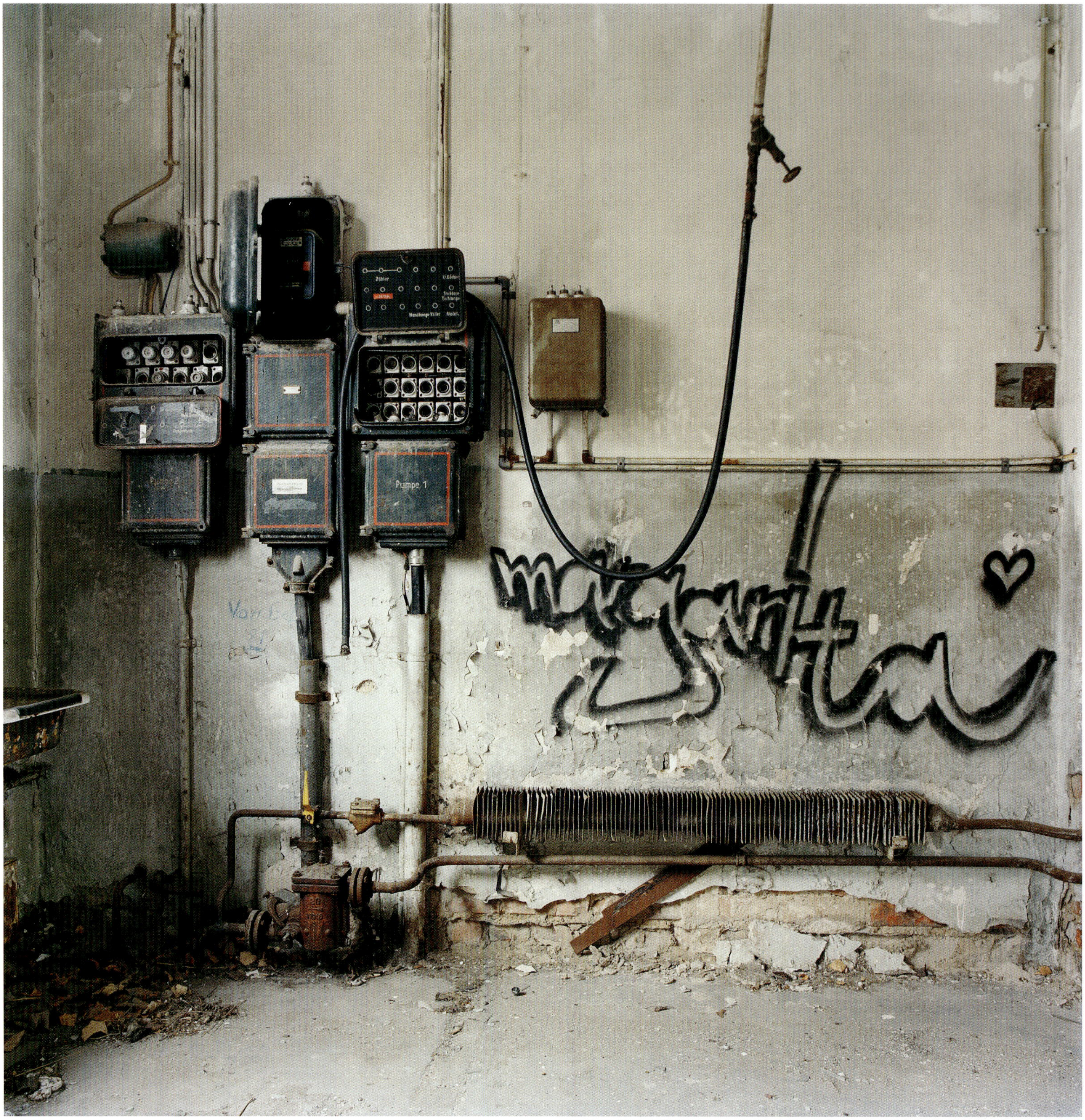

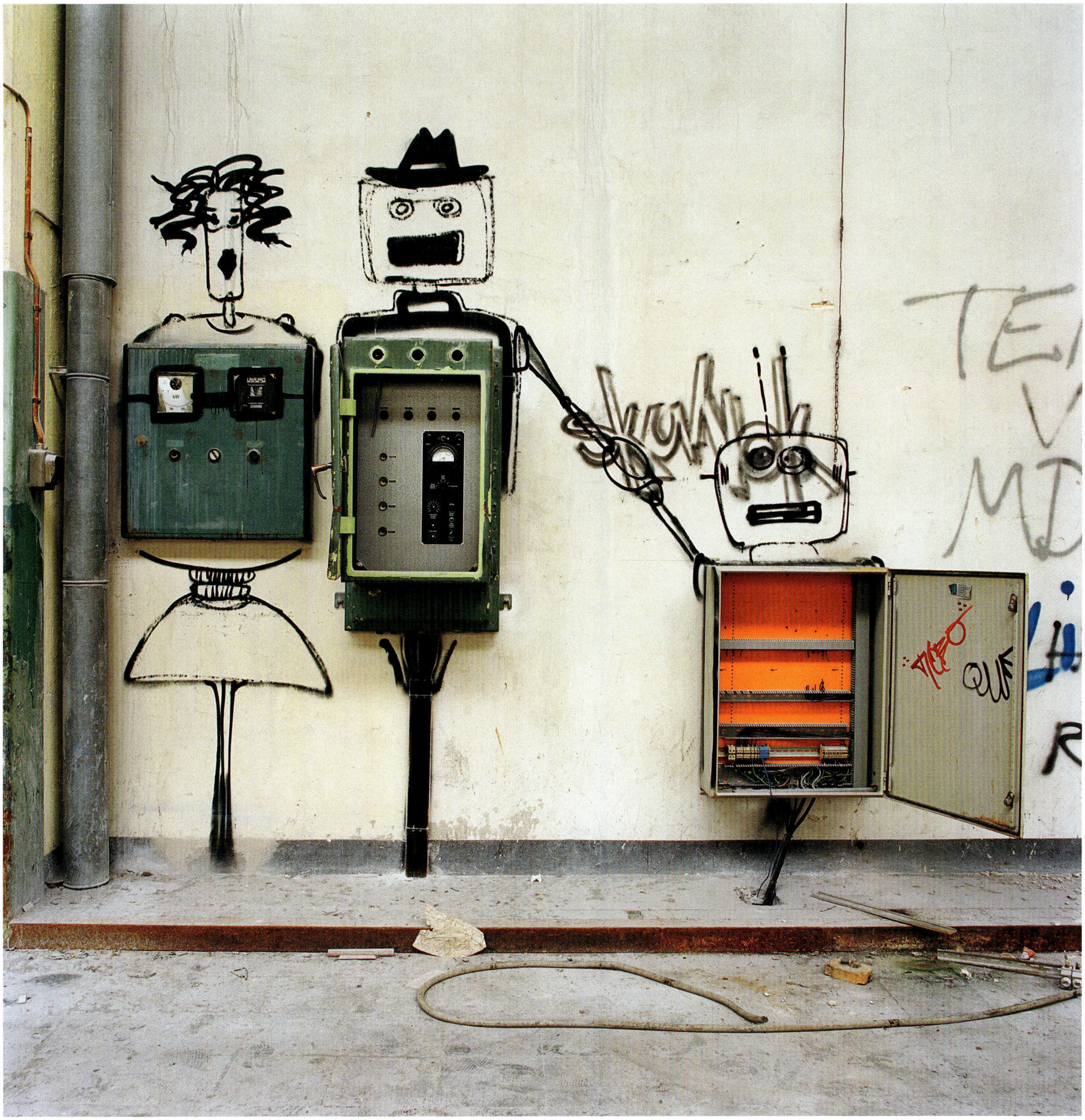

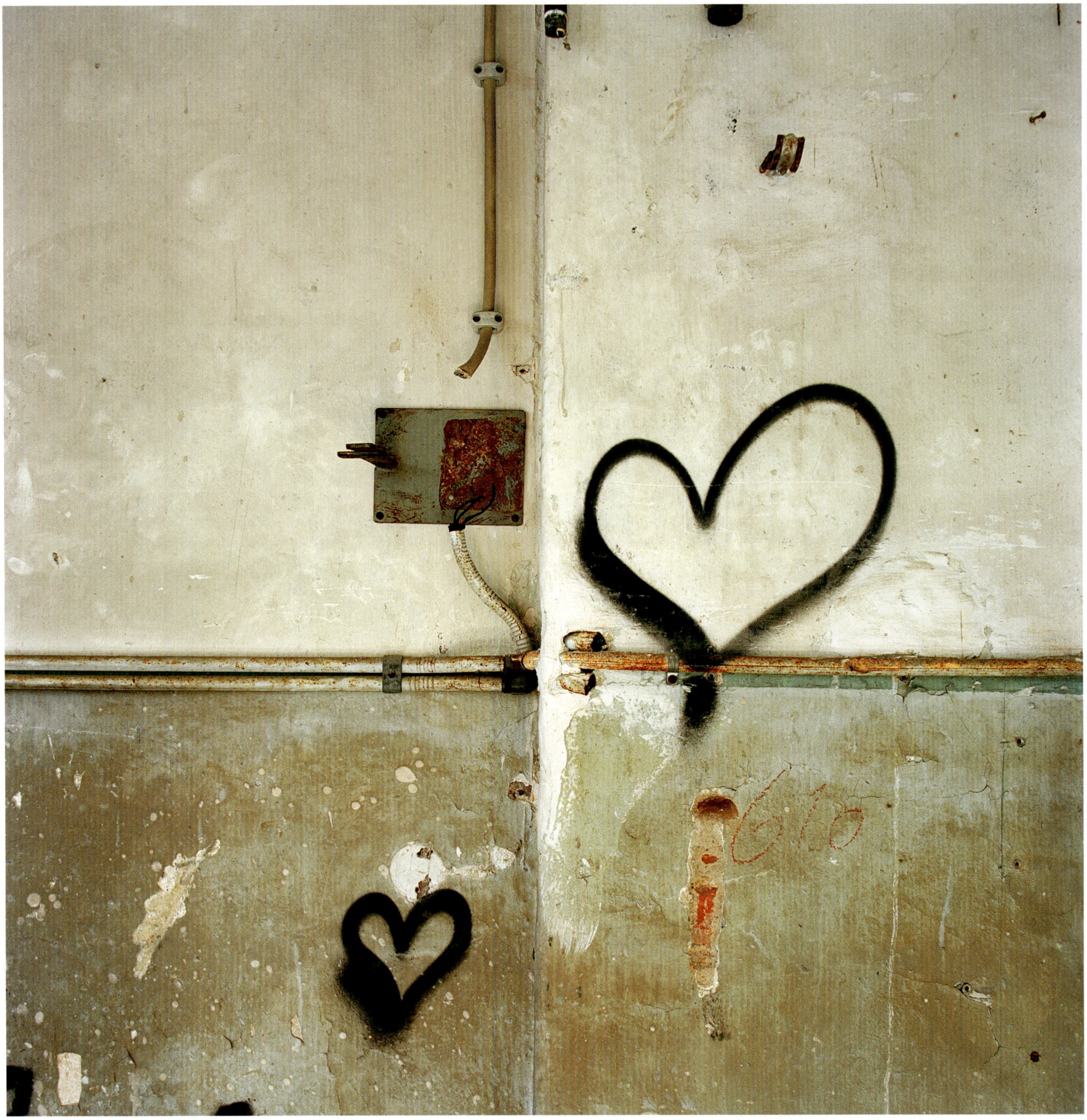

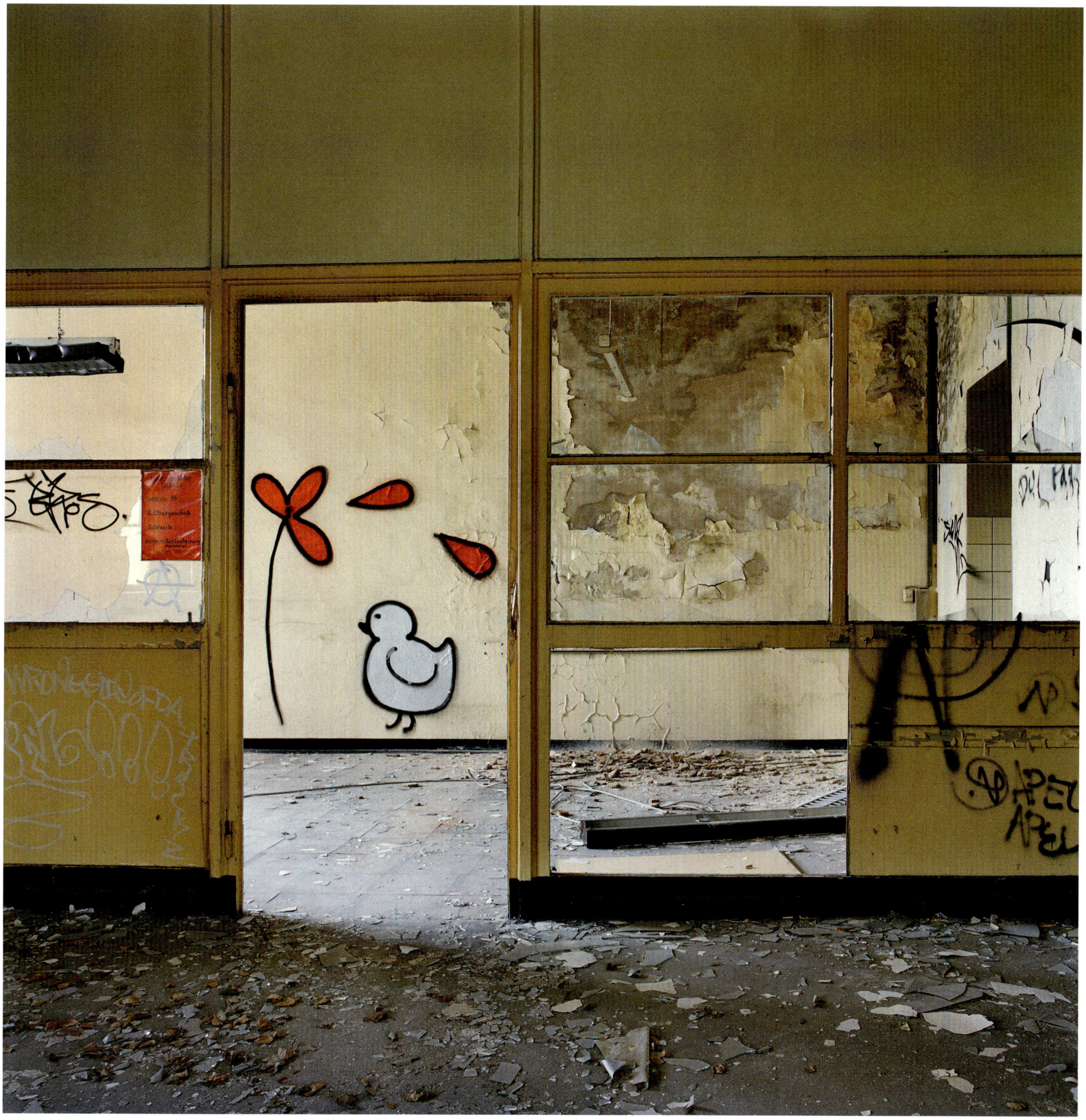

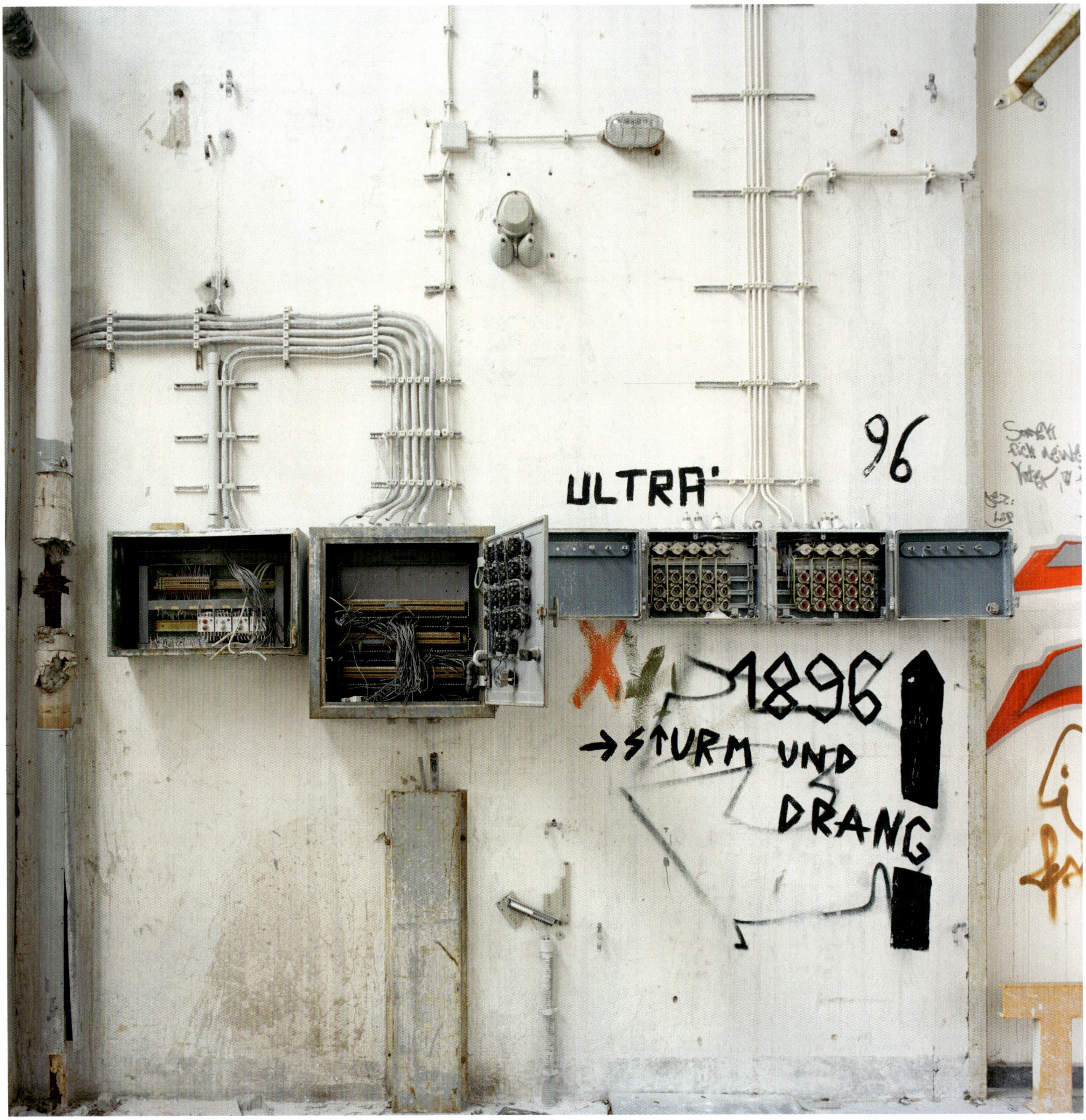
ULTRA'
96
1896
→STURM UND
DRANG

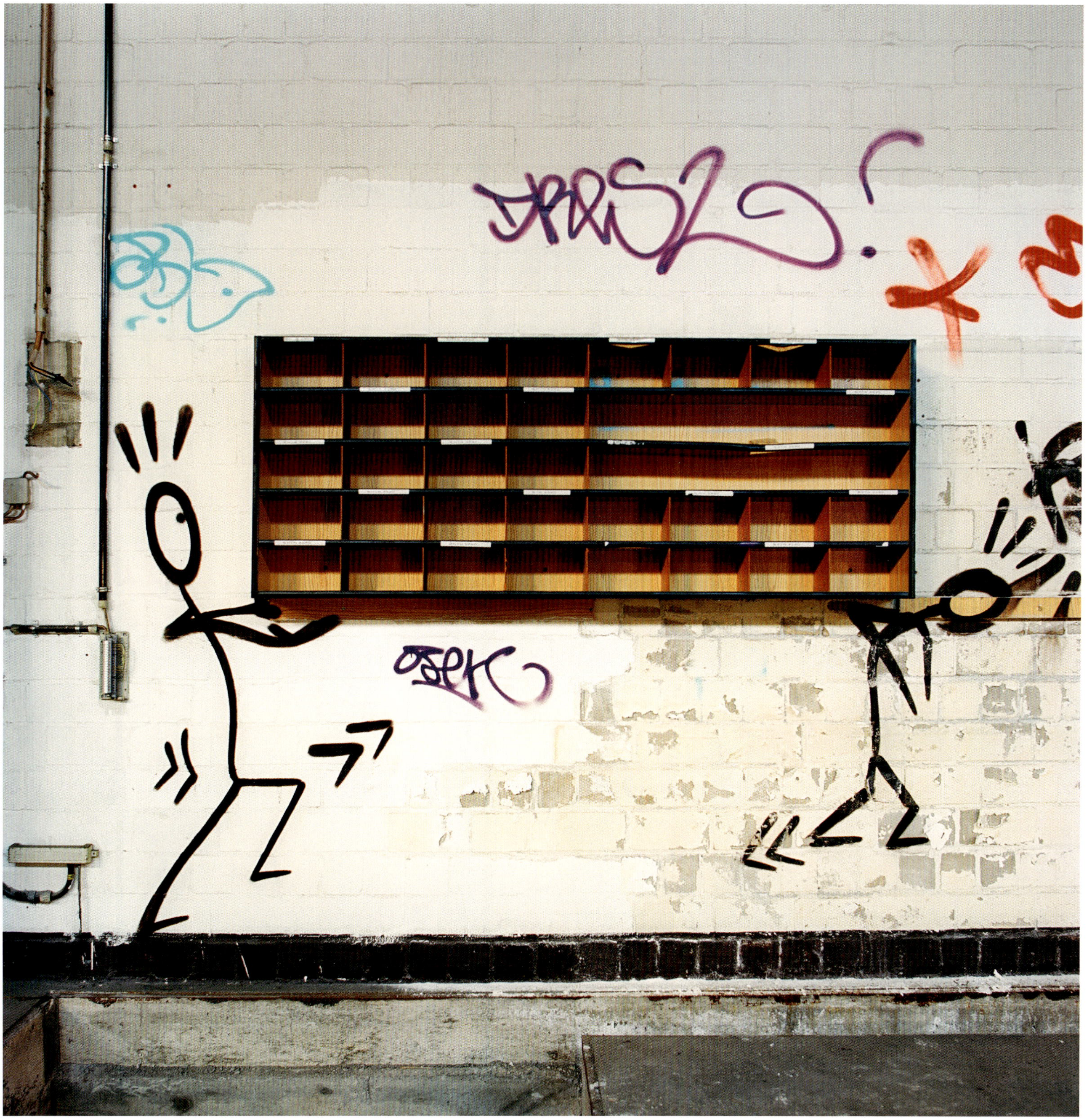

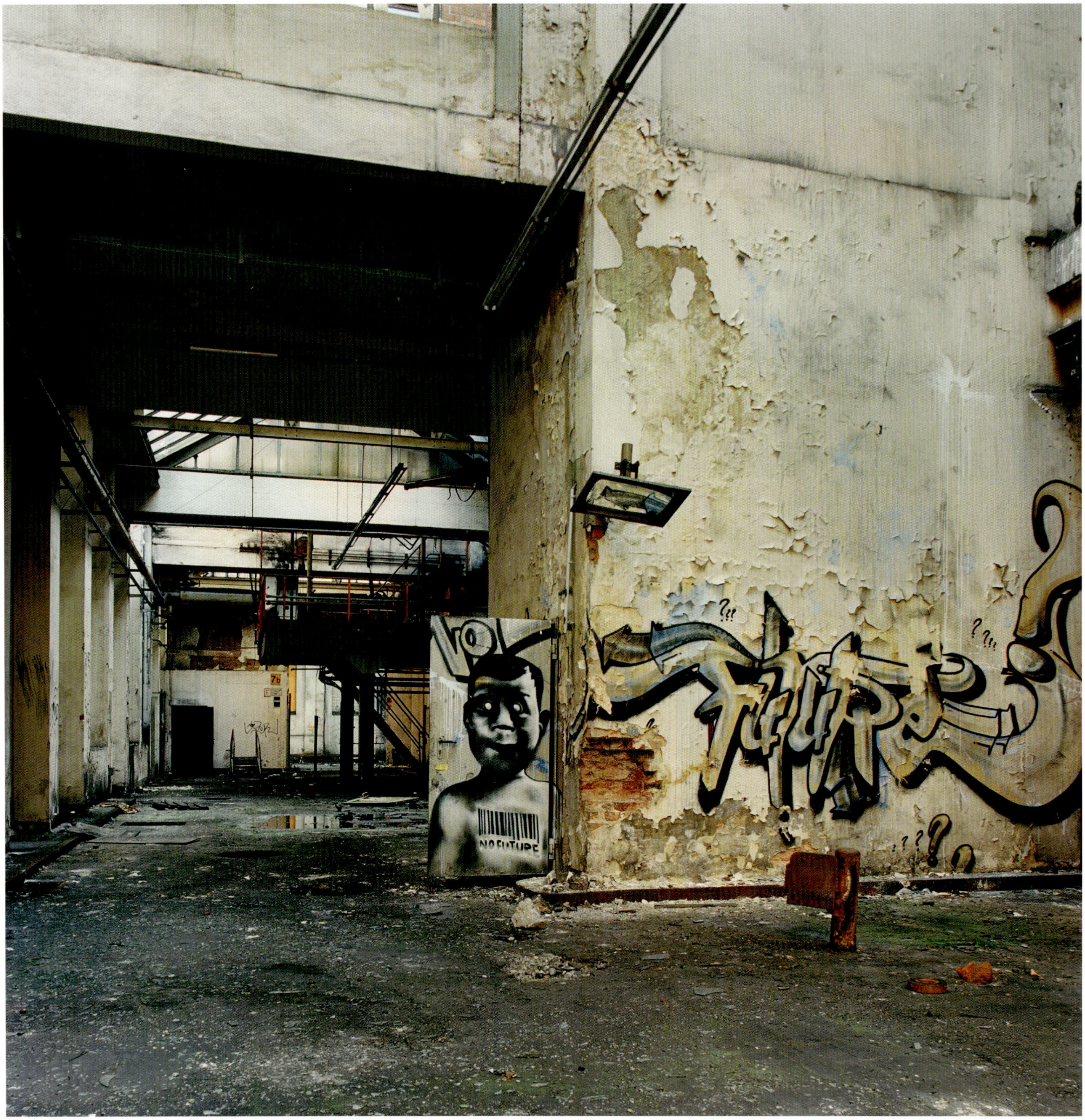
NO FUTURE

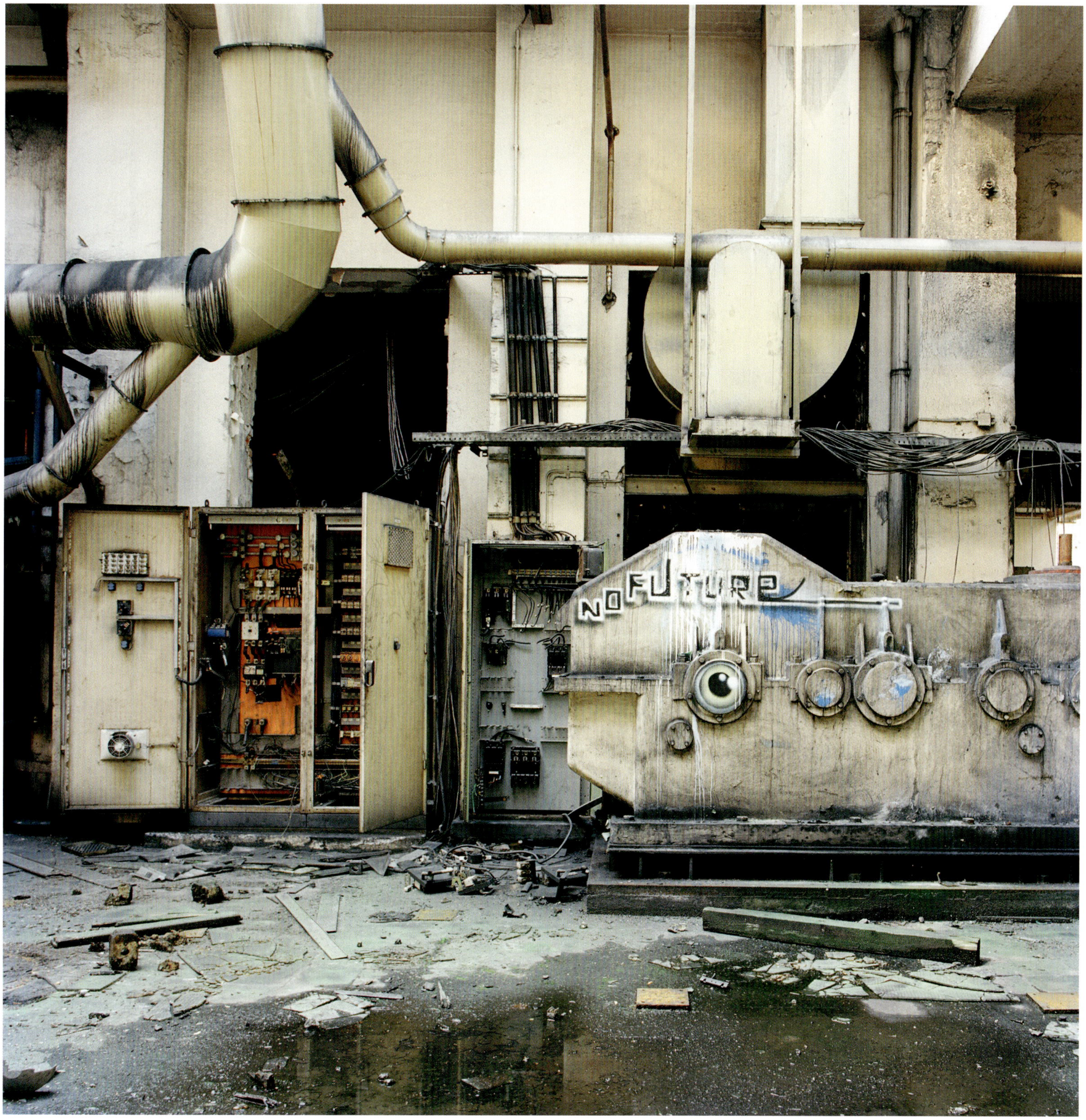
NO FUTURE

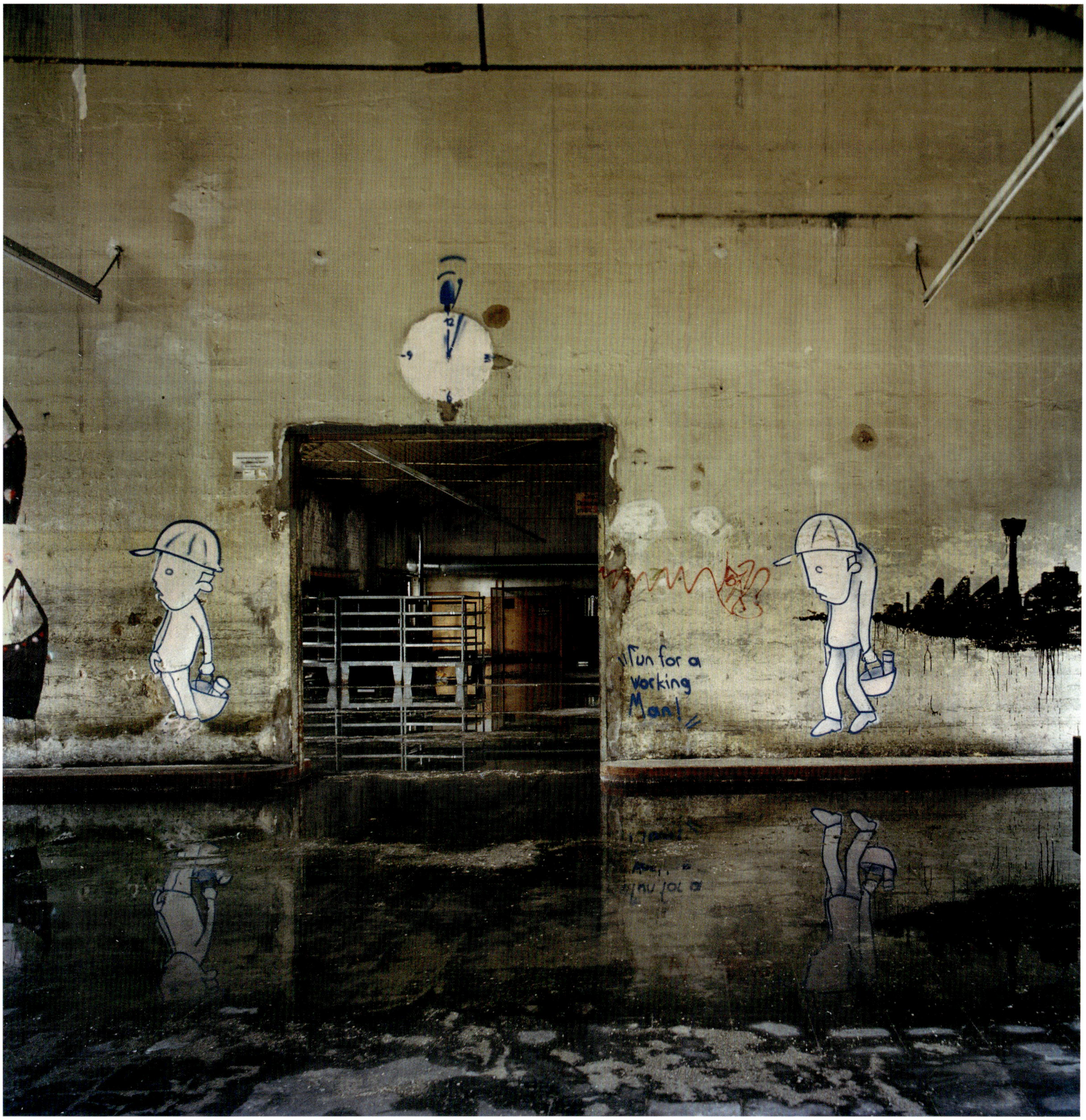
Fun for a
working
Man!

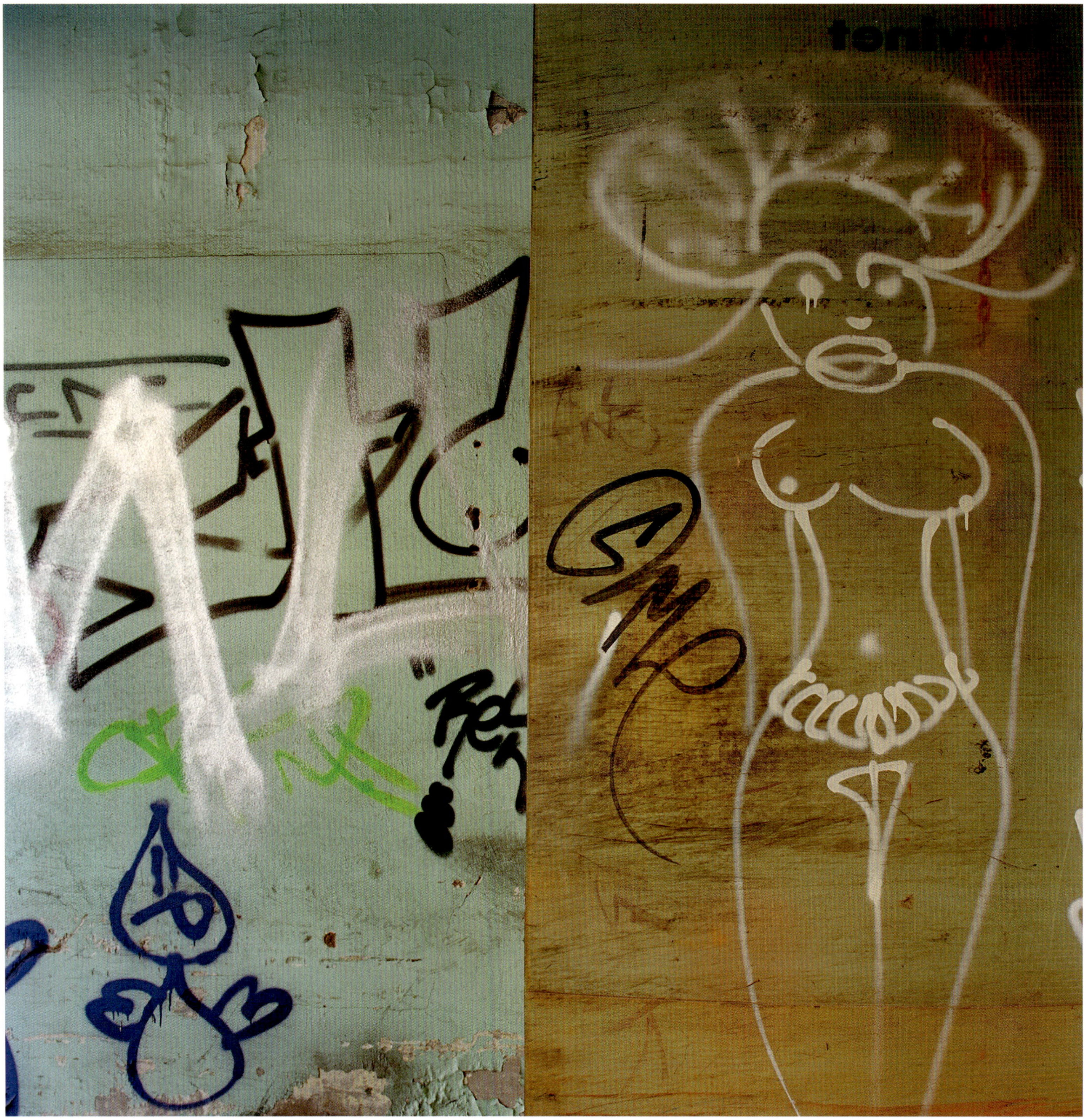

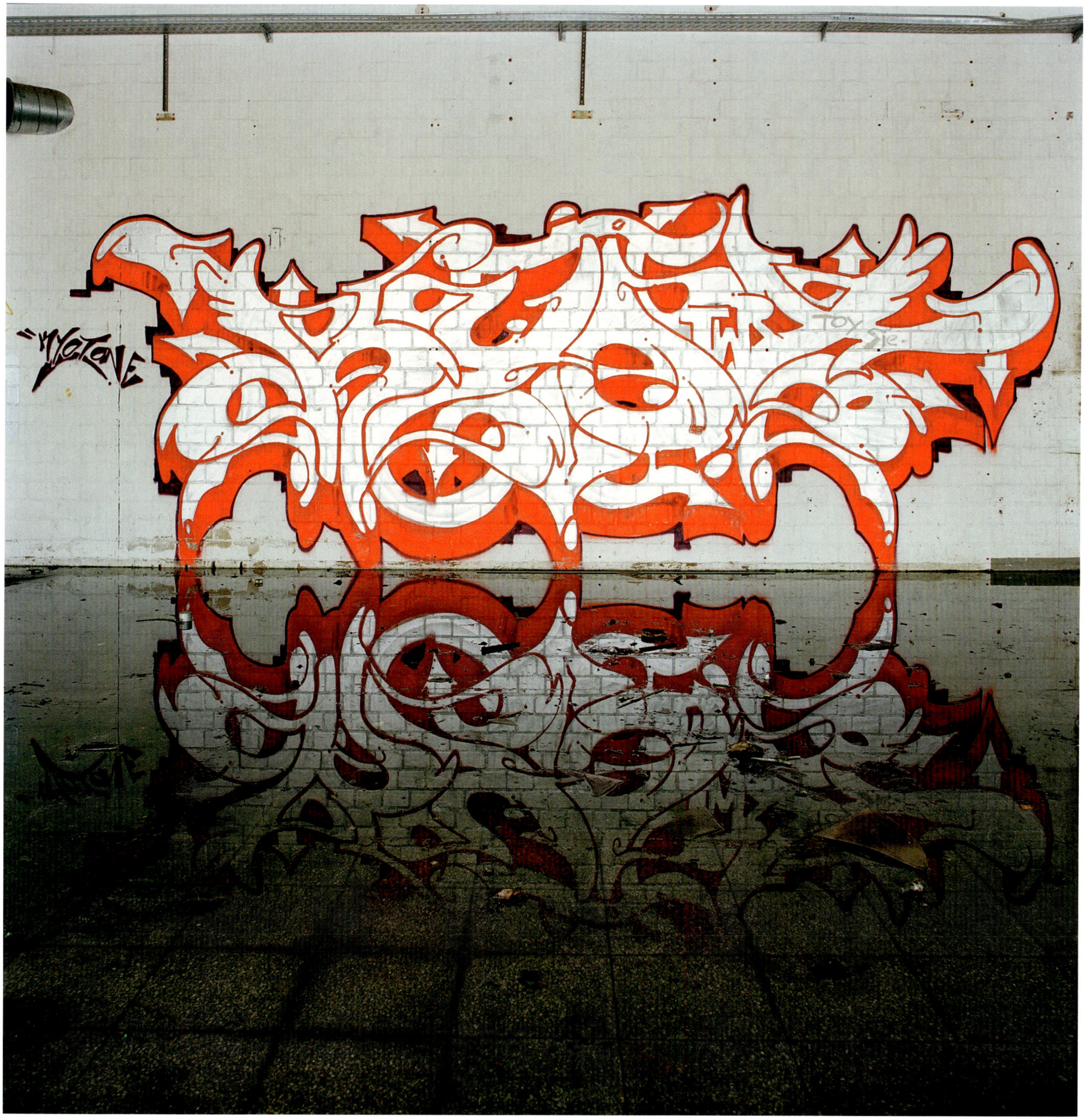

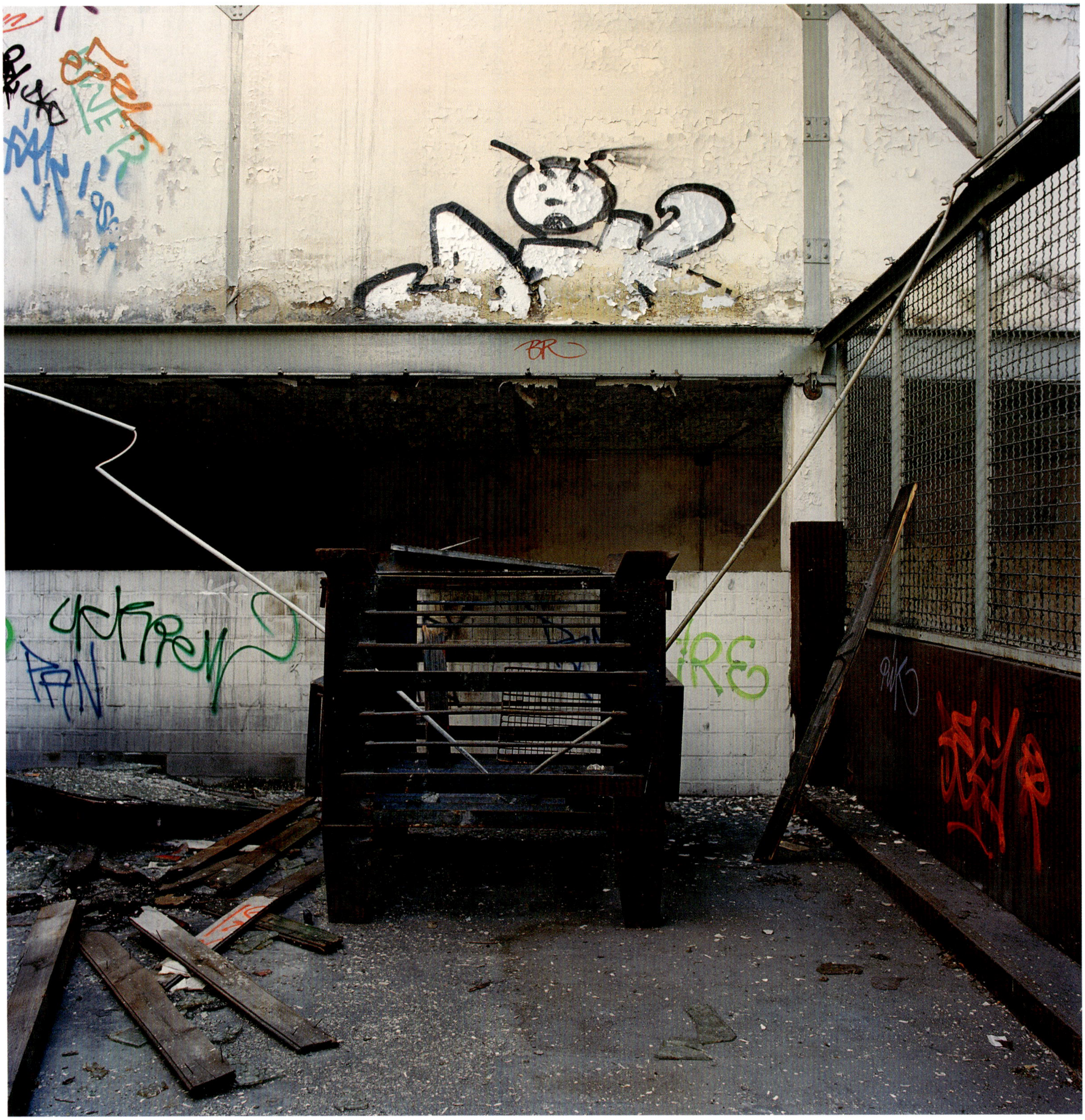

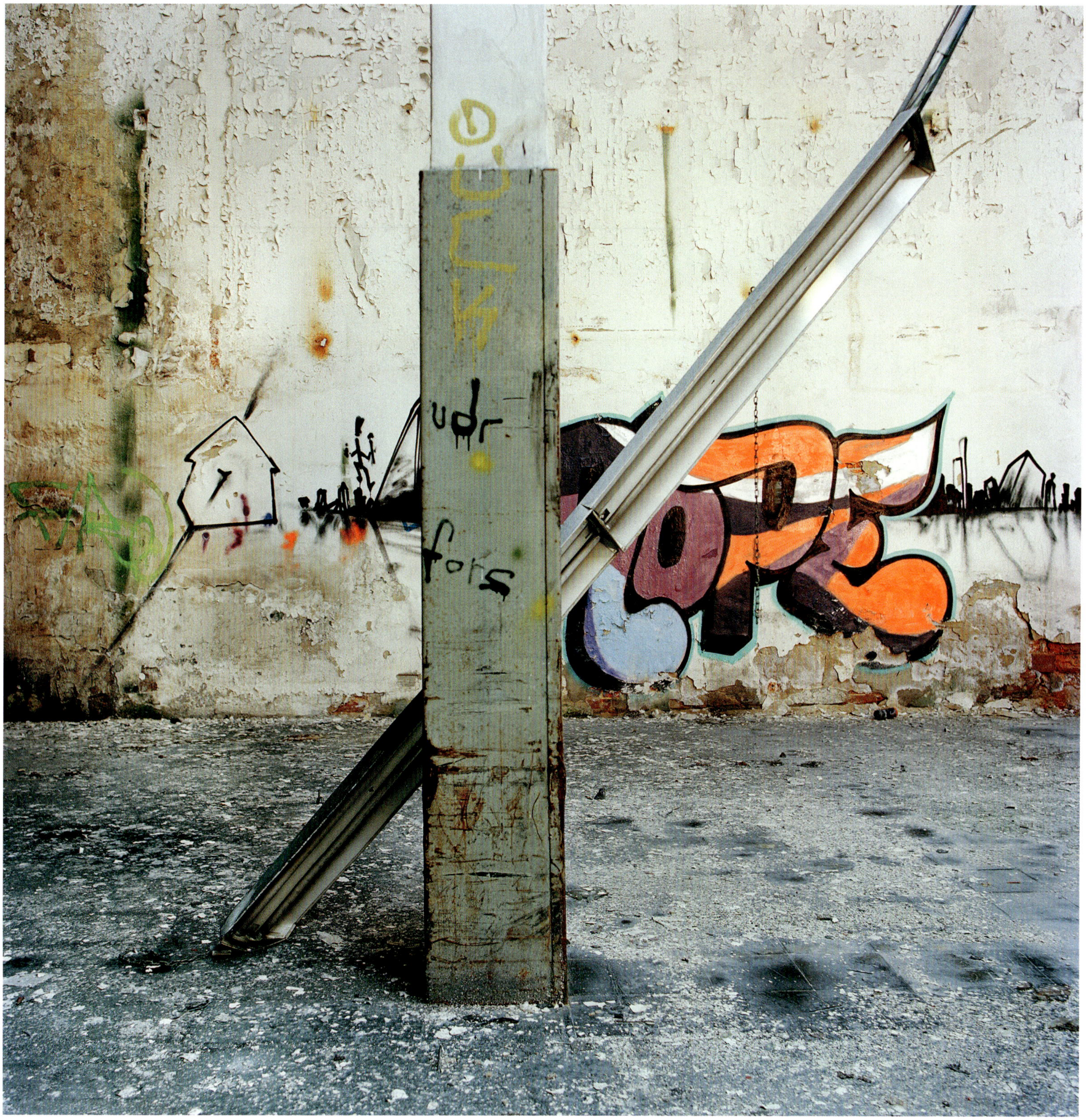
udr
fors

	Filter		
Betrieb	Außer Betrieb	in Ordnung	Defekt

Abreinigung		Druckdifferenz	
Betr. Reinigung		in Ordnung	Überschritten

Schnecke		Zellenrad	
Betrieb	Störung	Betrieb	Störung

Staubaustrag		Ventilheizung	
in Ordnung	Ansammlung	Betrieb	Störung

Ventilator Staubabsaugung		Ventilator Dunstabsaugung	
Betrieb	Störung	Betrieb	Störung

NOT-AUS

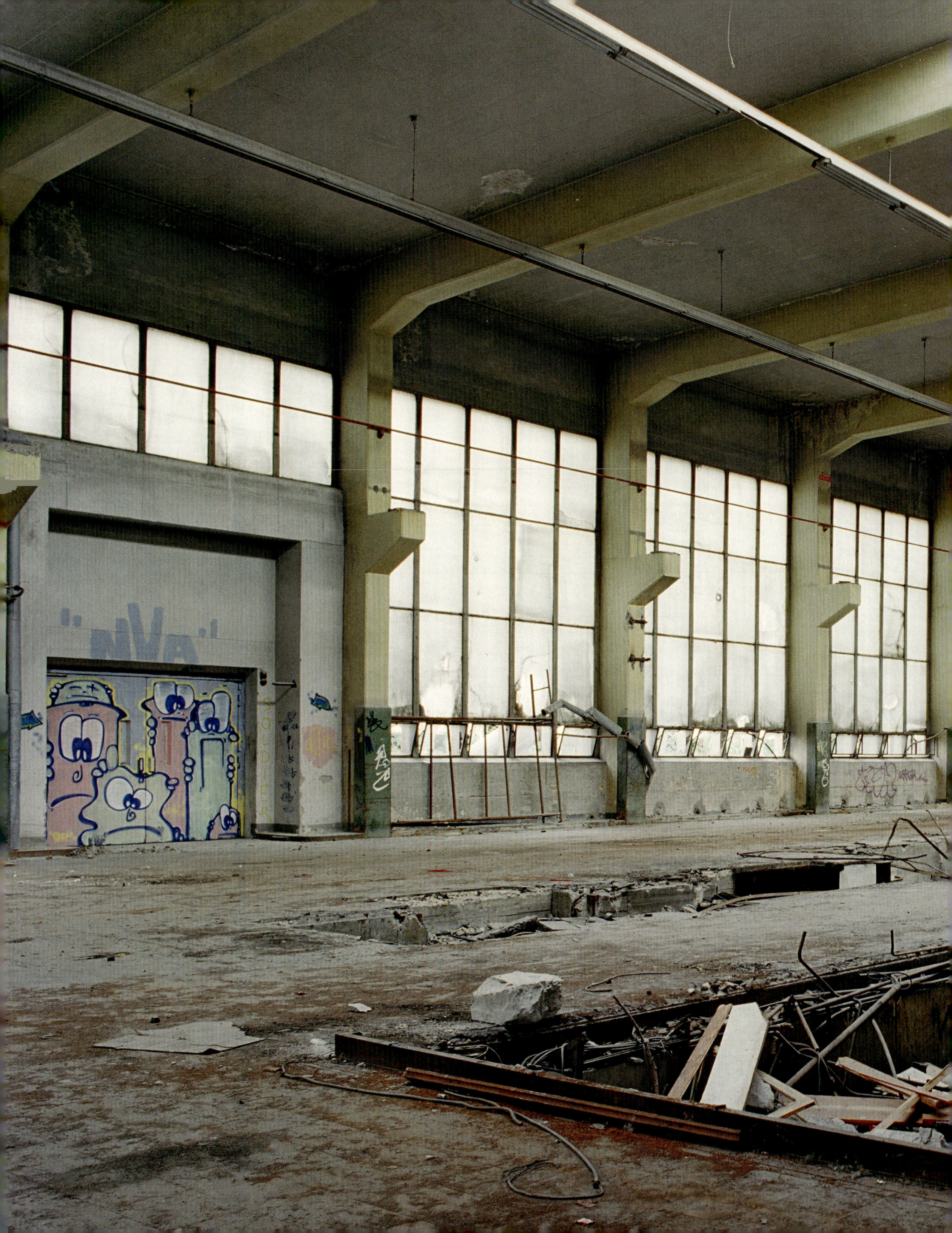
NVA

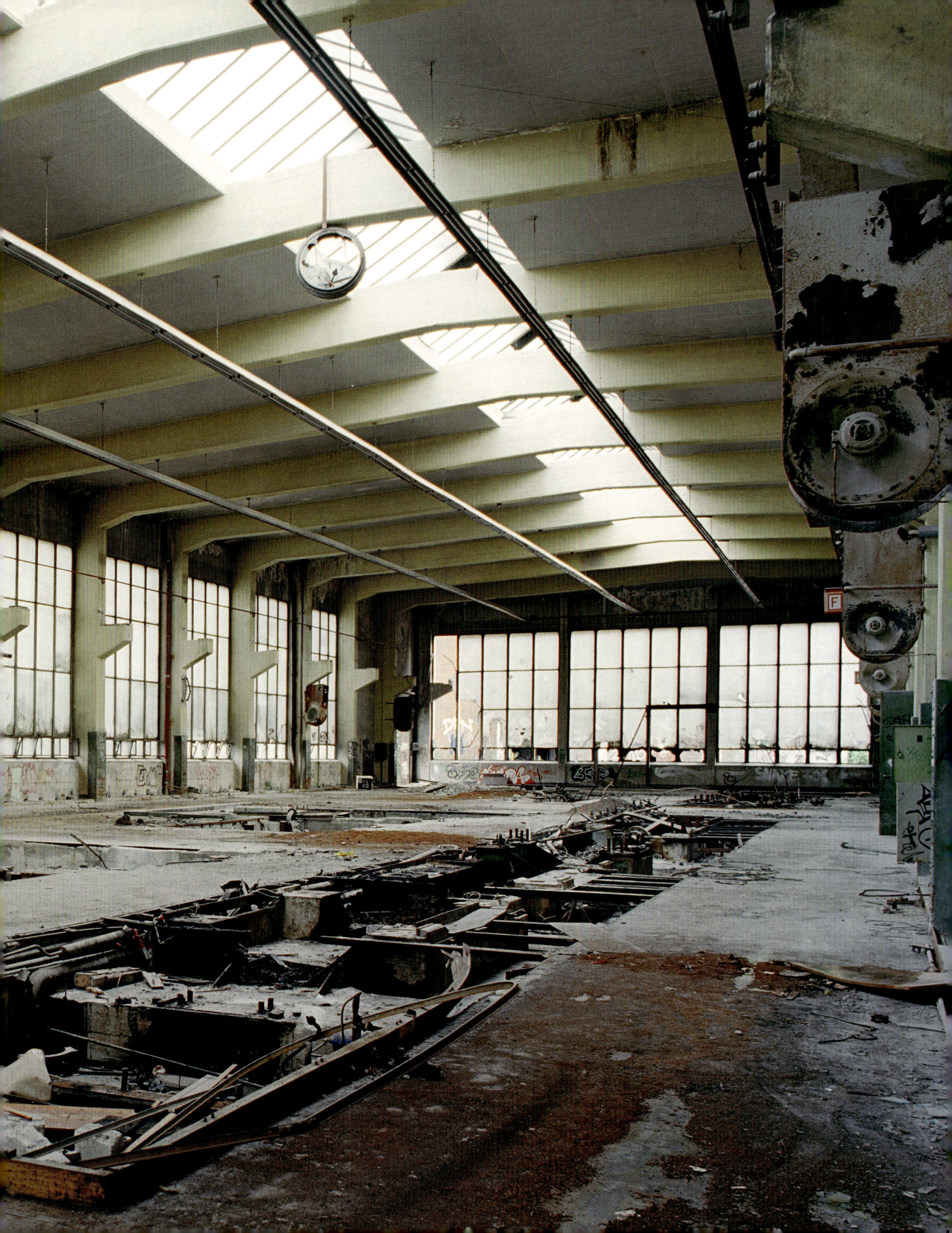
F

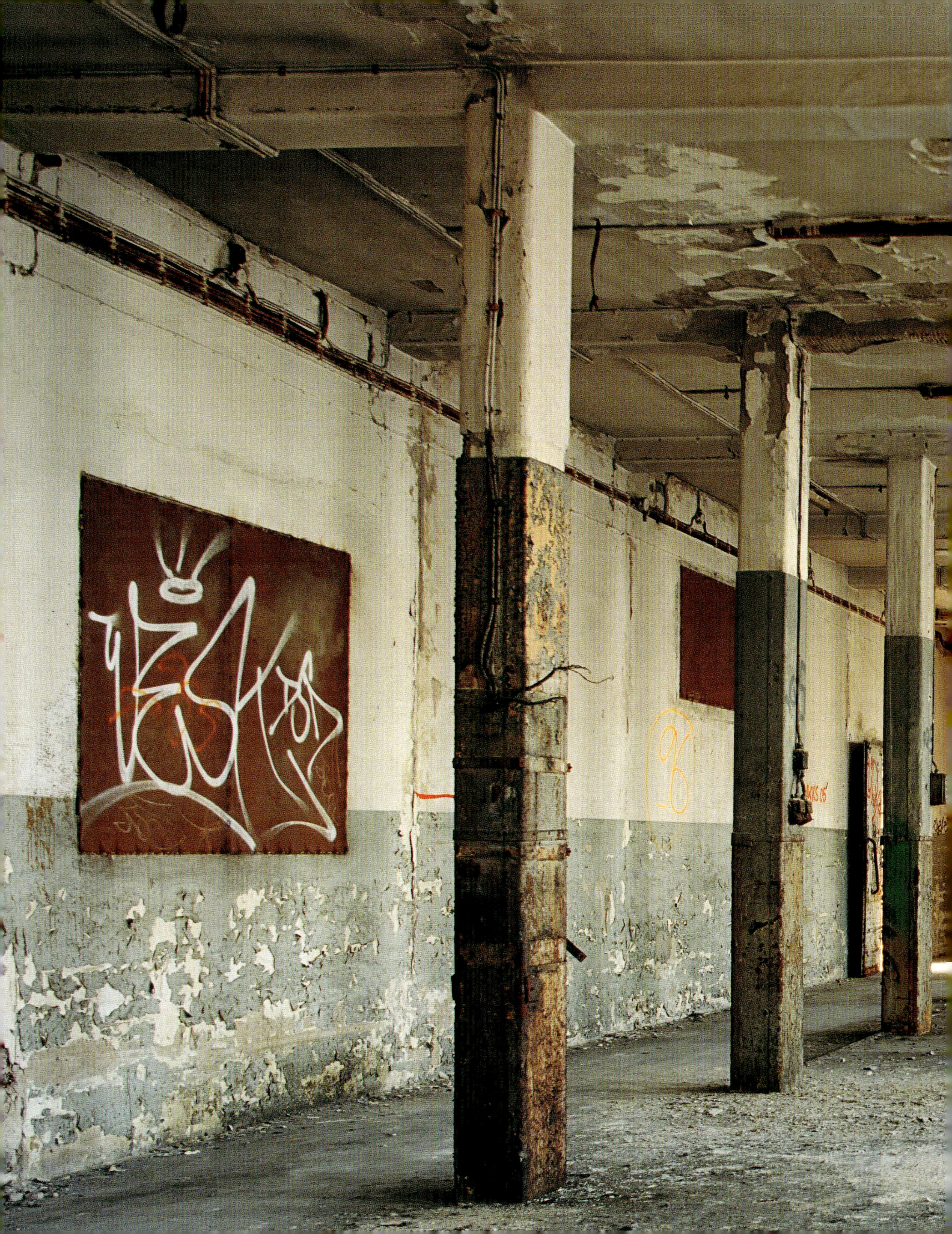

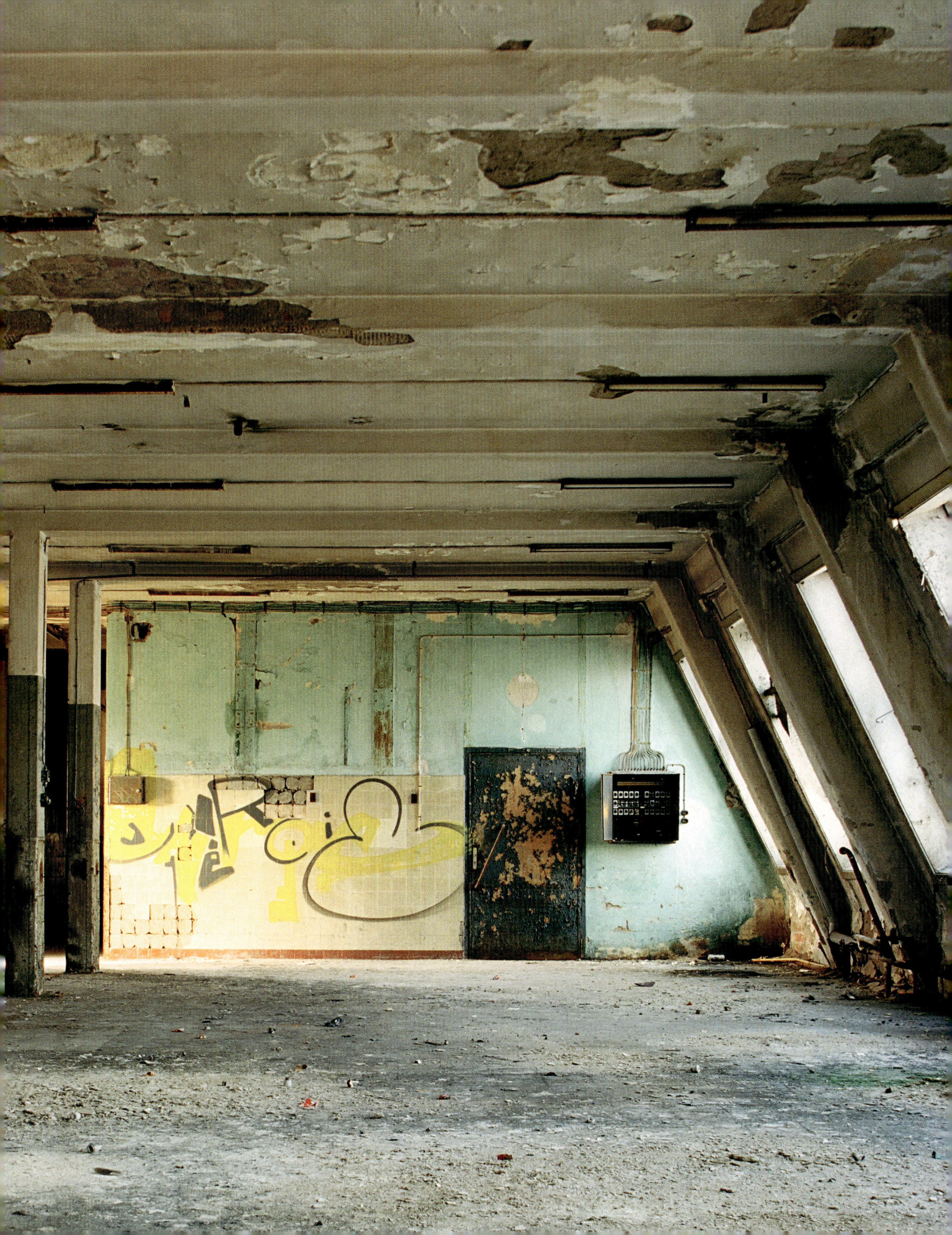

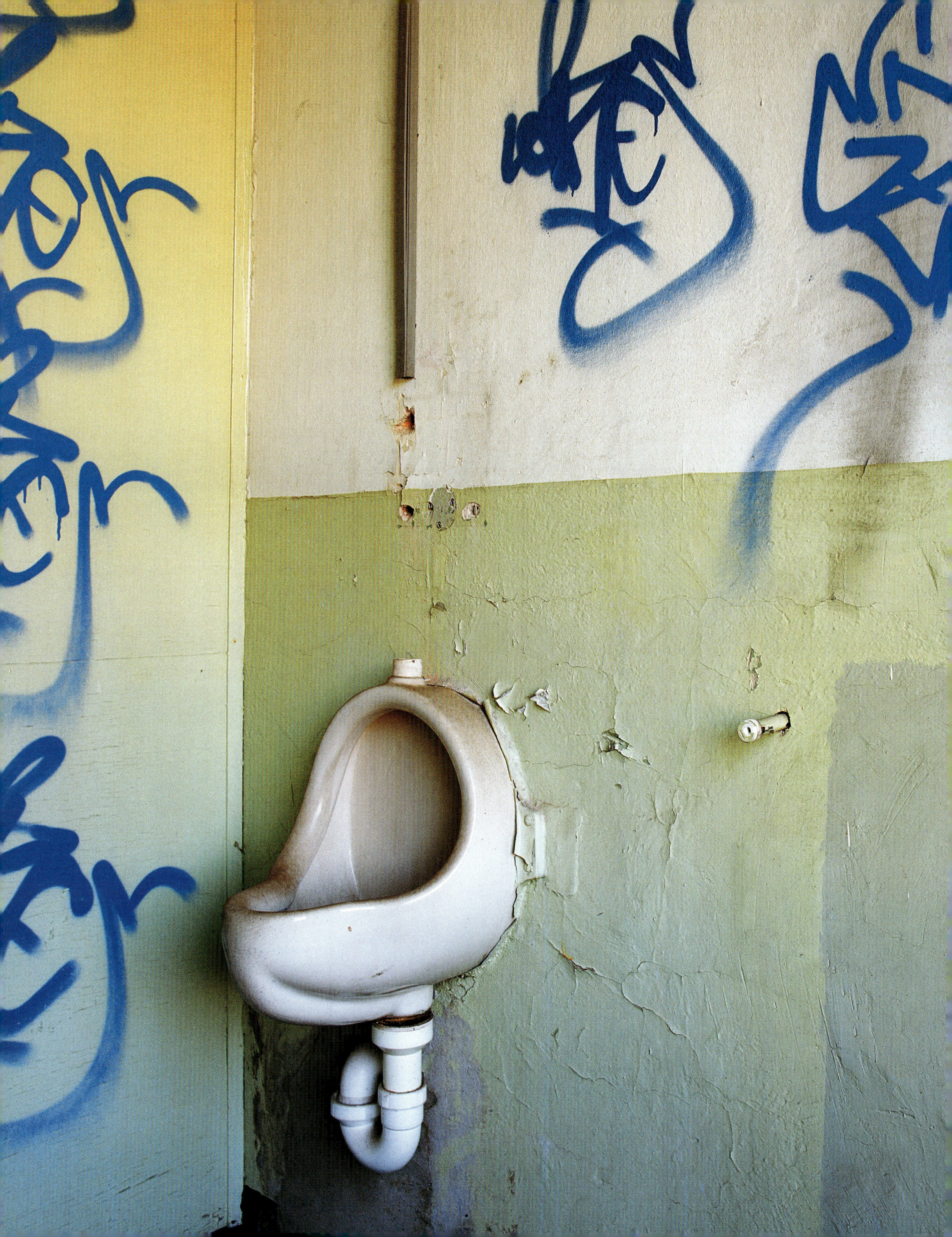

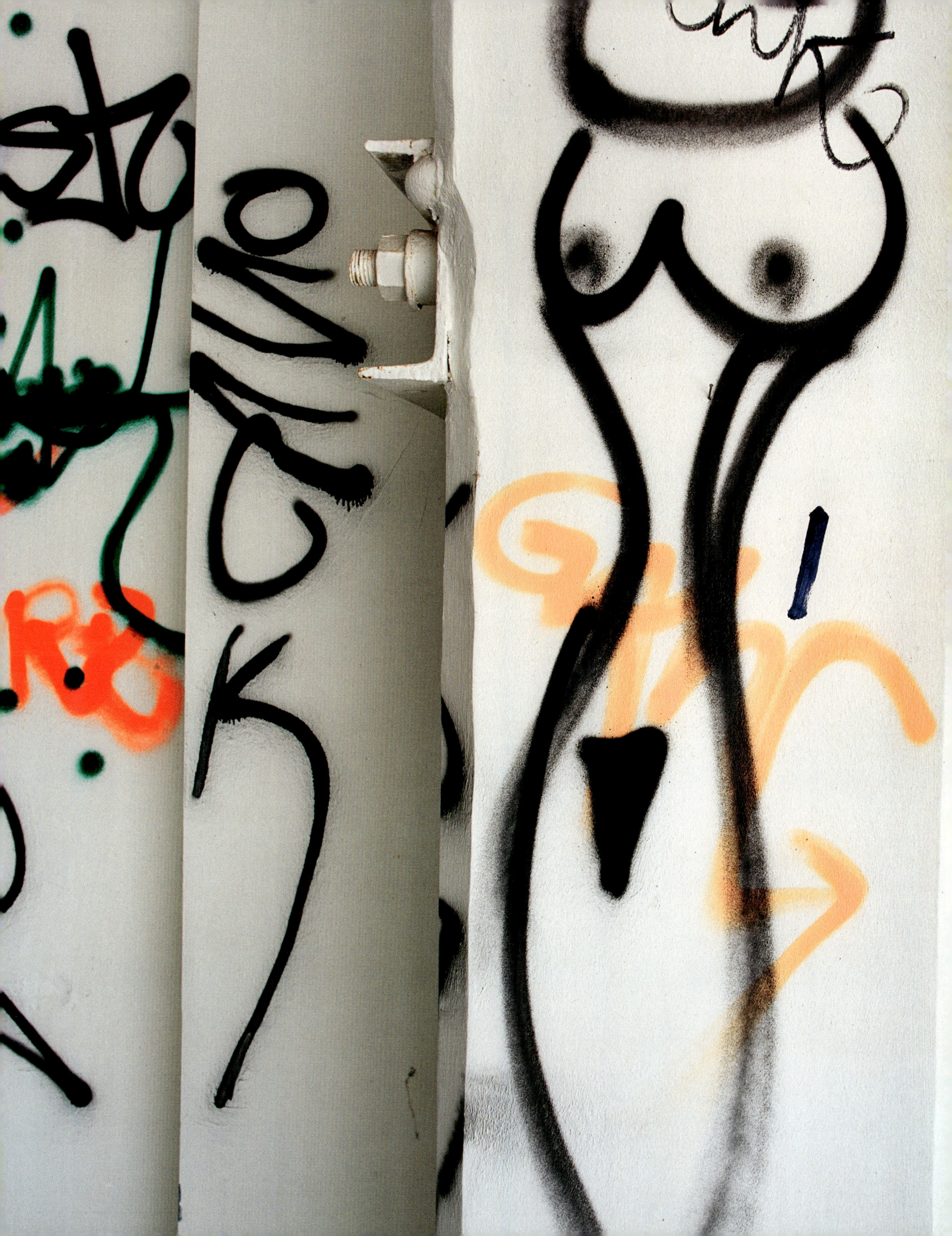

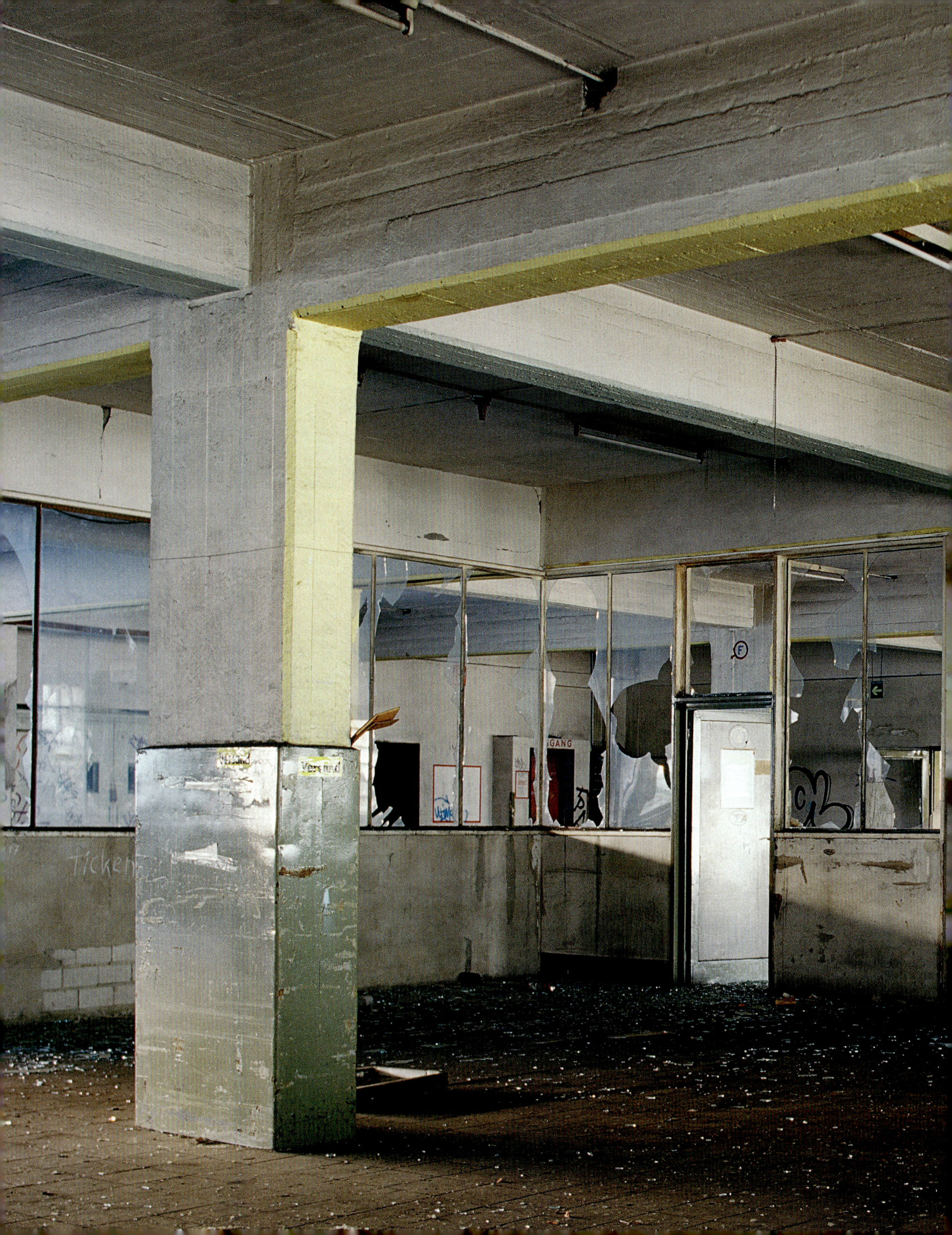
Versand

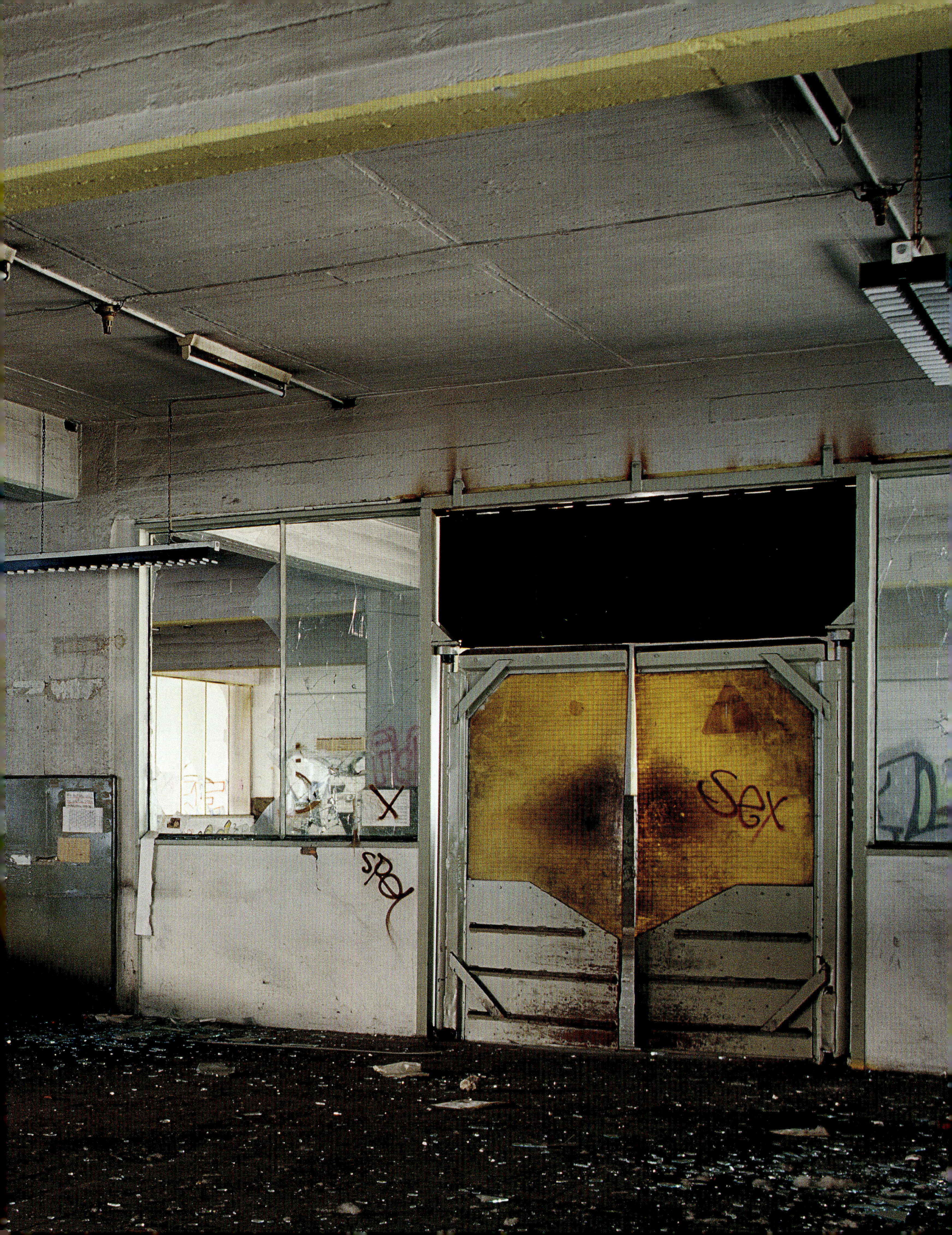
Sex

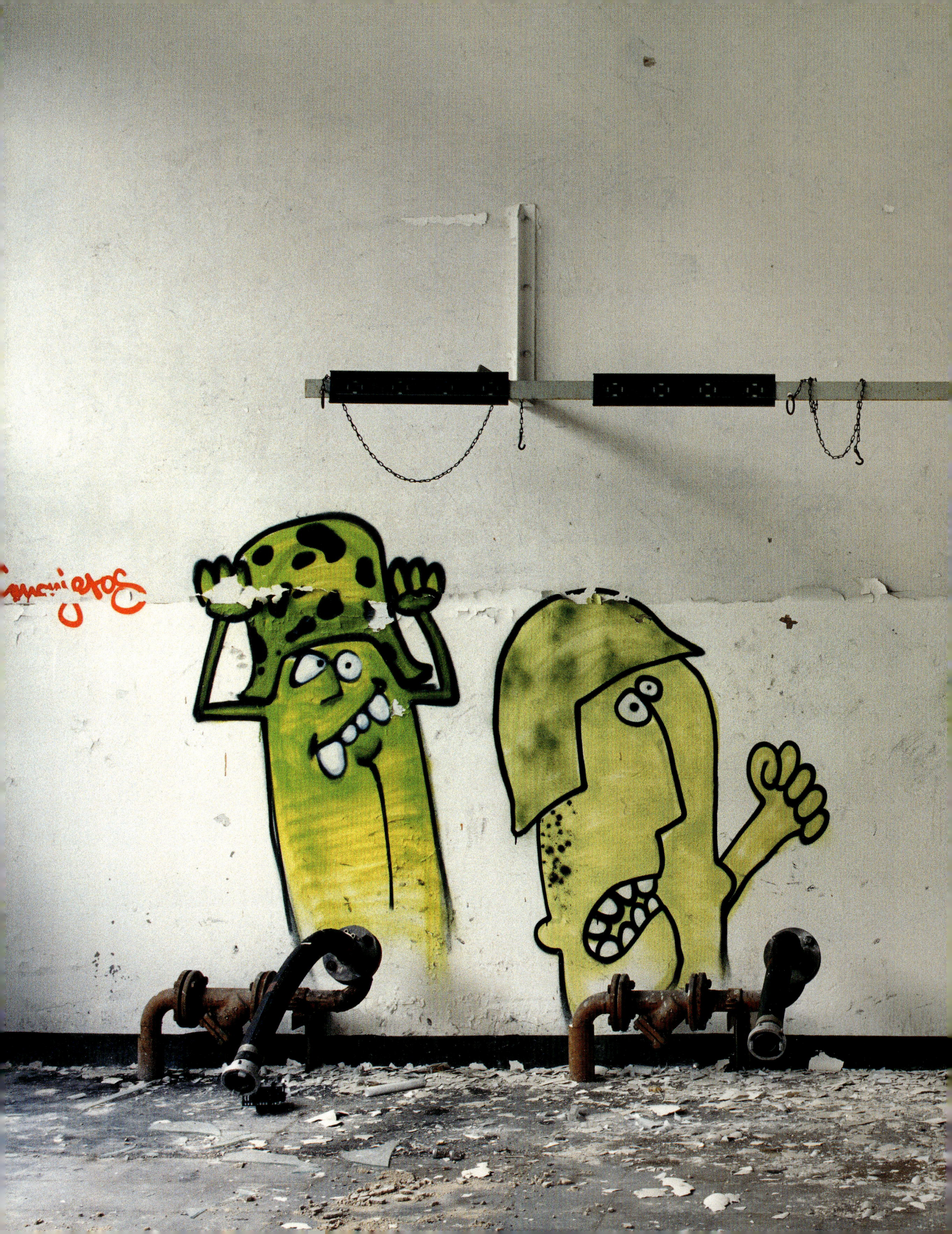

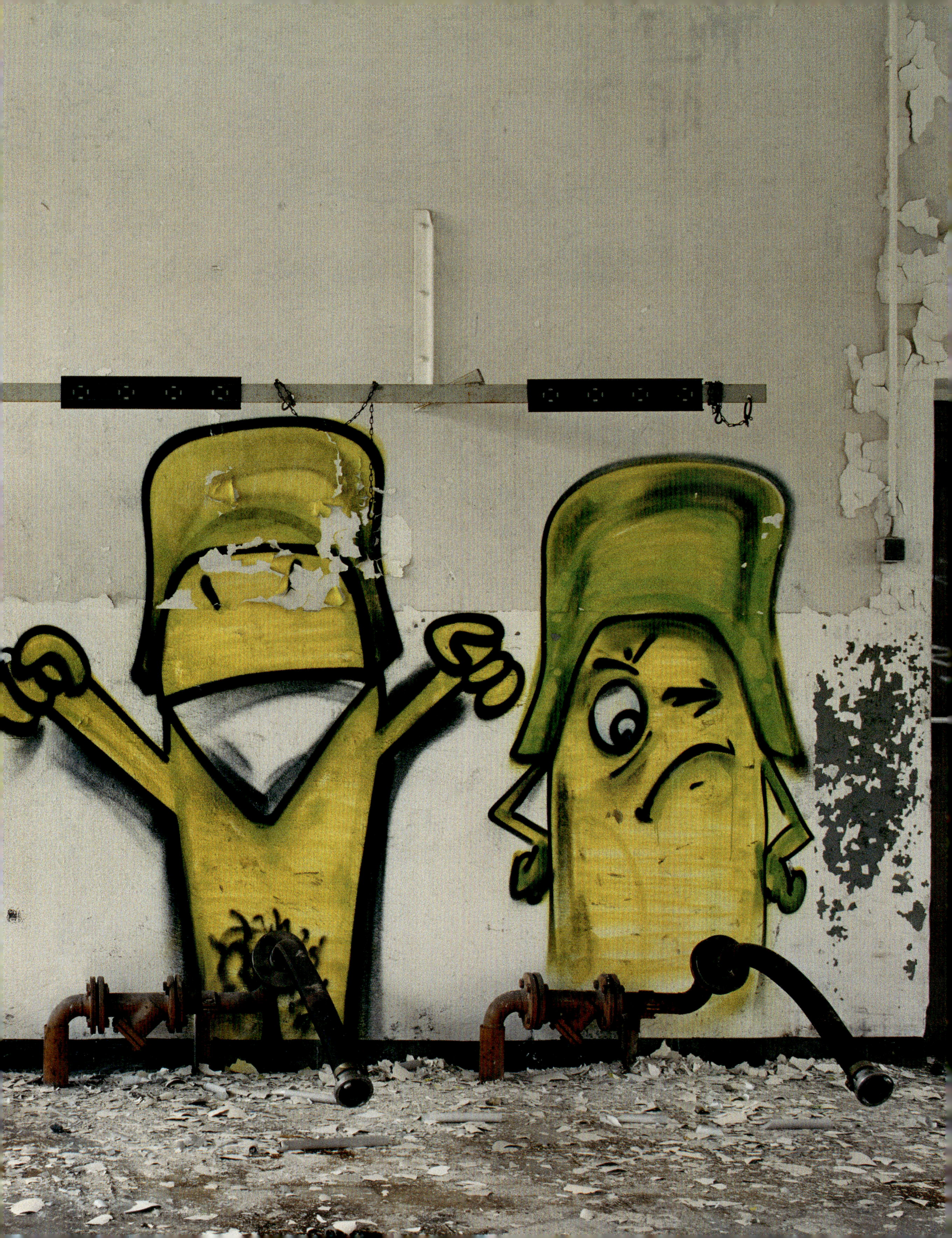

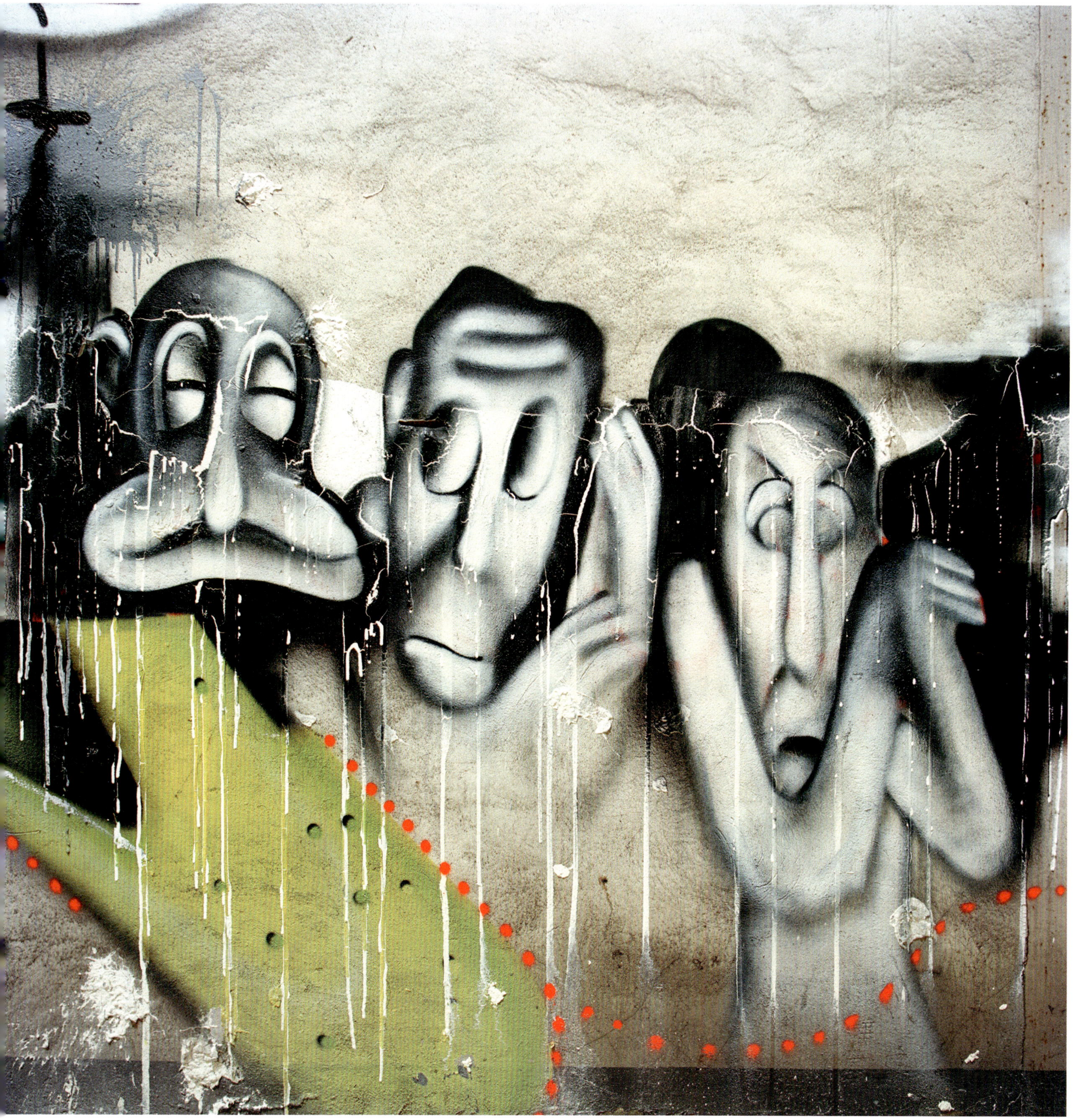

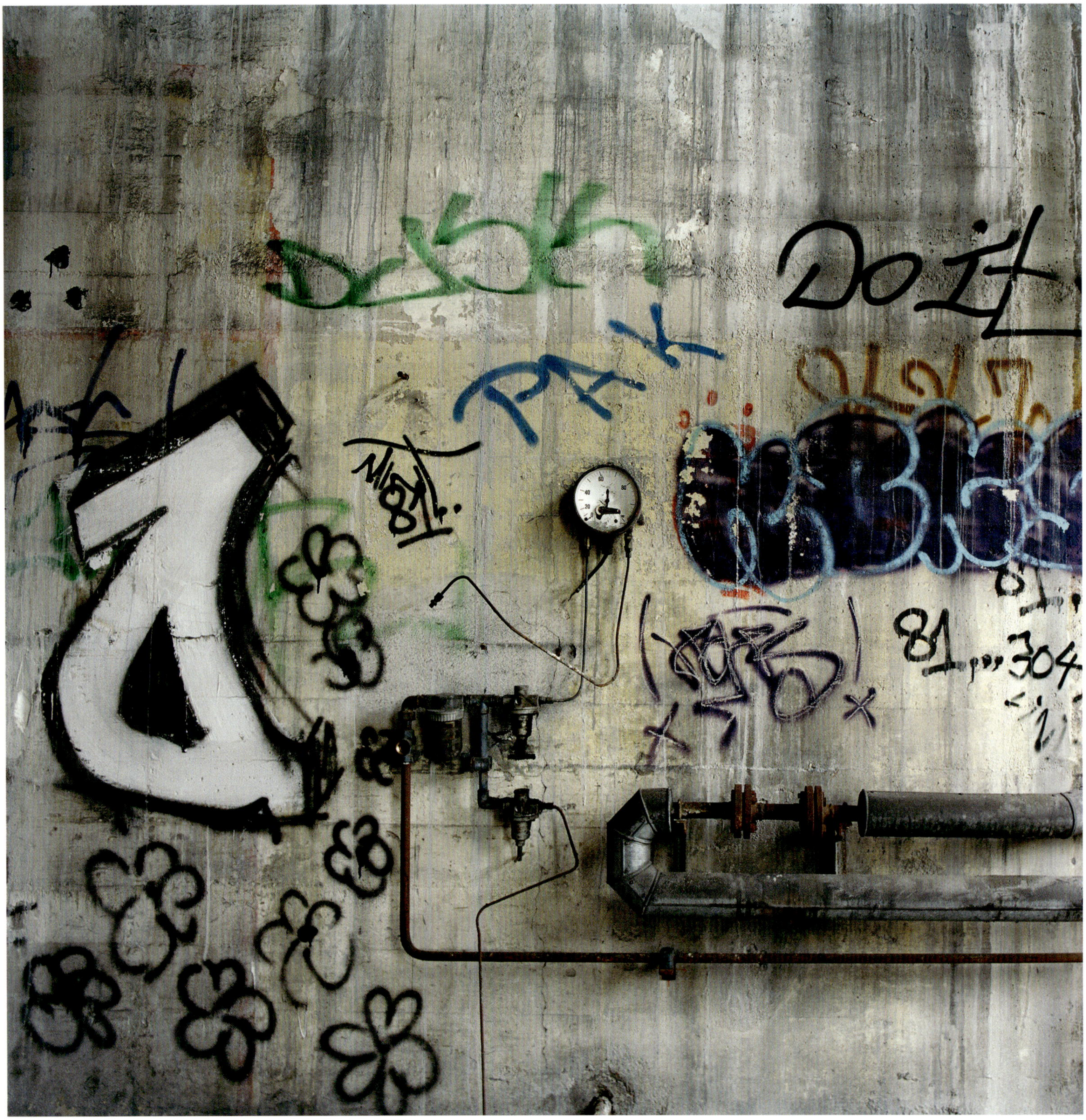

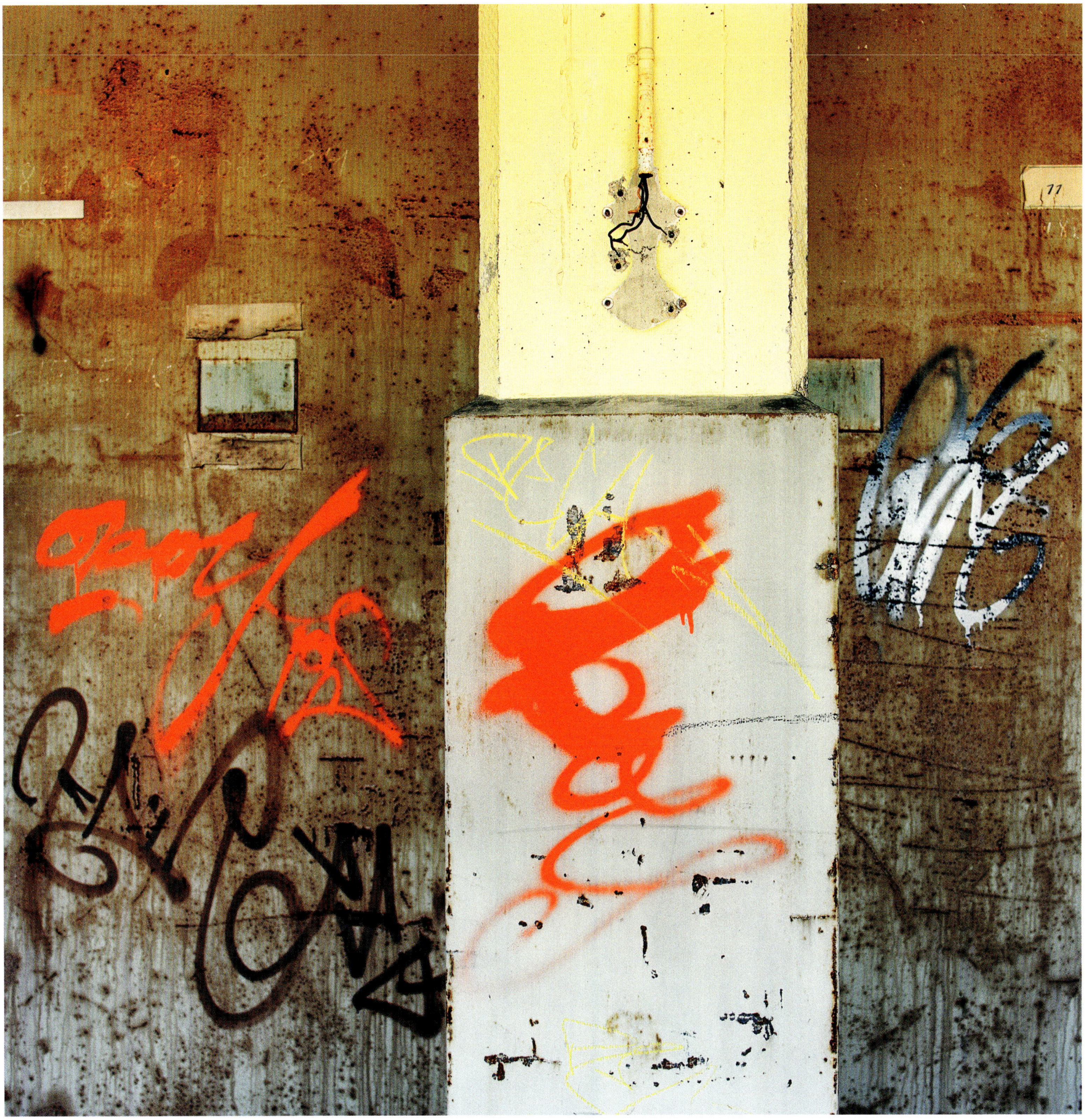

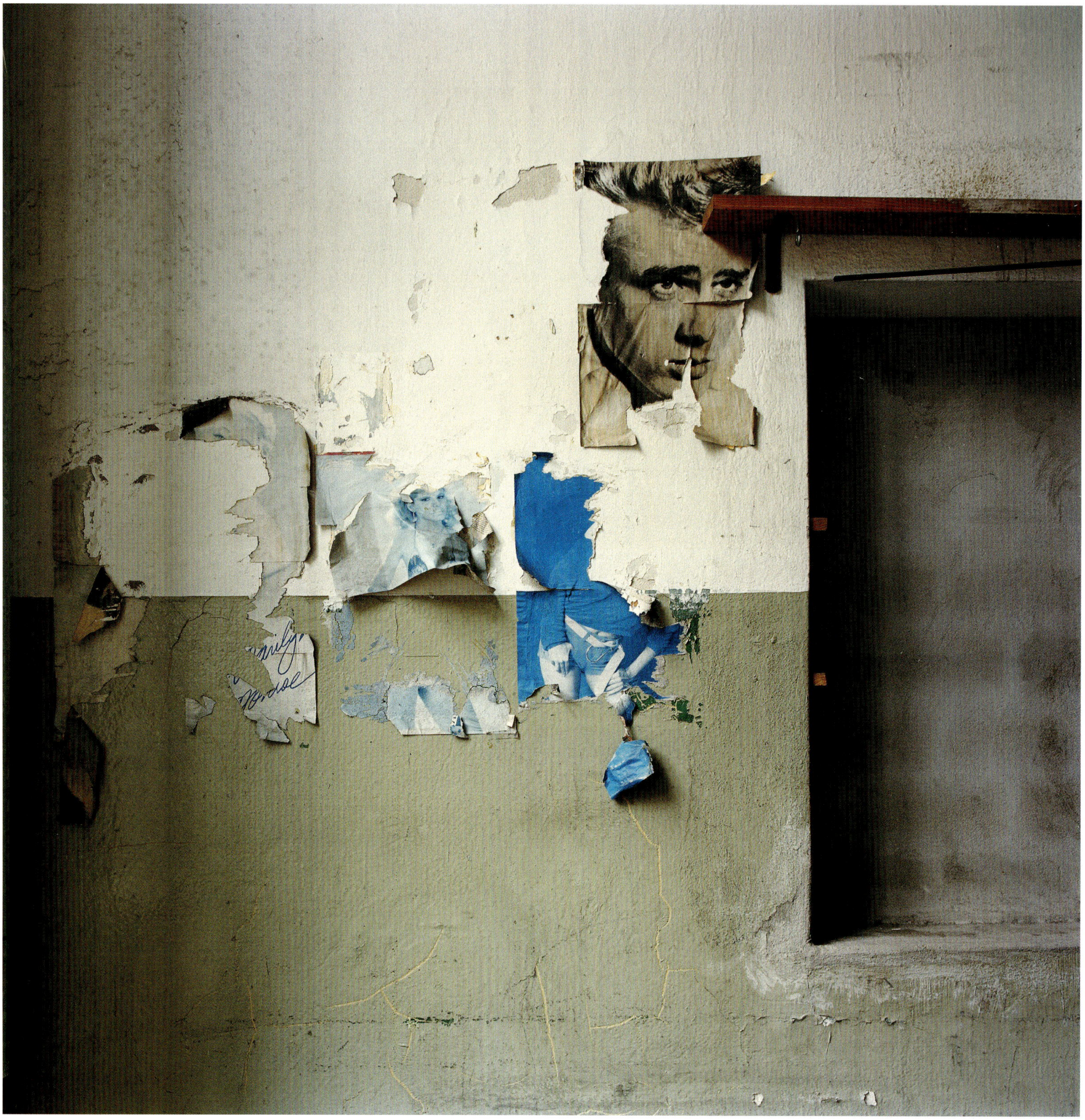

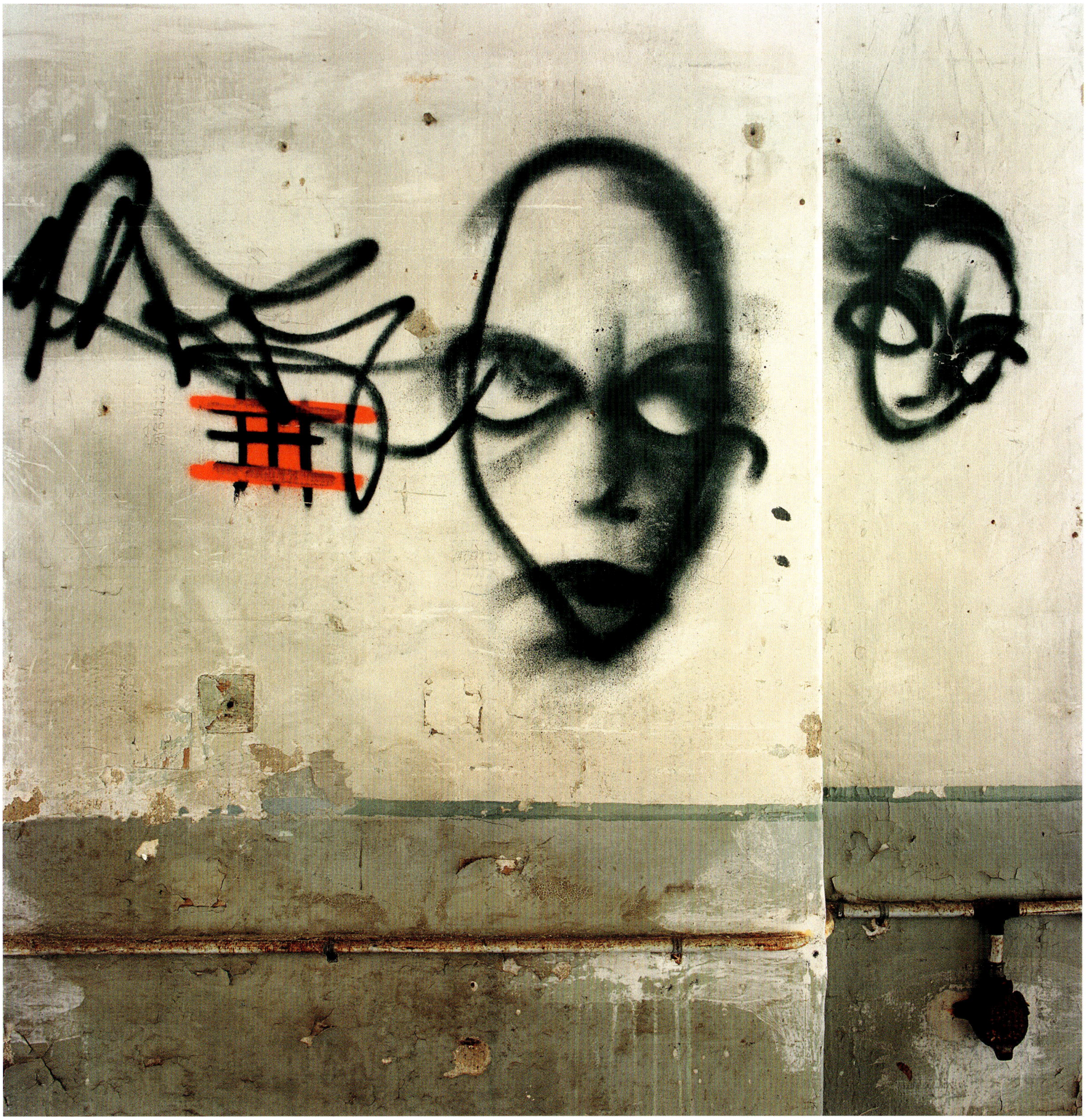

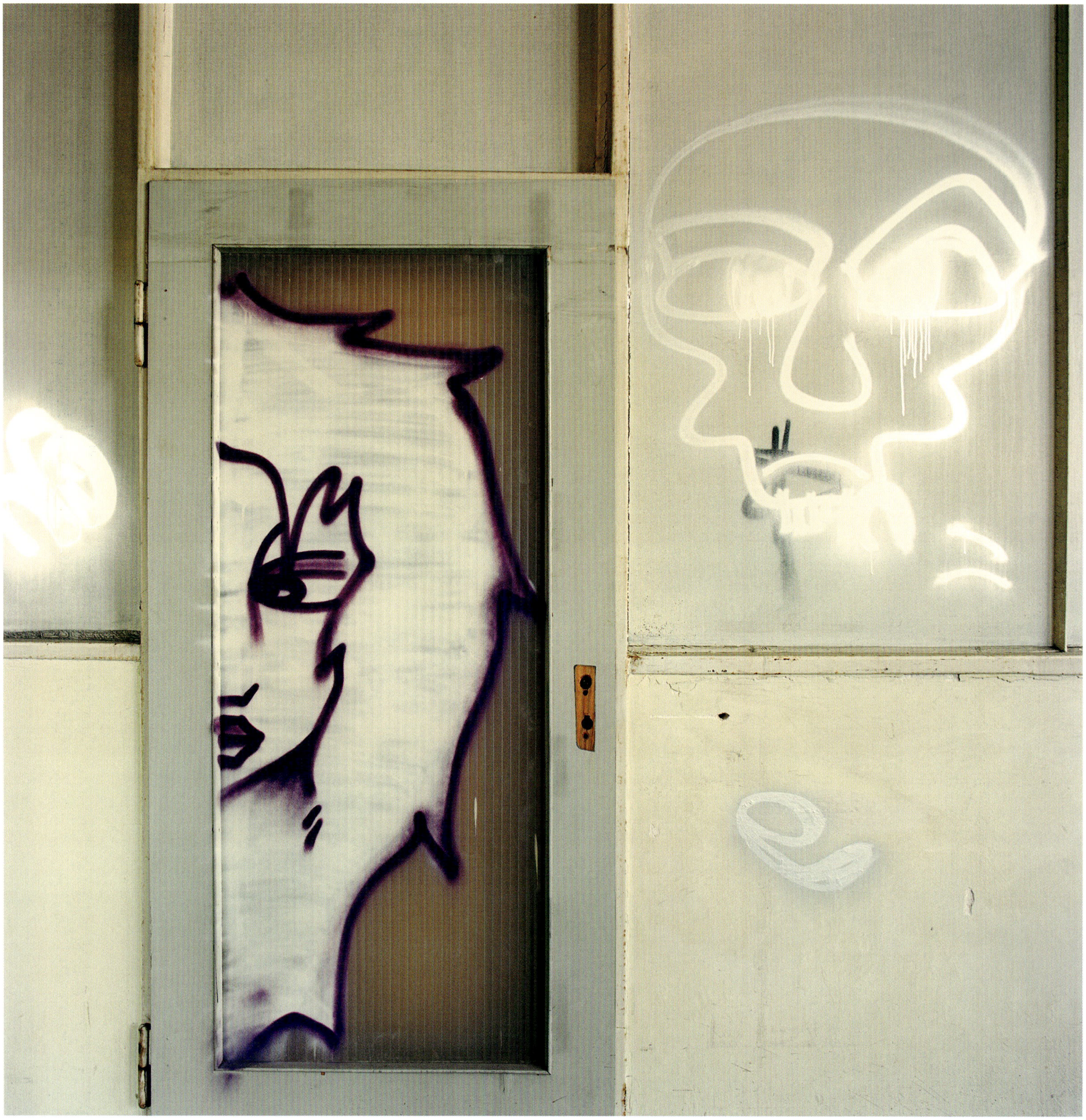

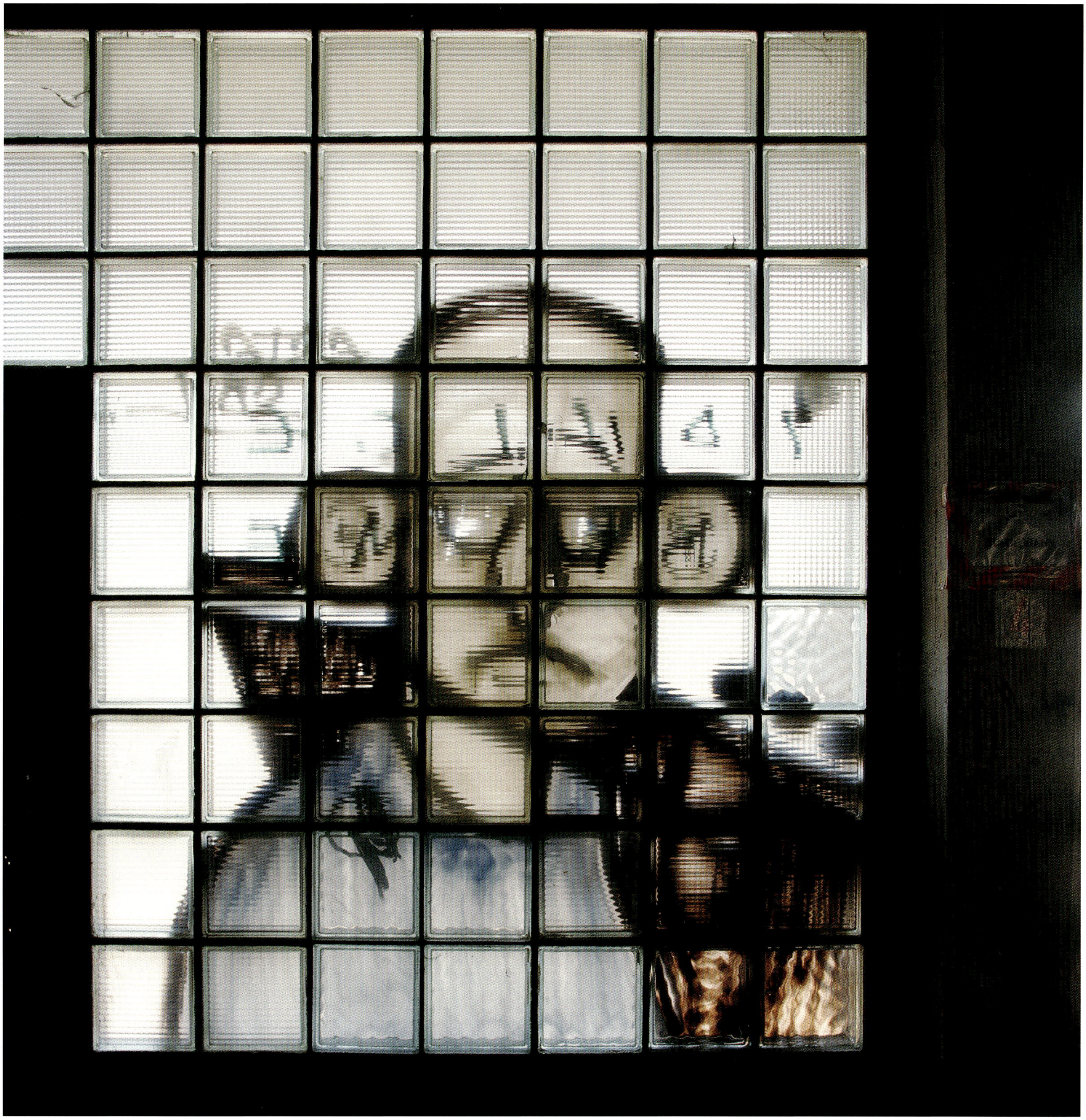

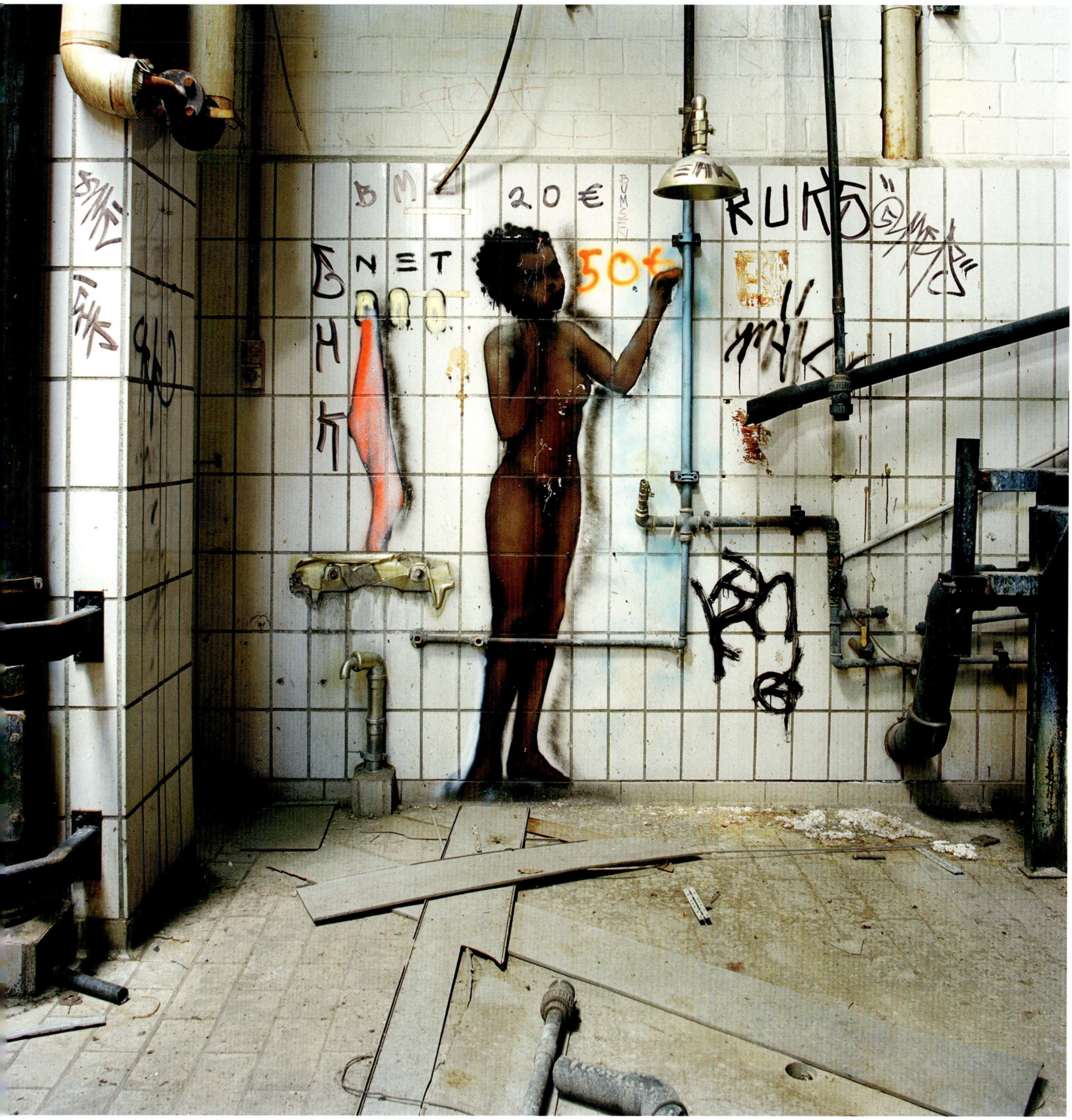
20 €
NET
50€

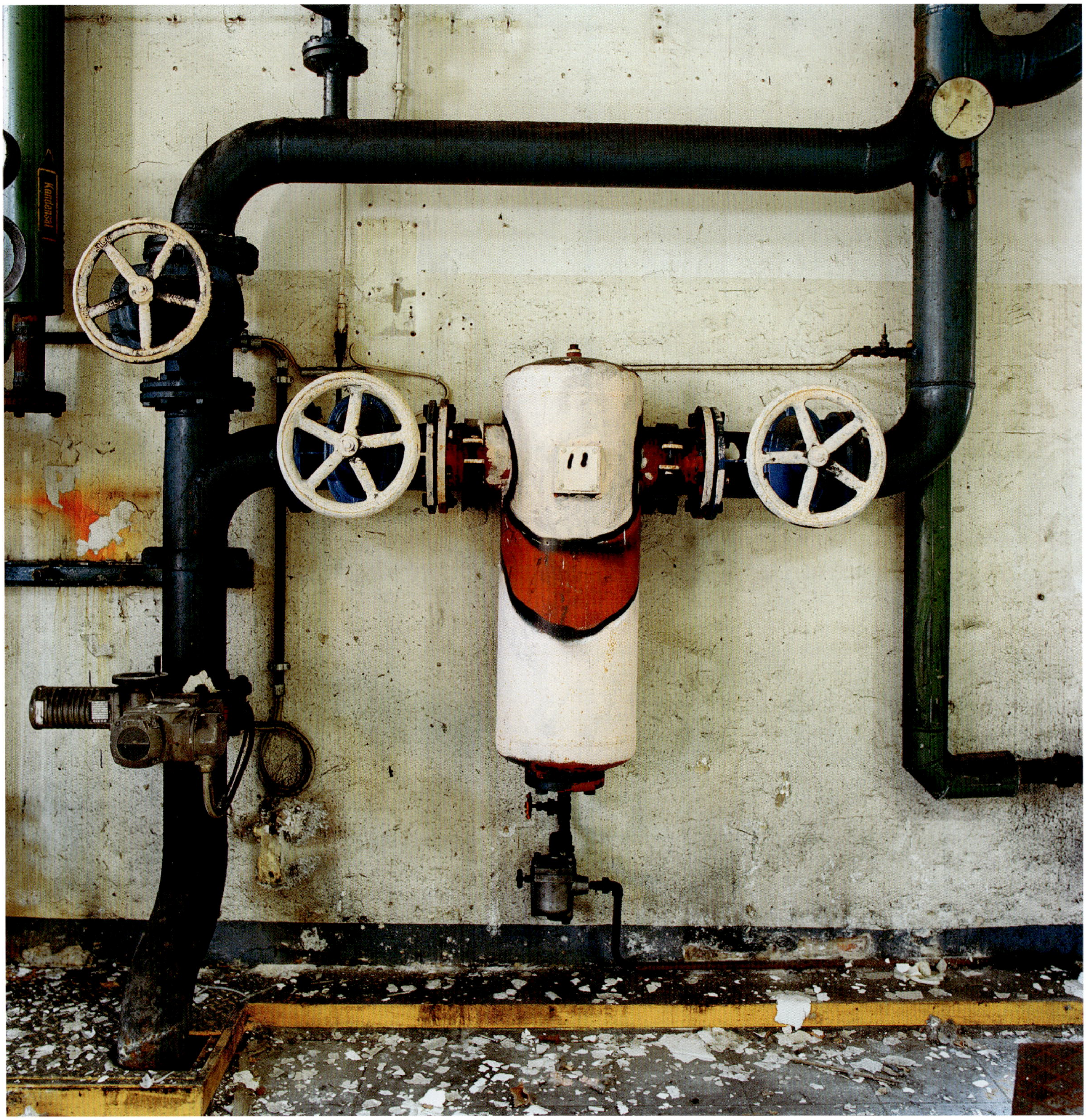

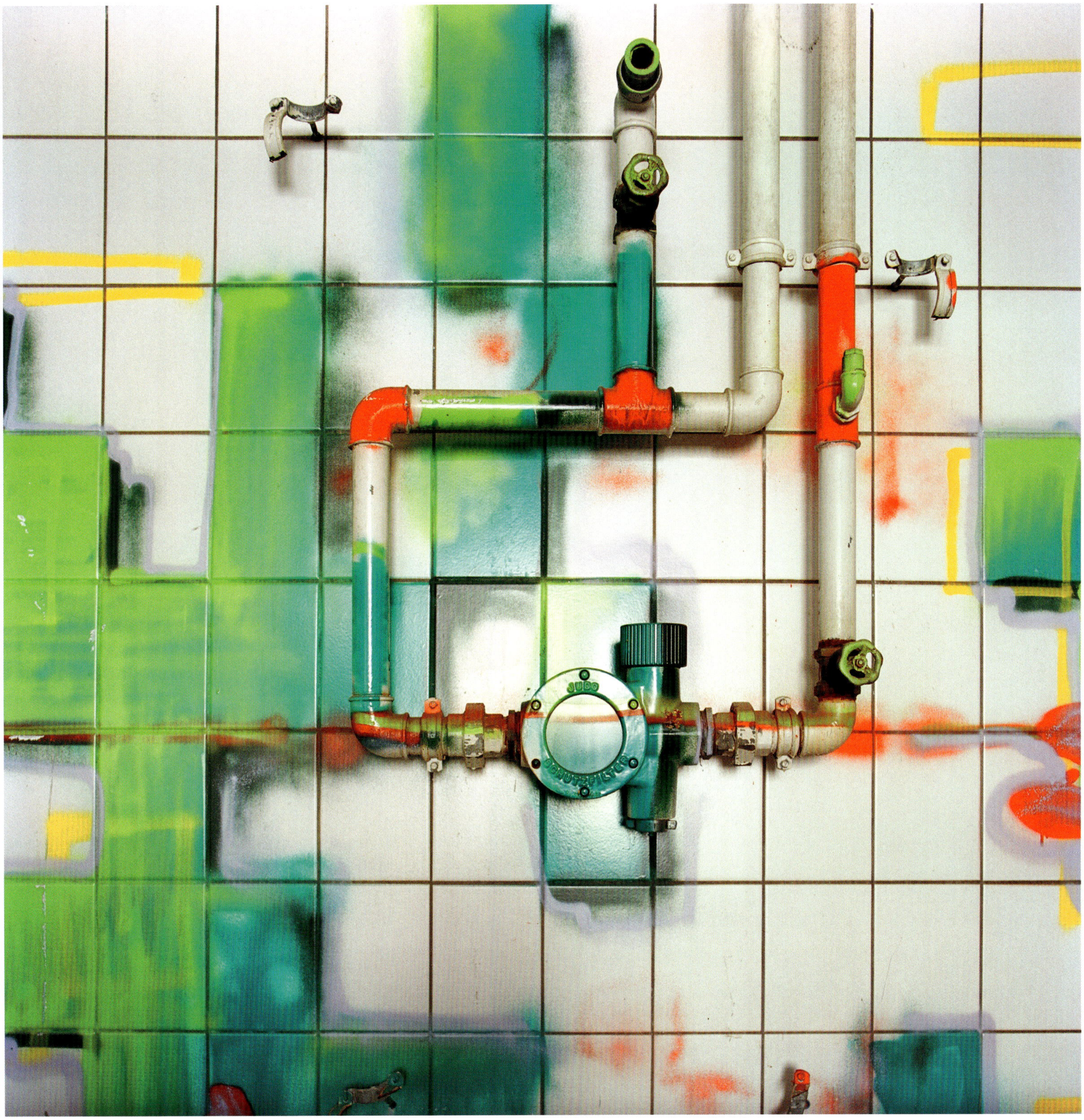
JUDO
SCHUTZFILTER

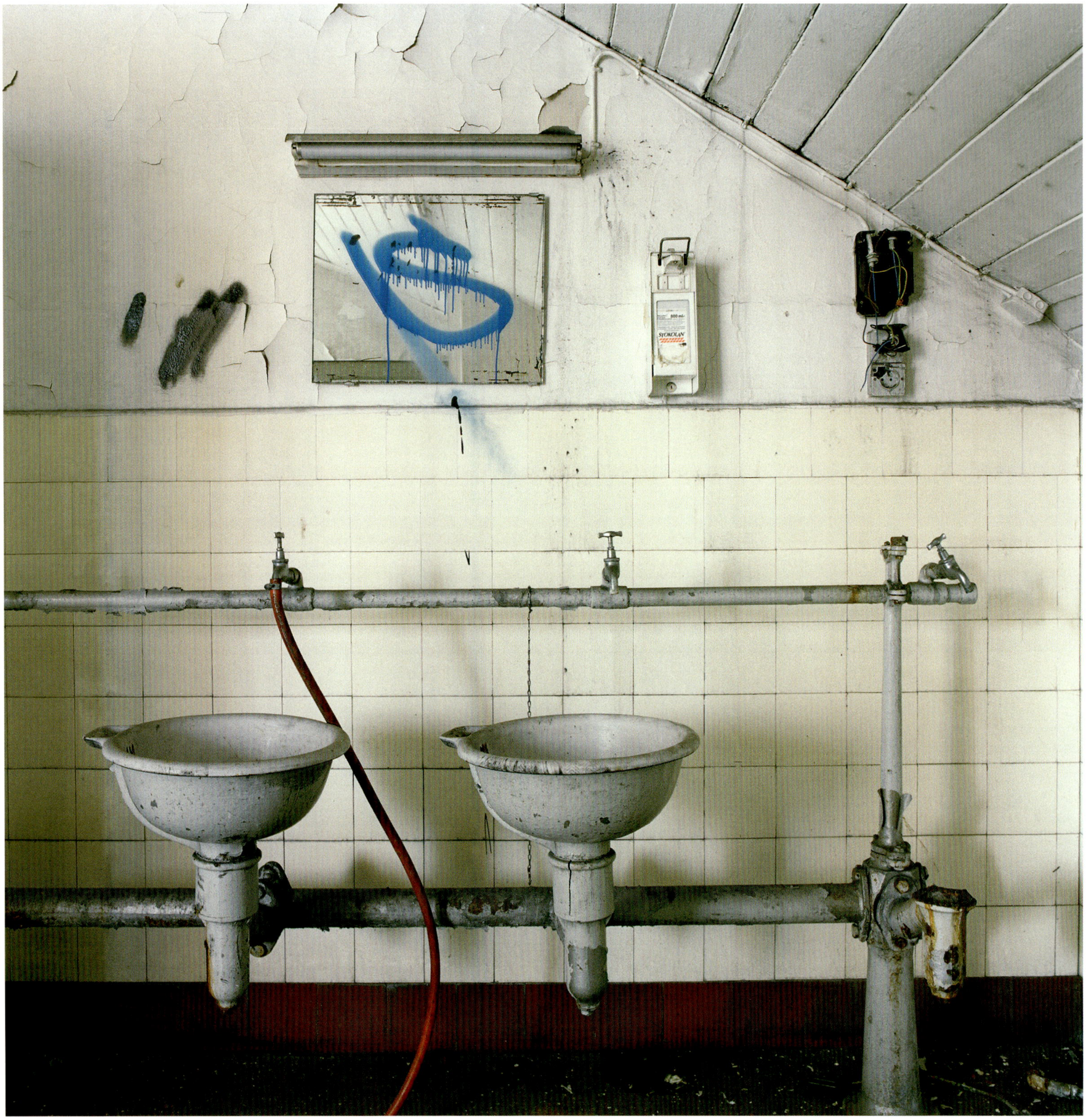

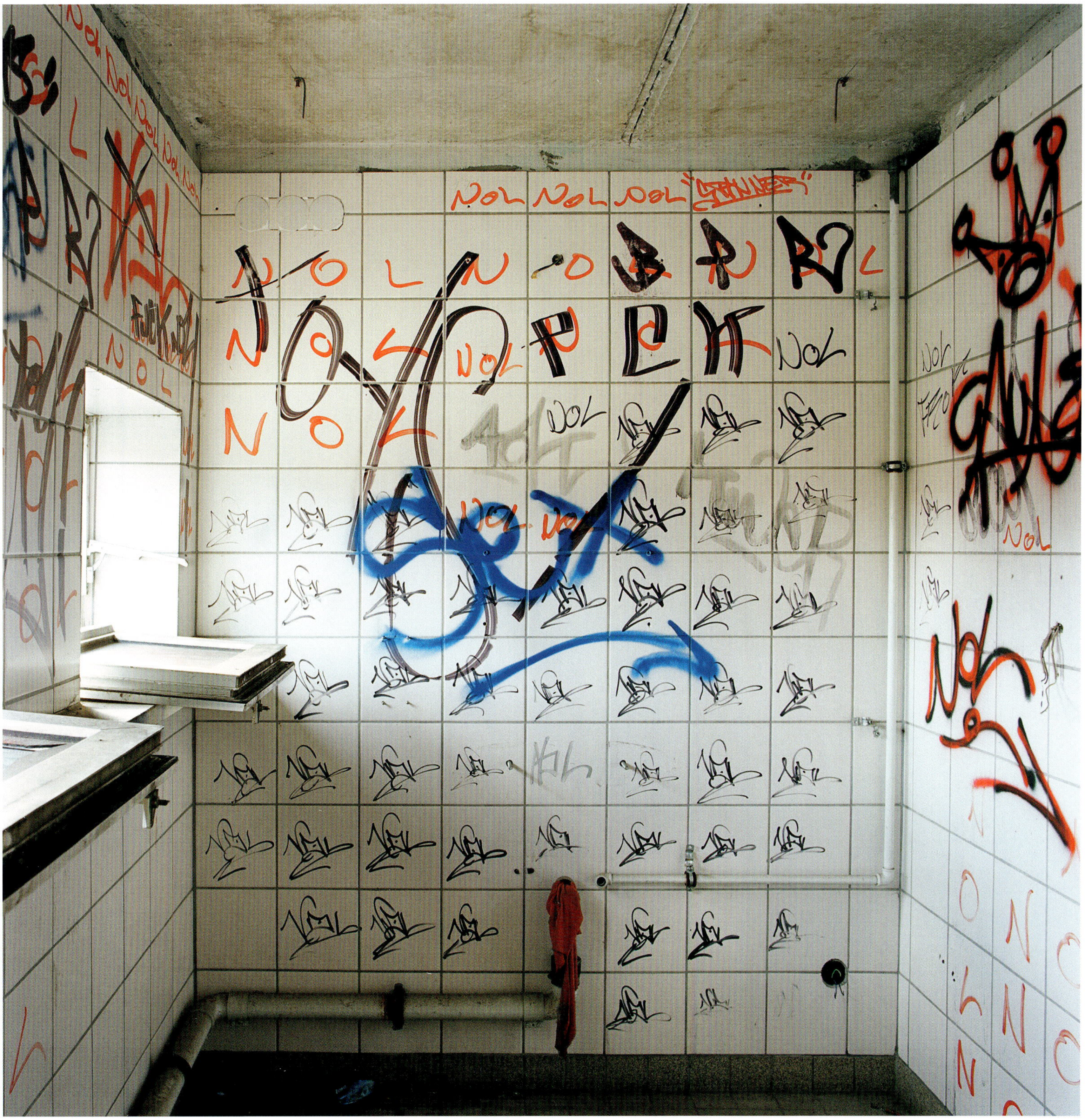

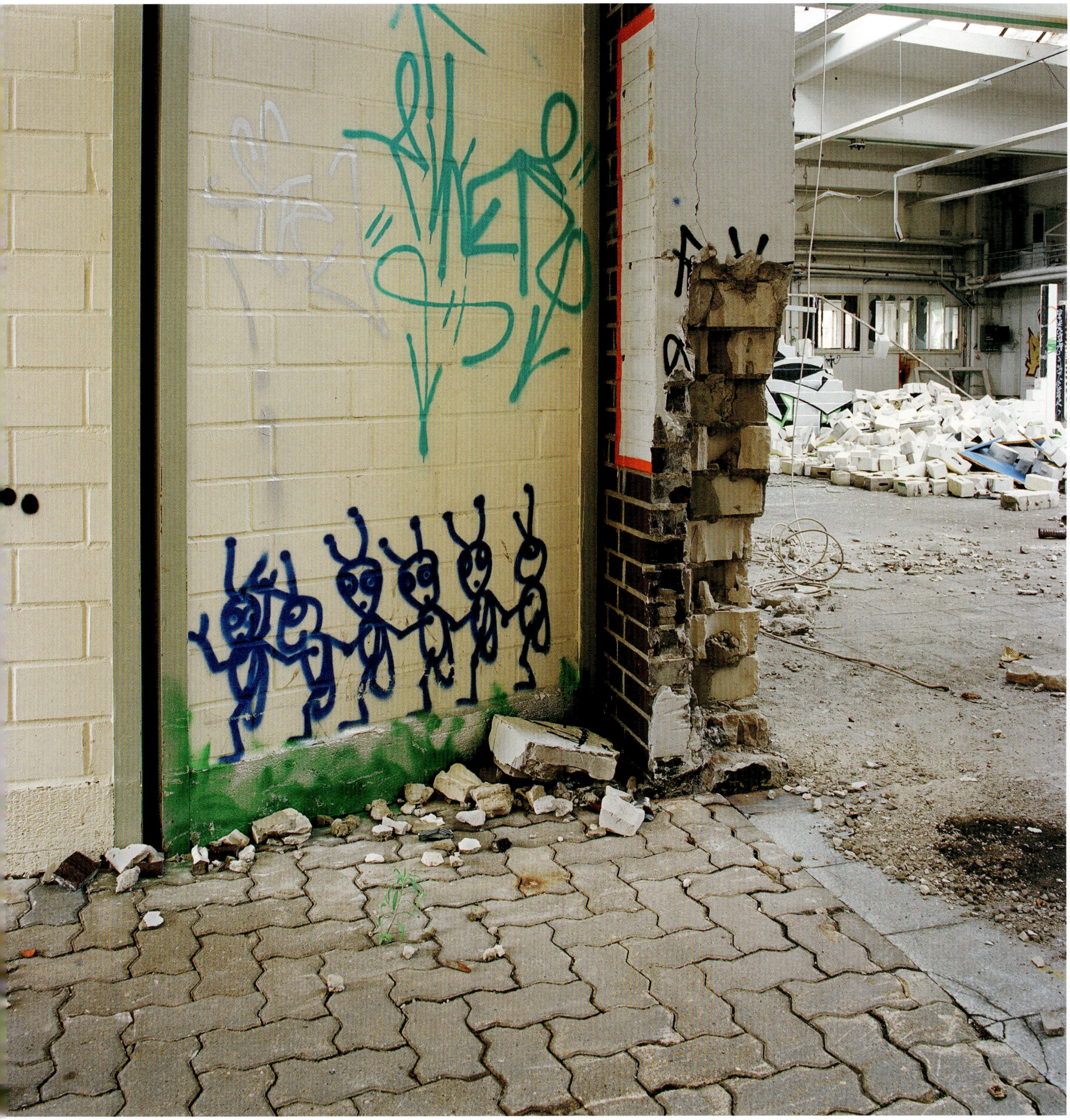

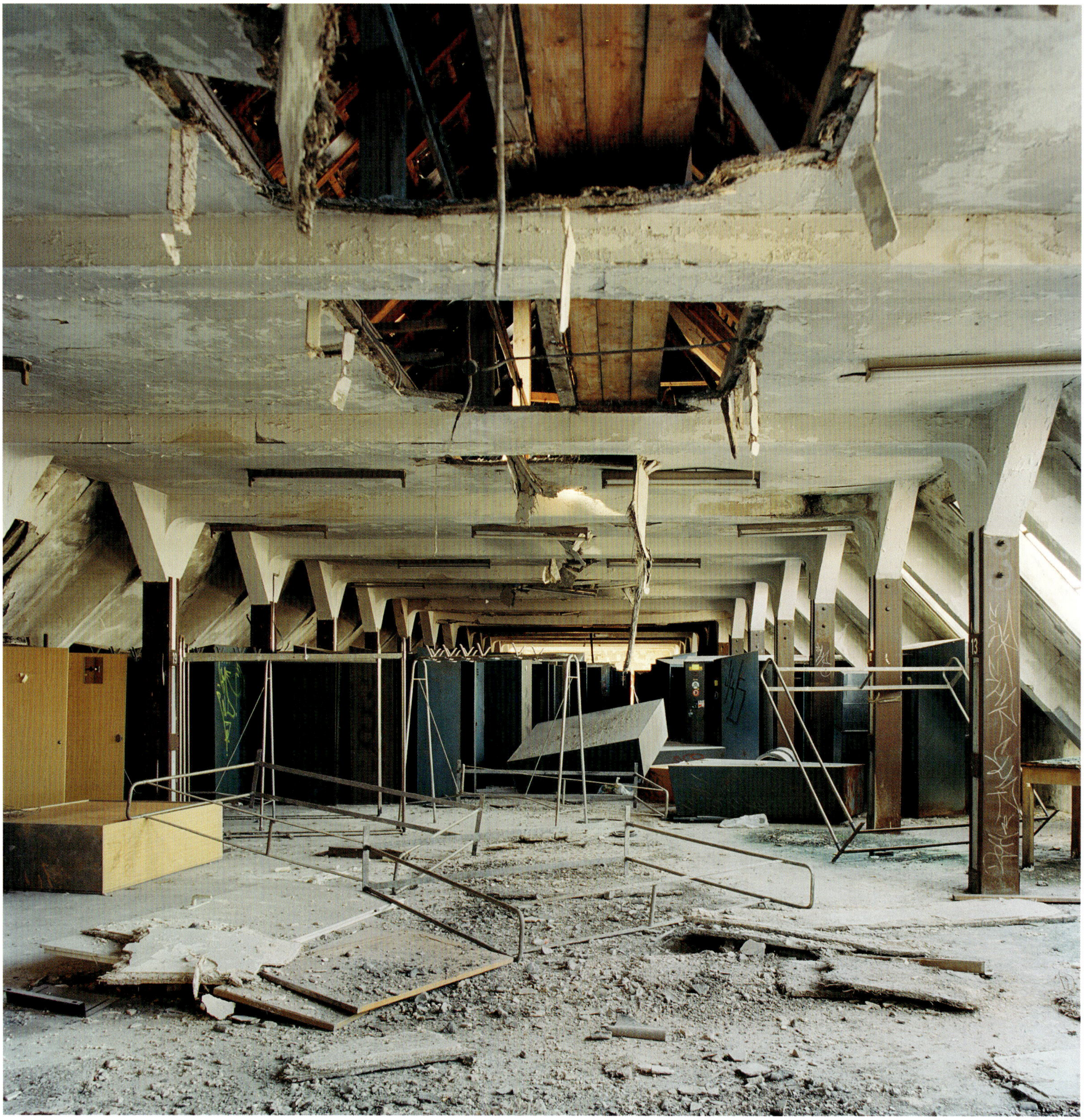

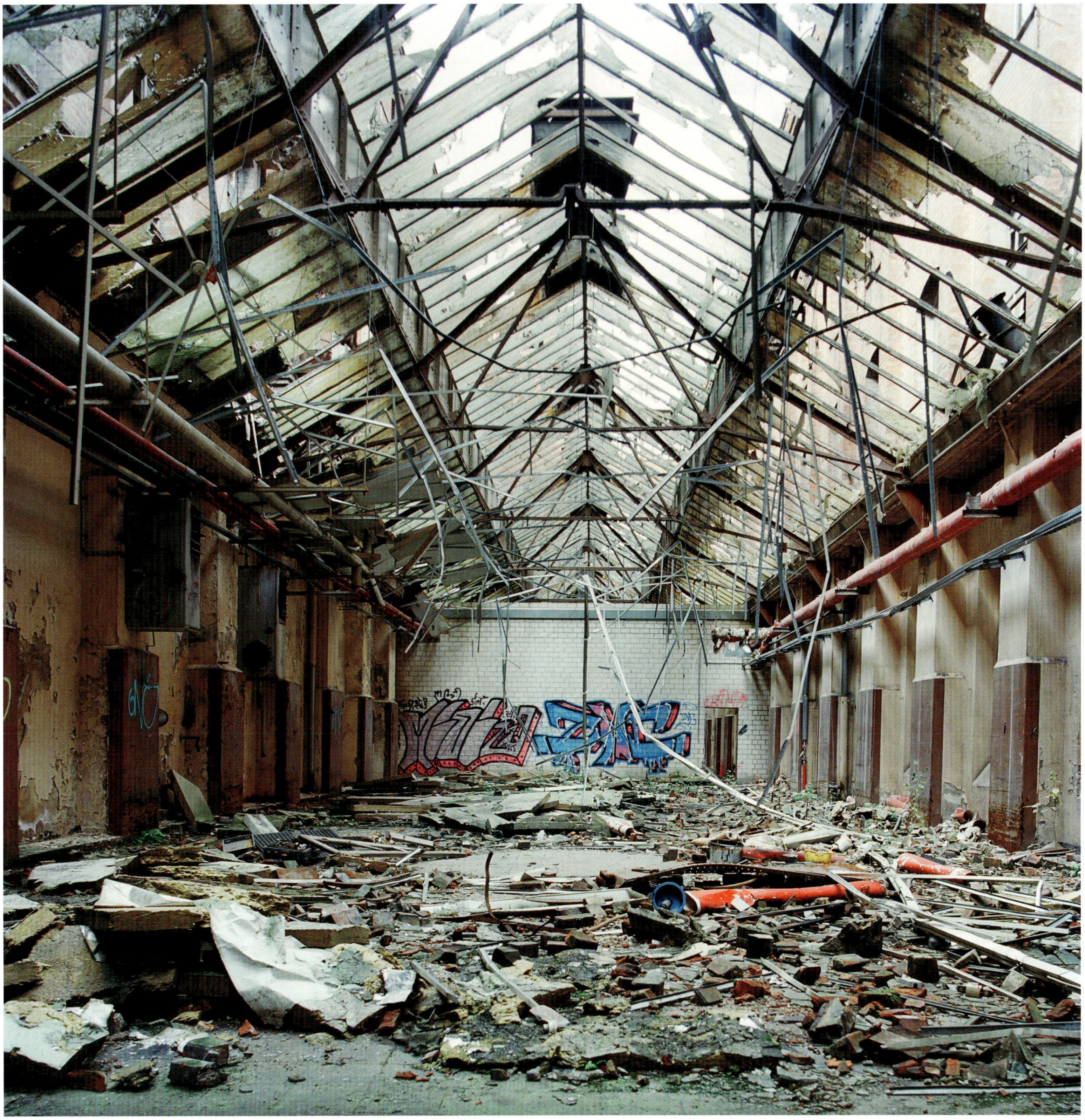

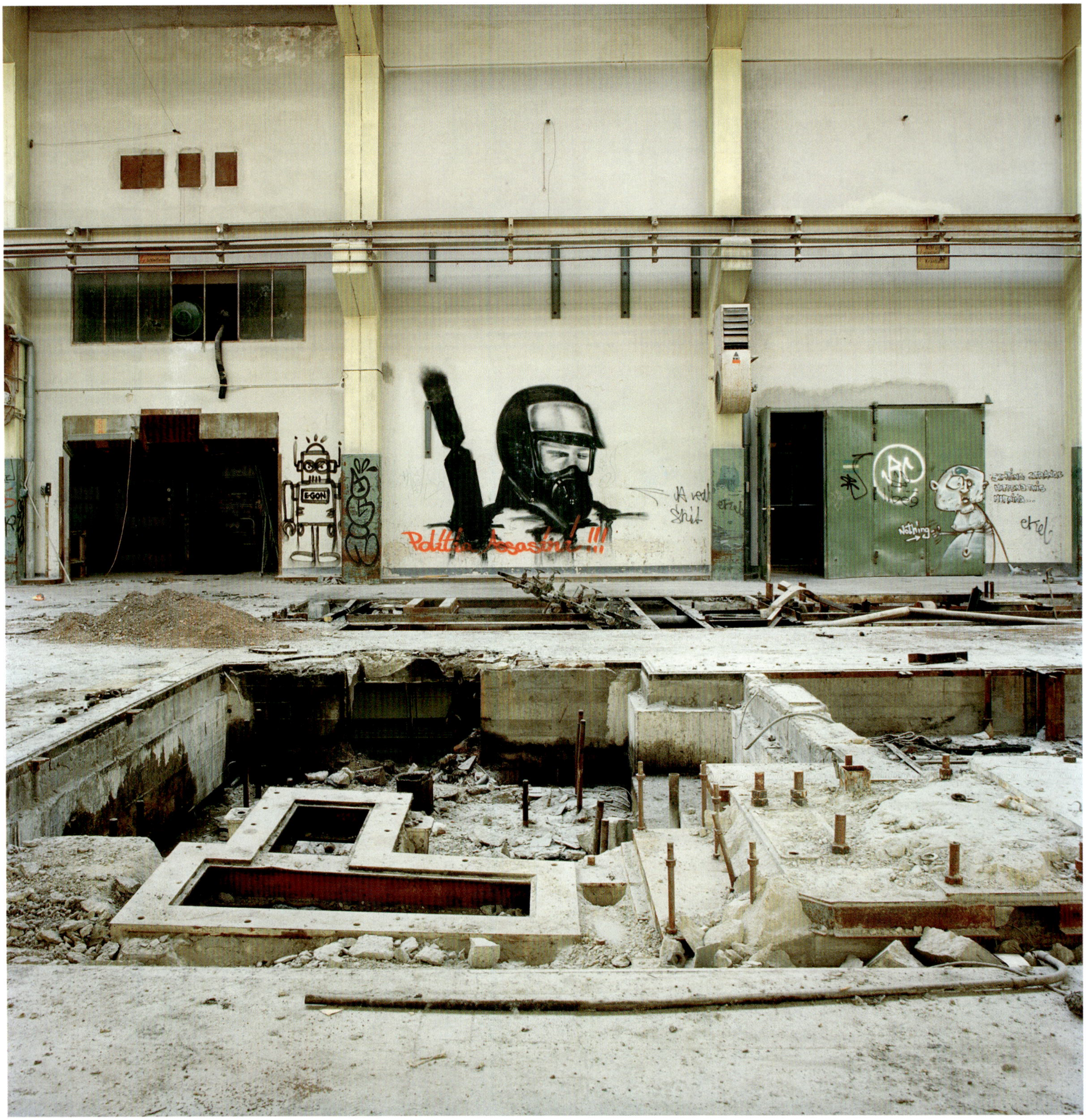

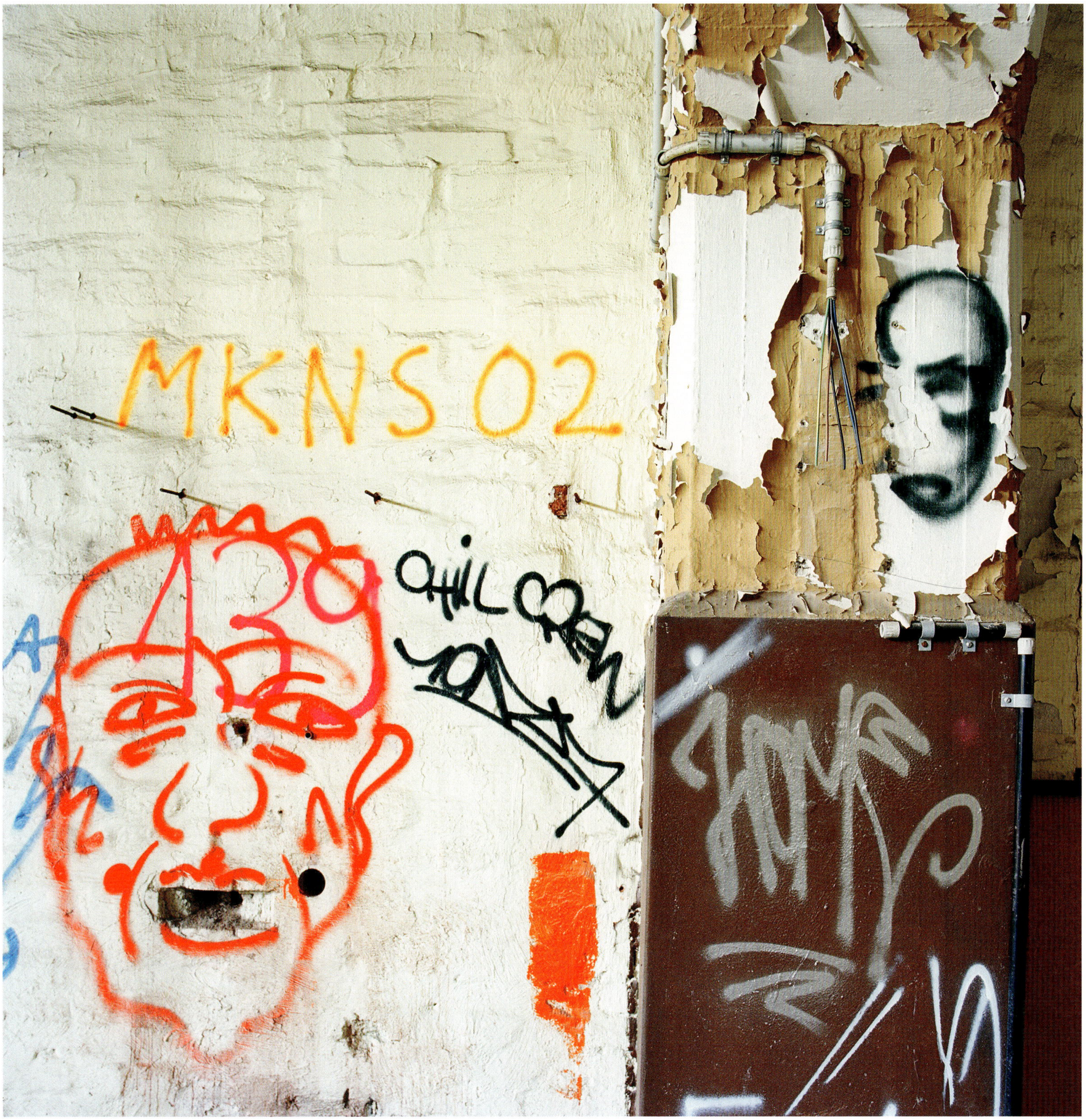
MKNS 02
CHIL CREW

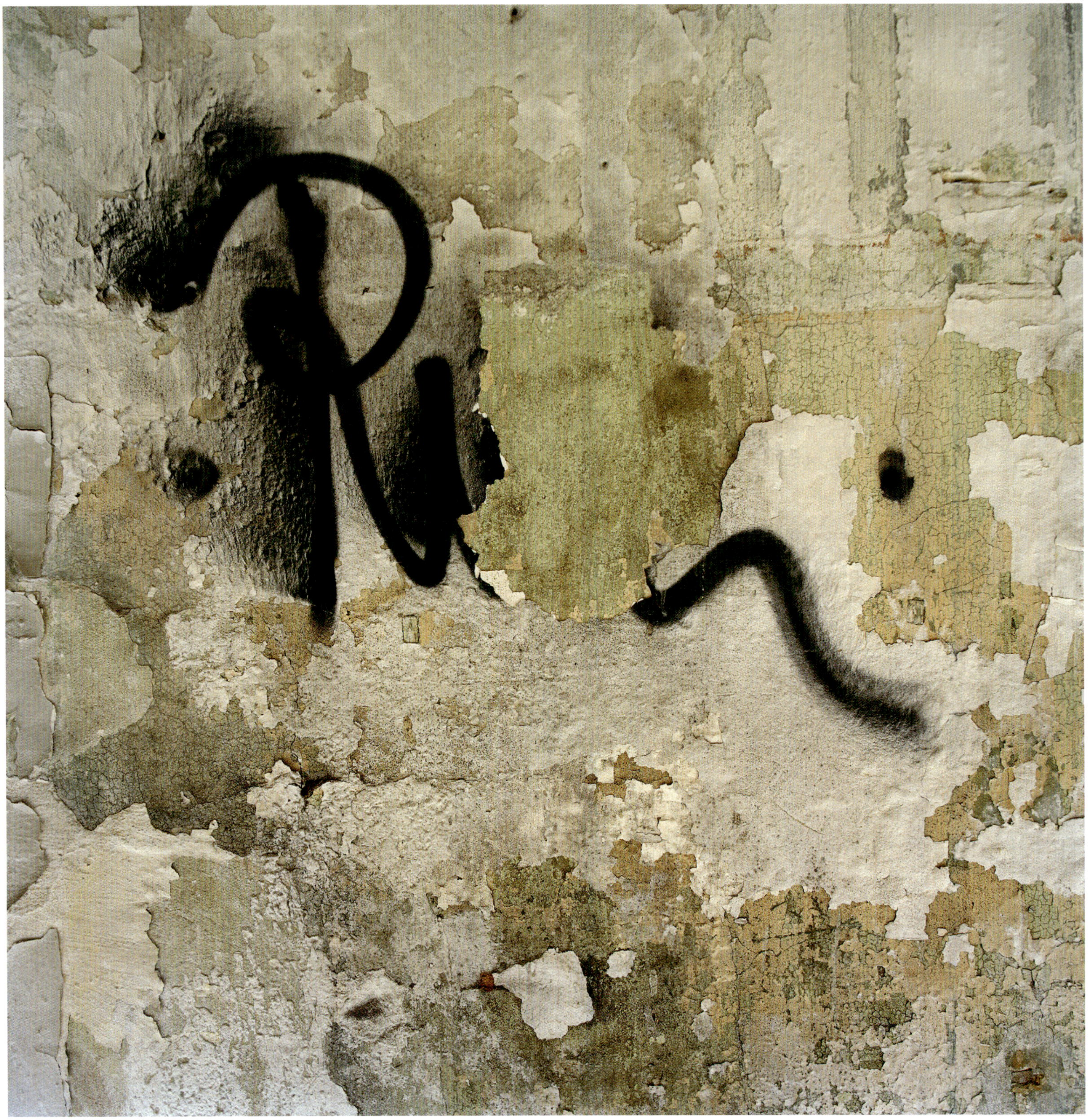

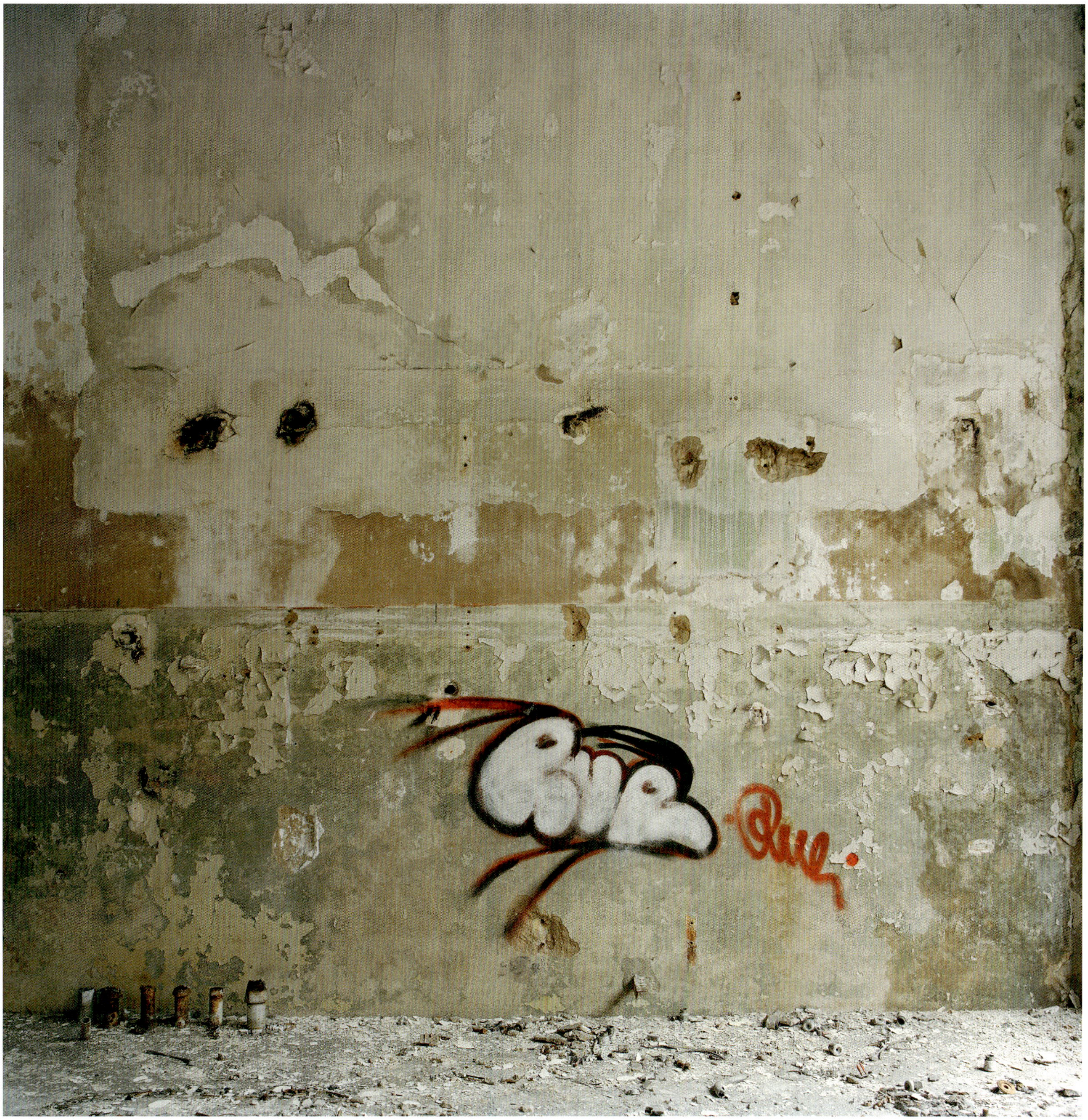

94

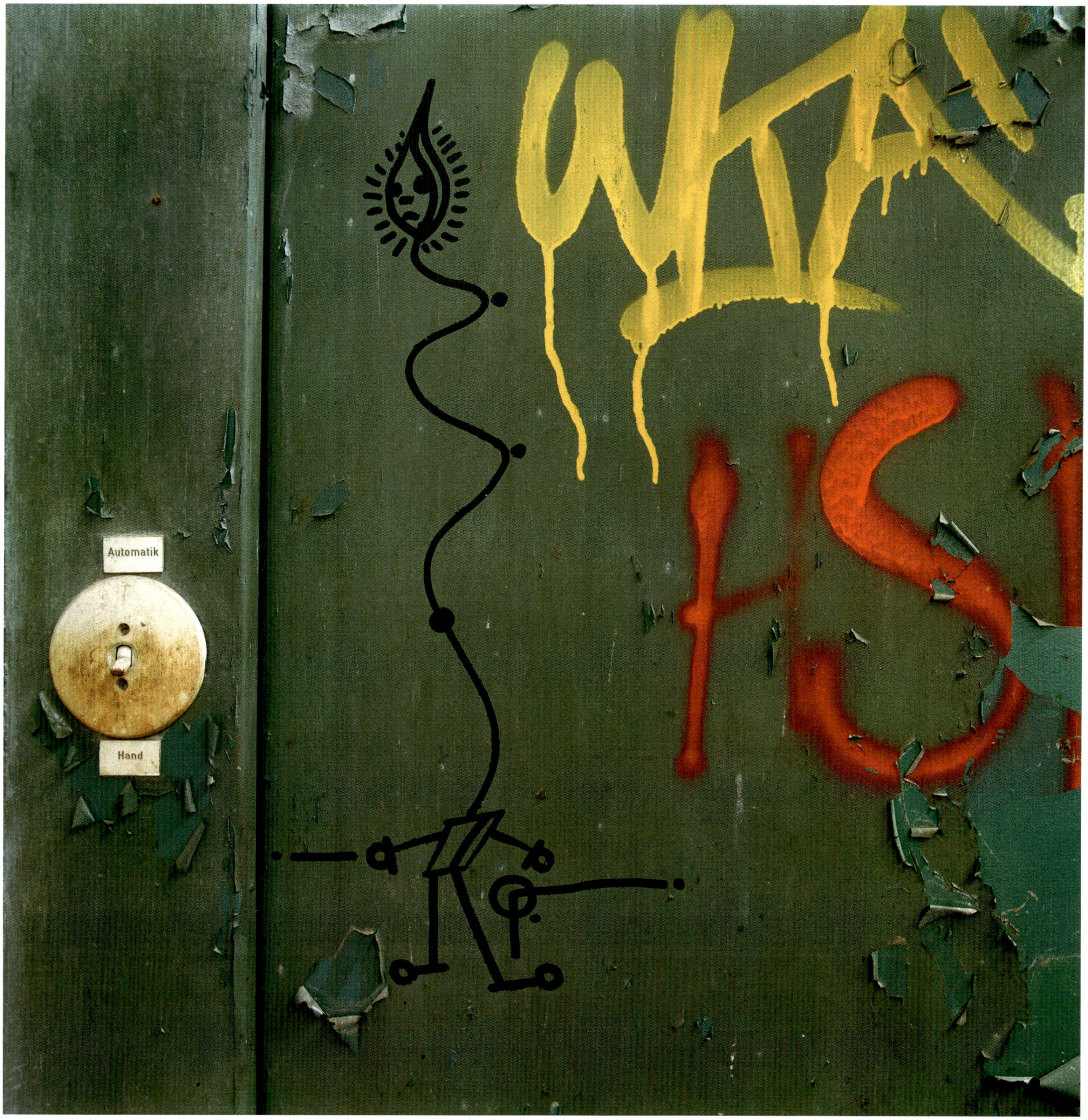
Automatik
Hand

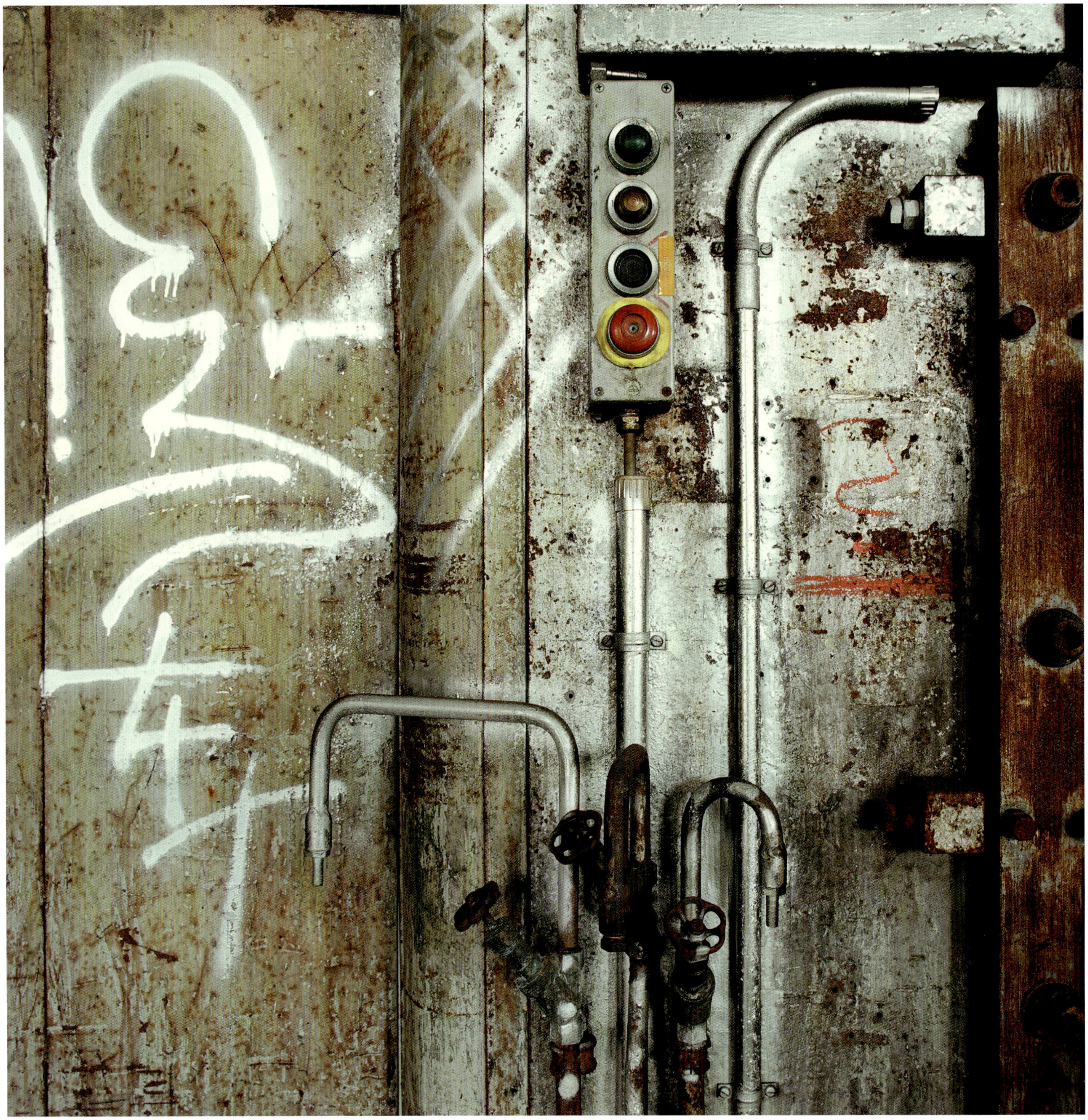

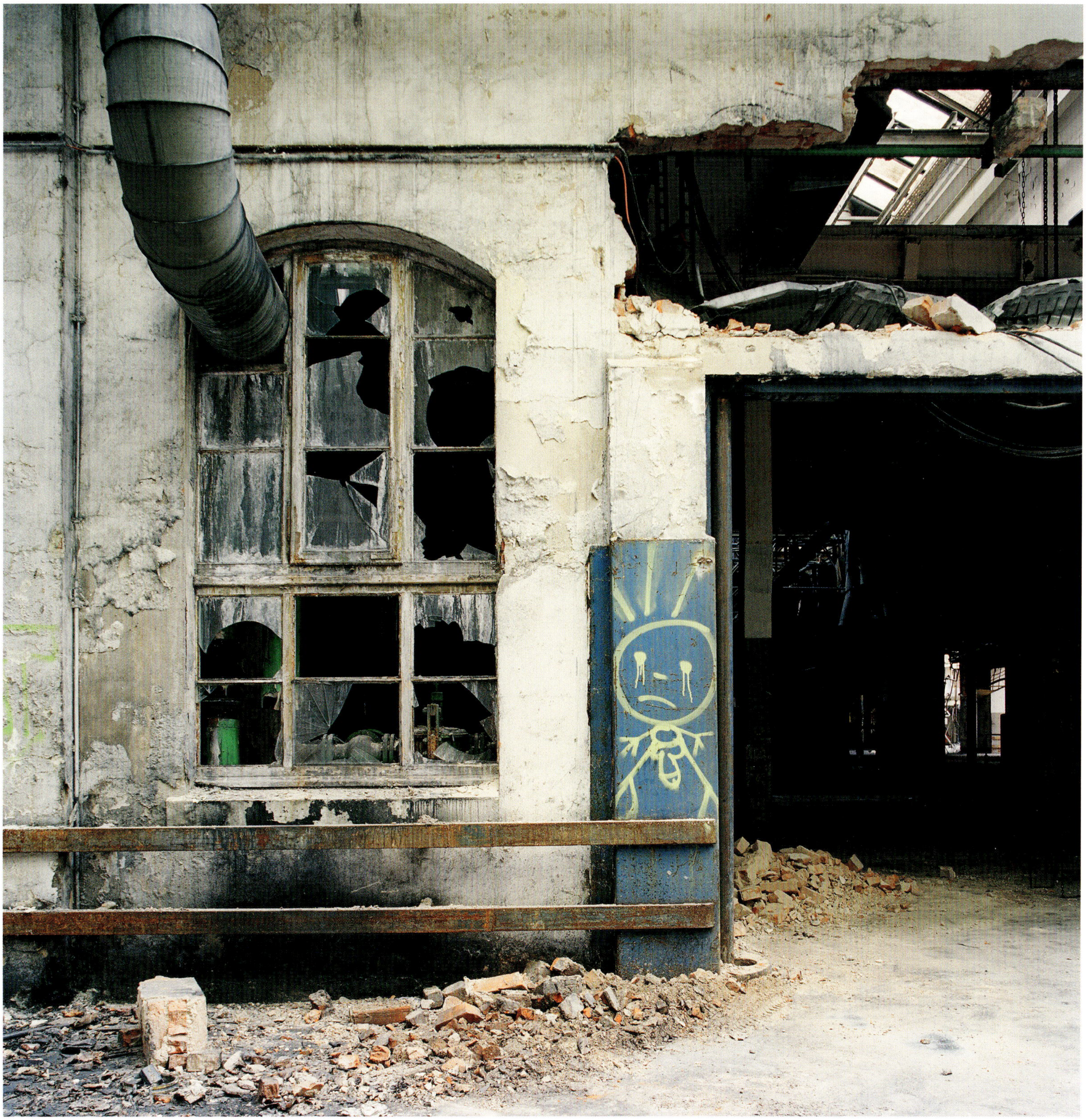

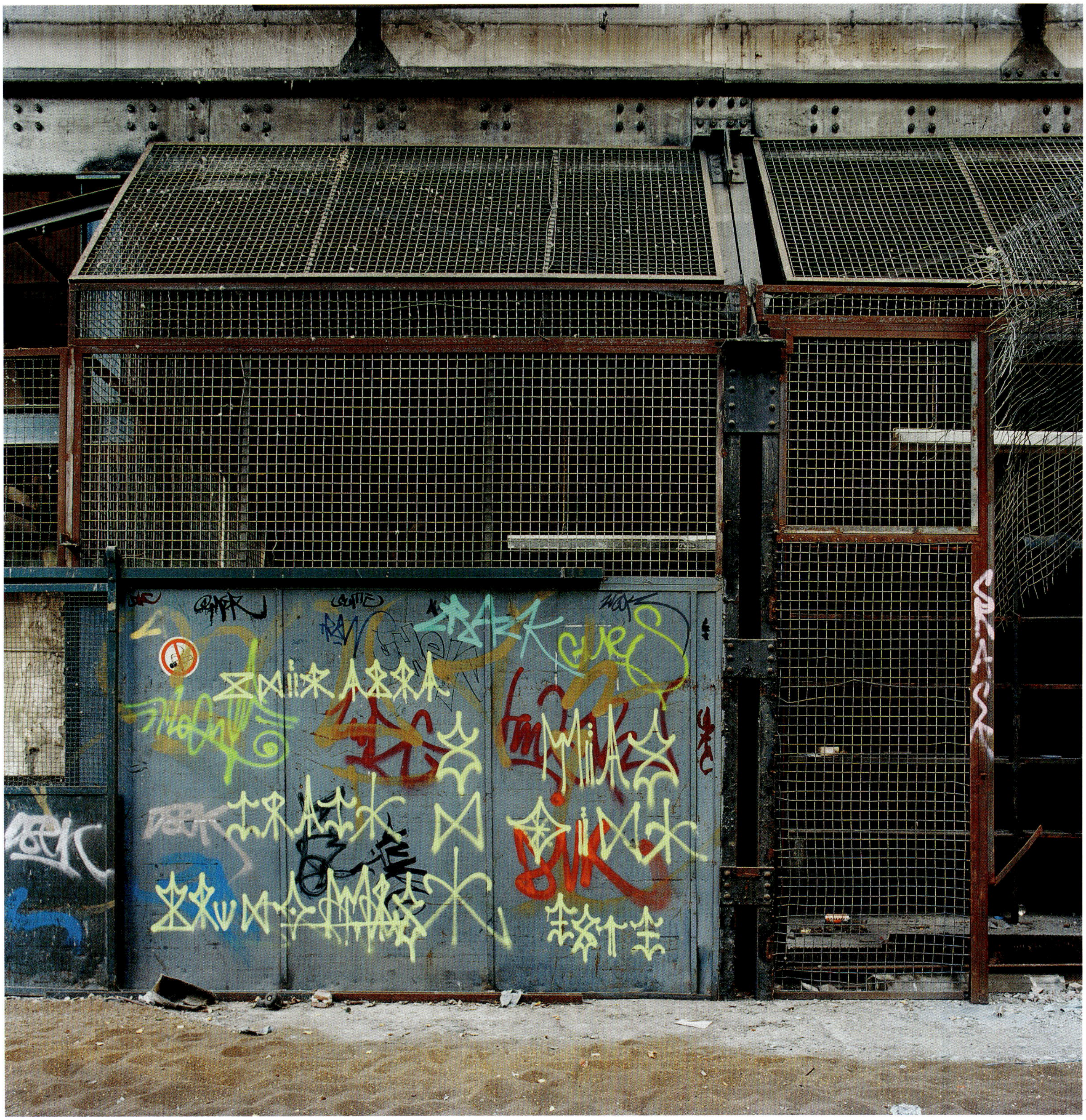

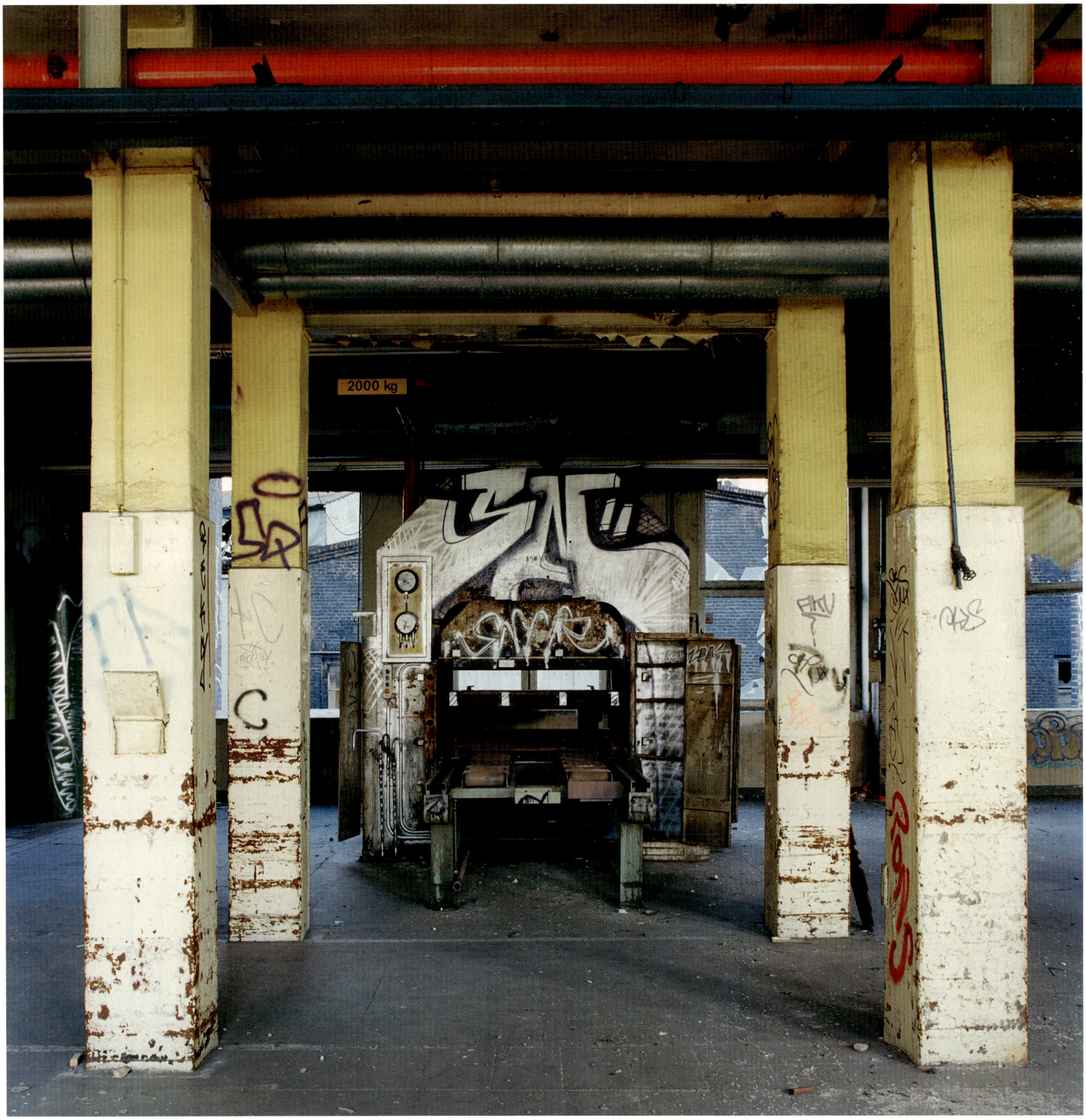
2000 kg

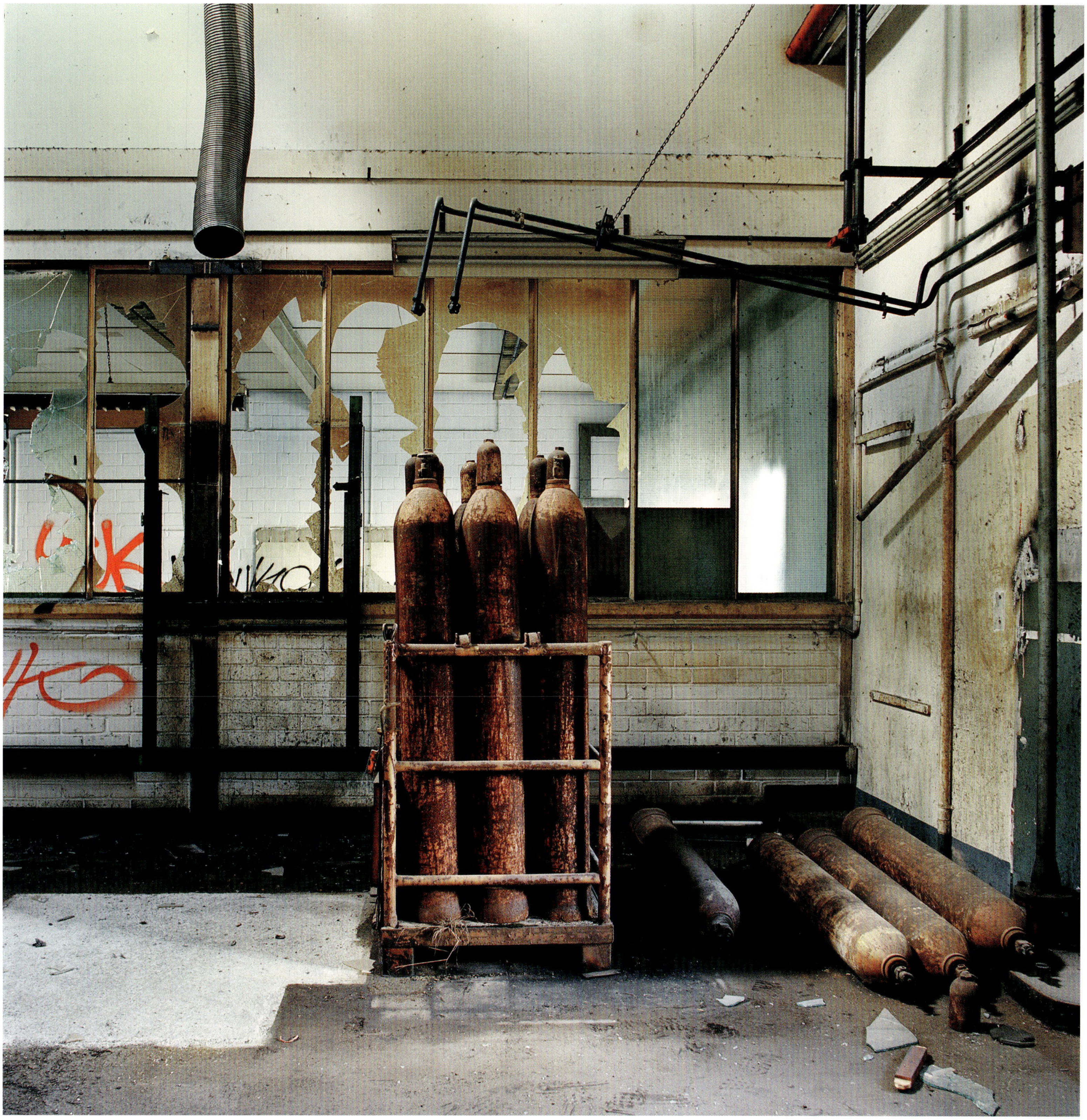

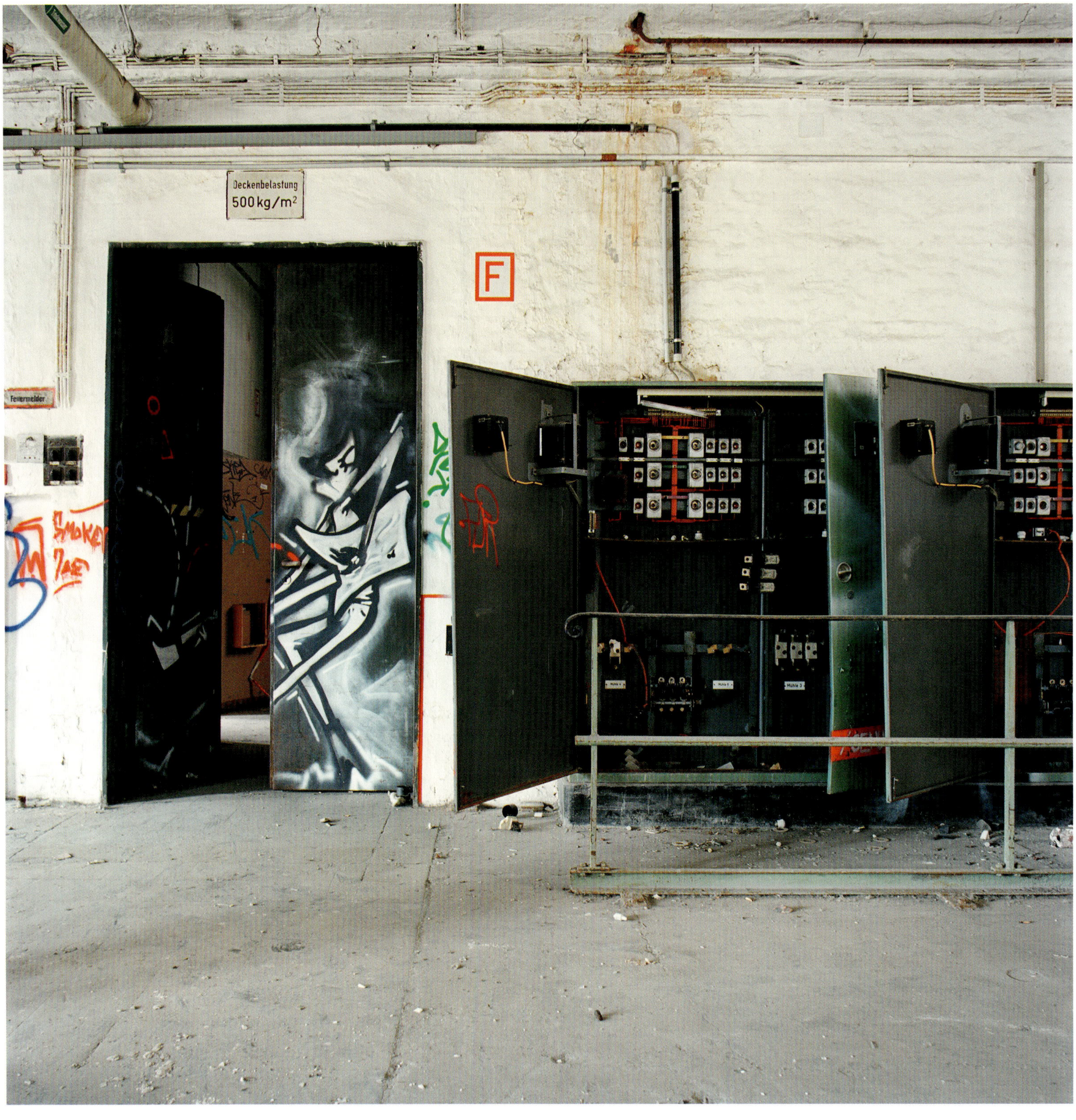
Deckenbelastung
500 kg/m²
F
Feuermelder

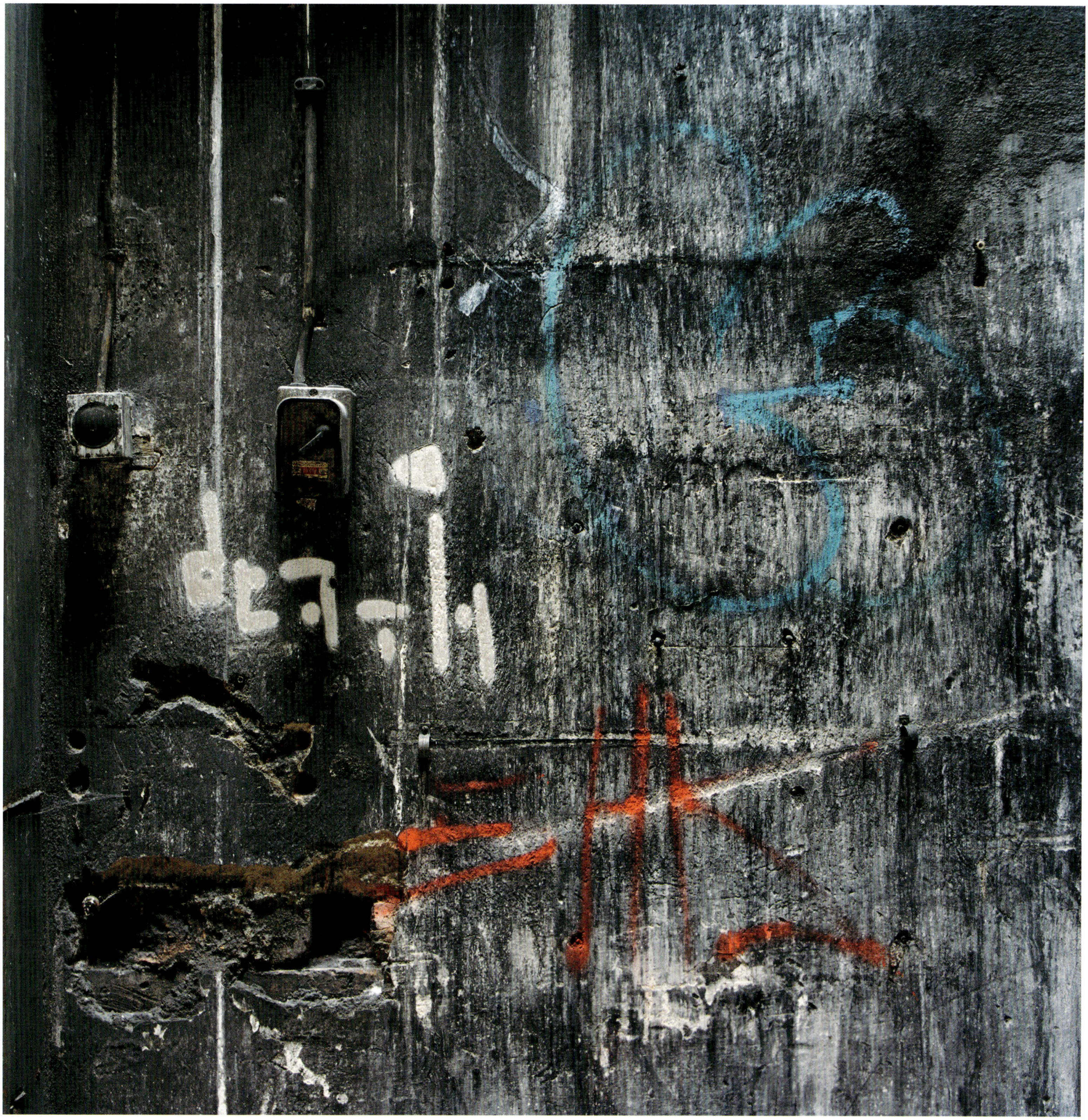

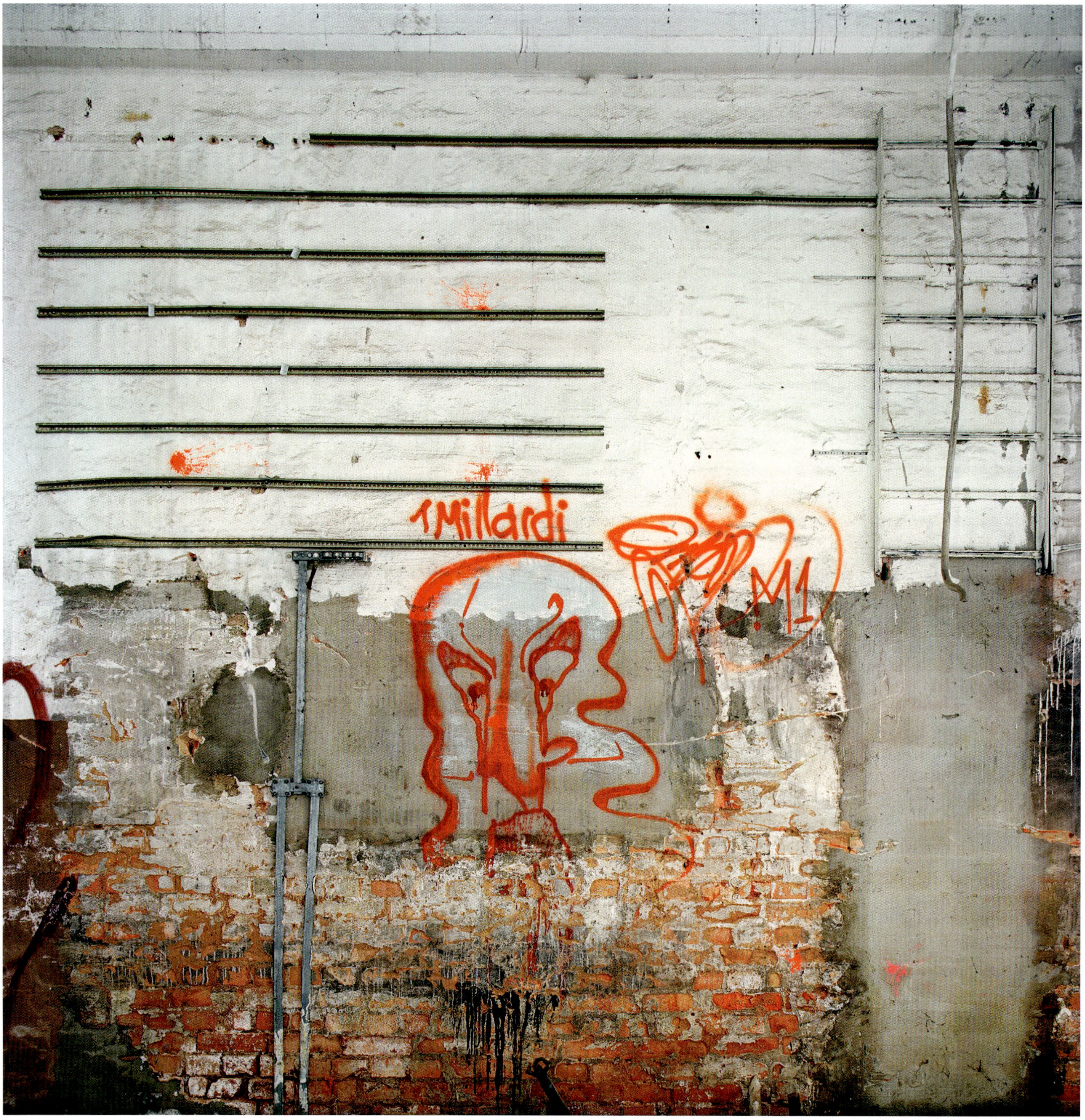
1 Millardi
M1

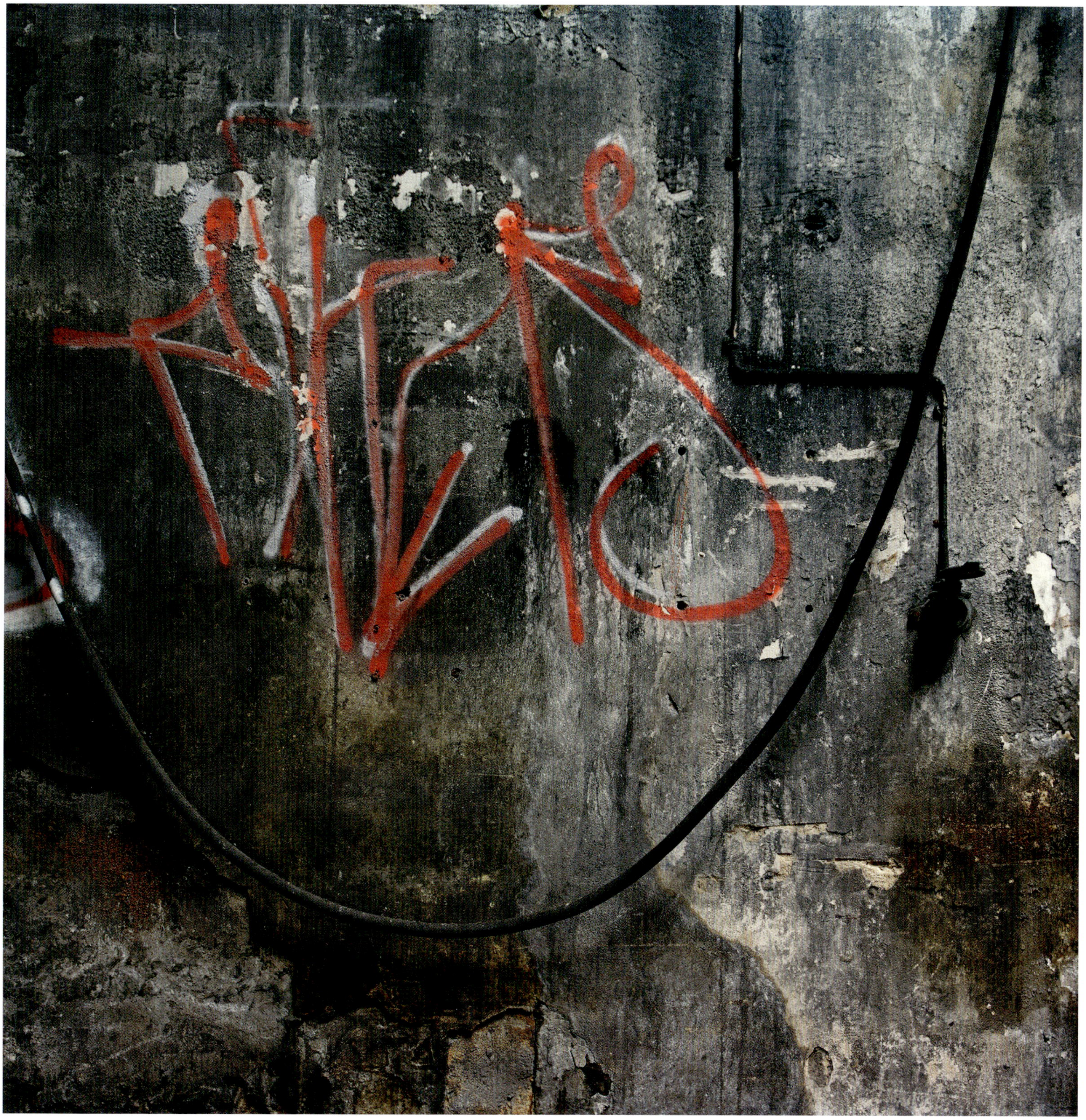

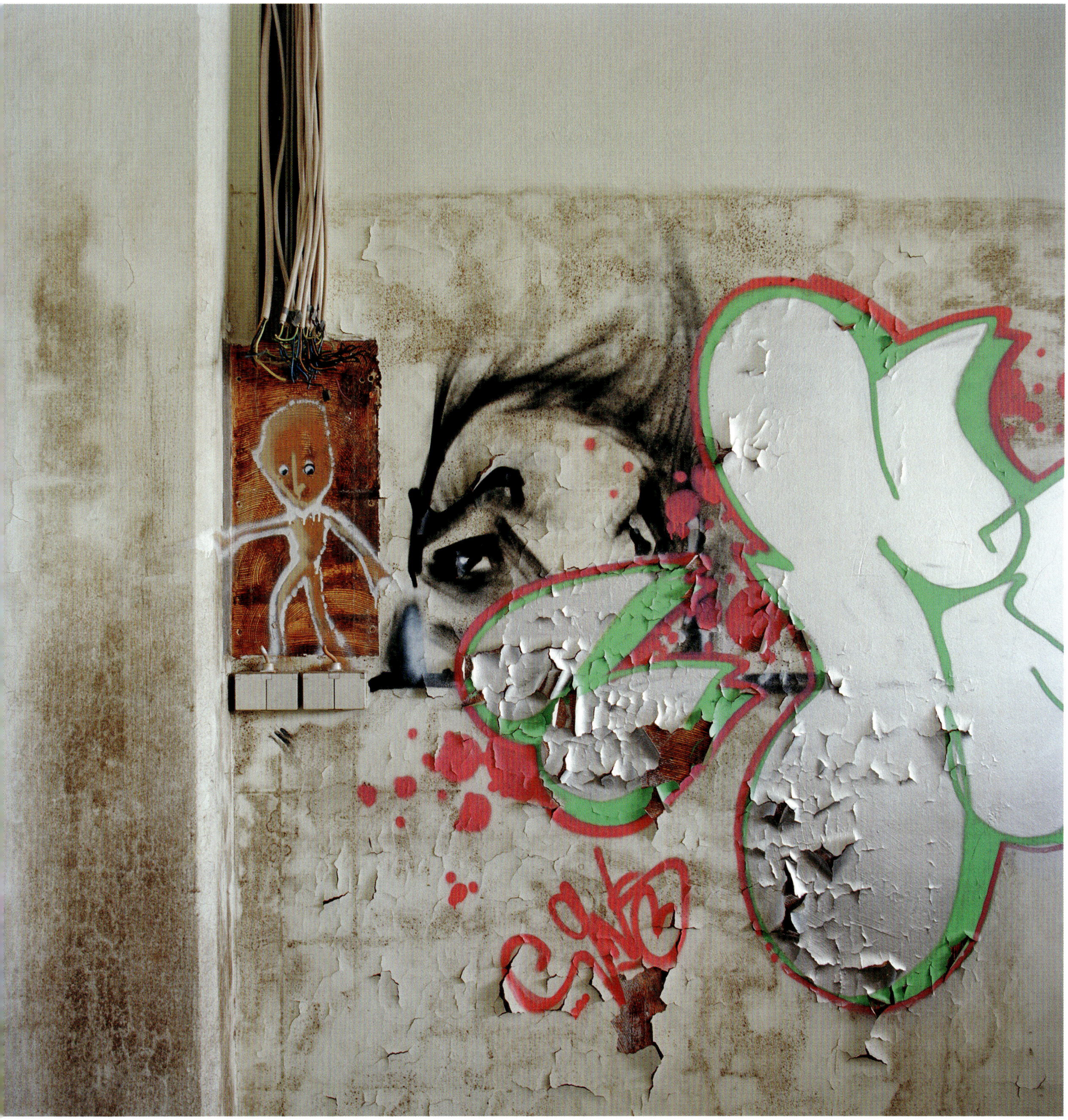

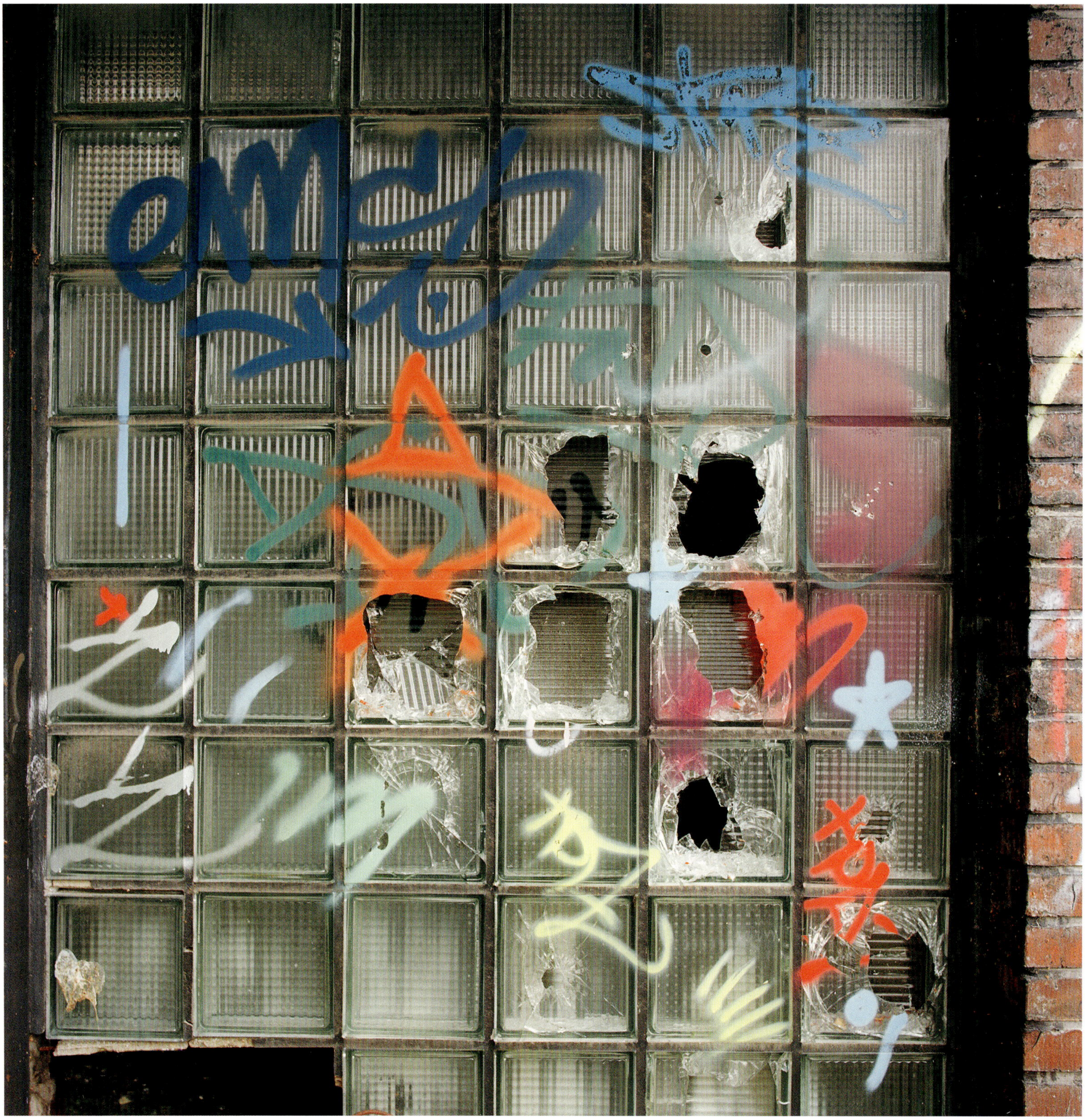

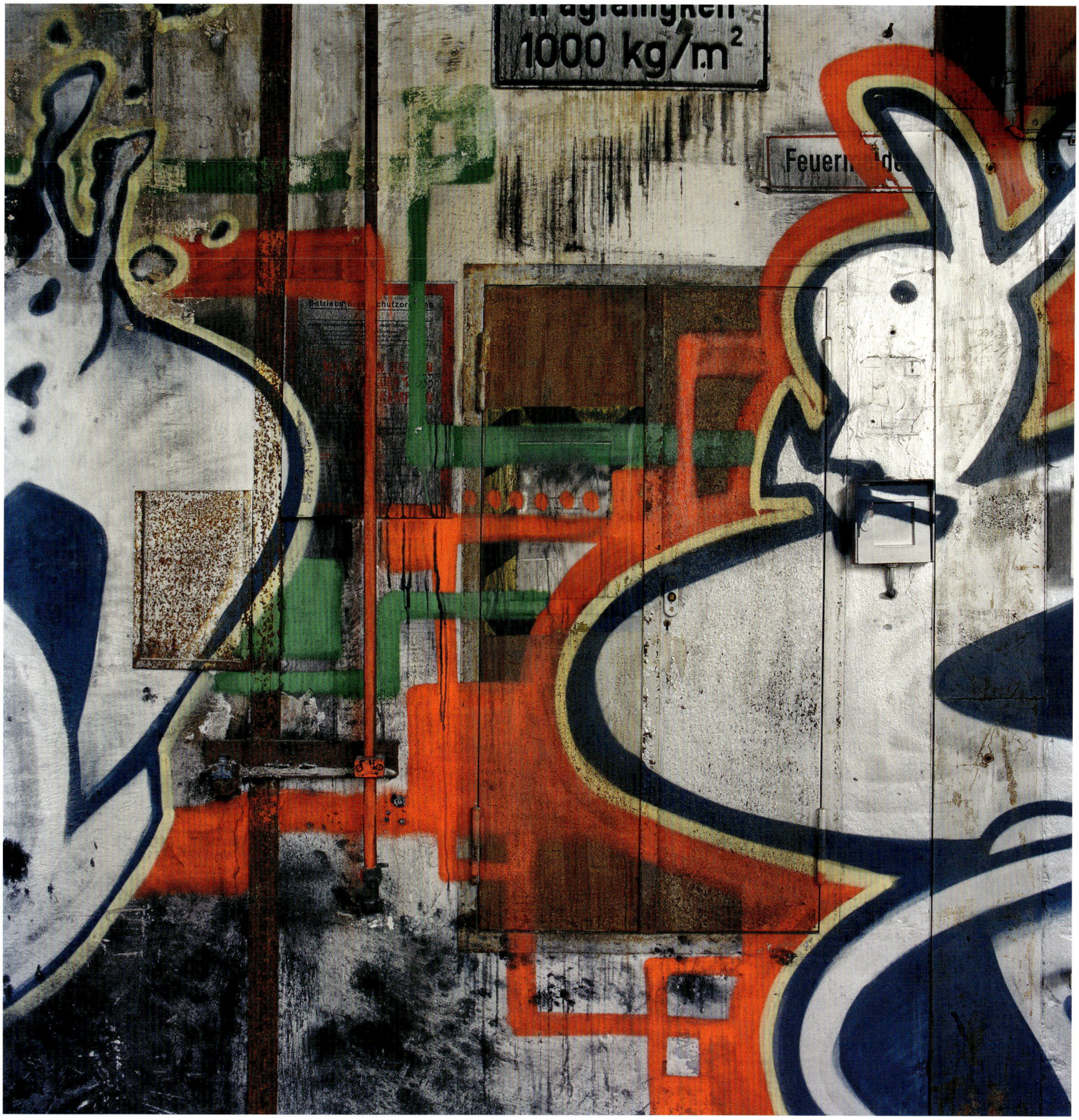
1000 kg/m²

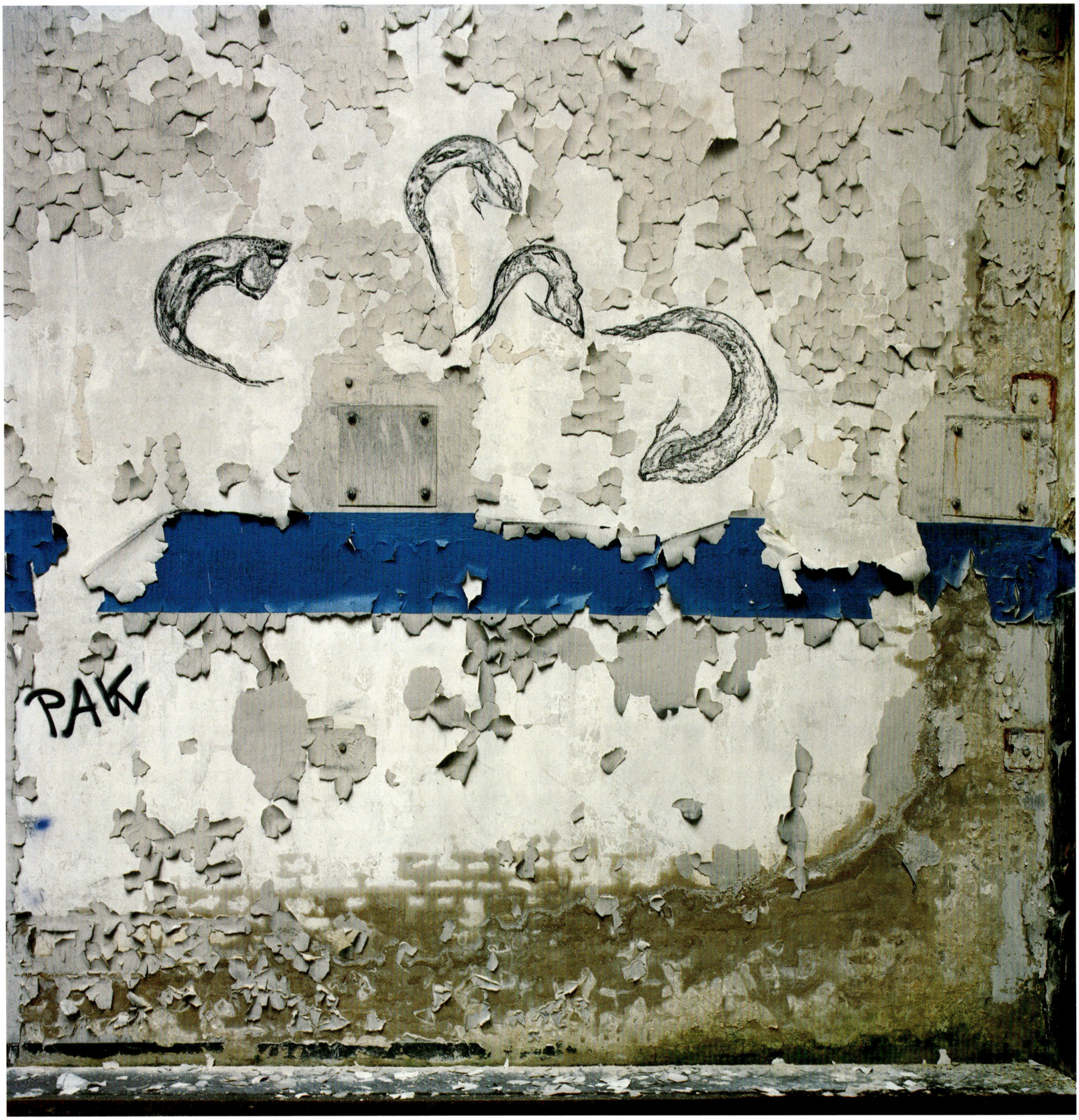
PAK

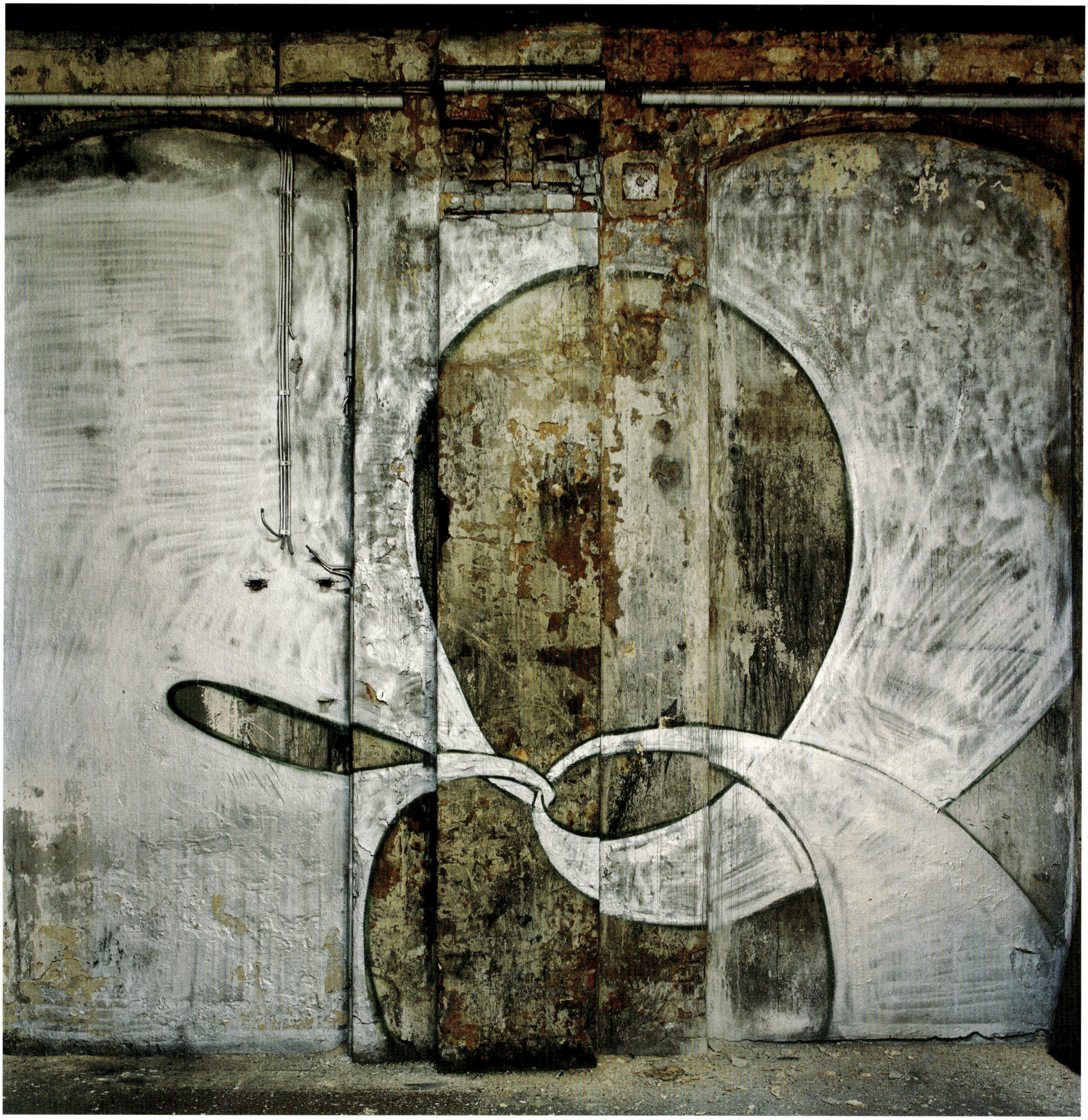

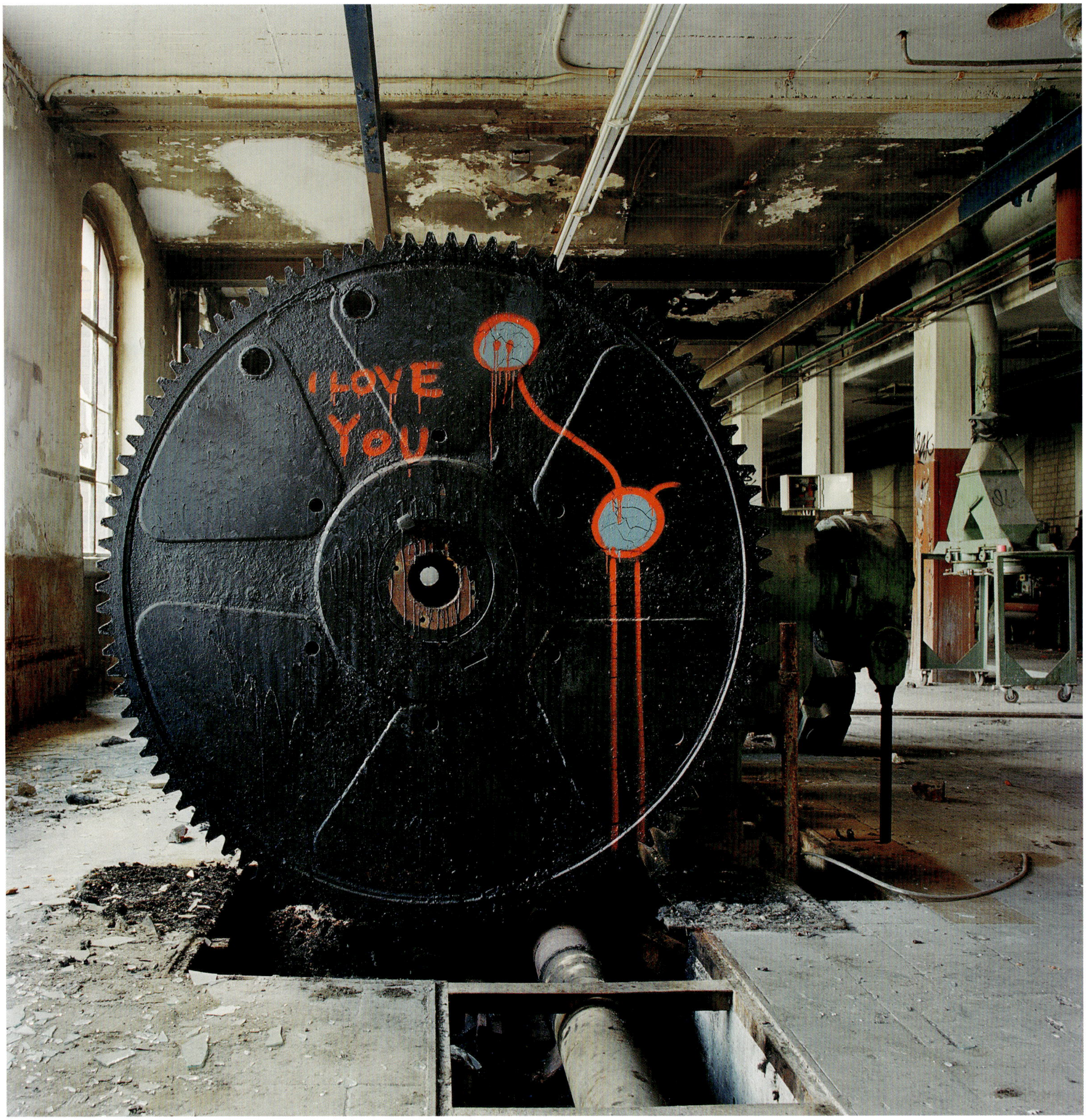
I LOVE
YOU

SCHNELL-
KLÄRER

PUFFER
6

PUFFER
7

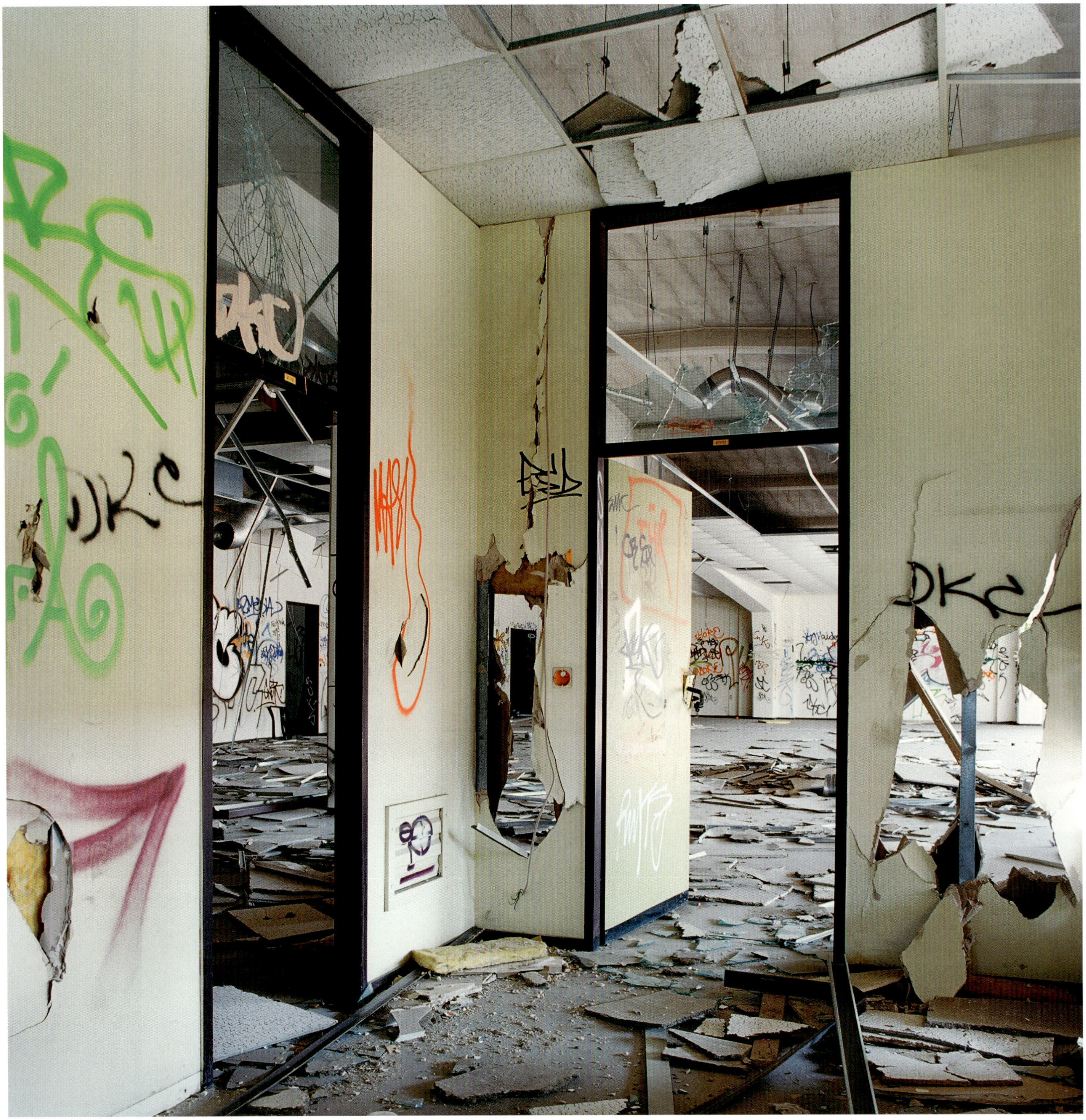

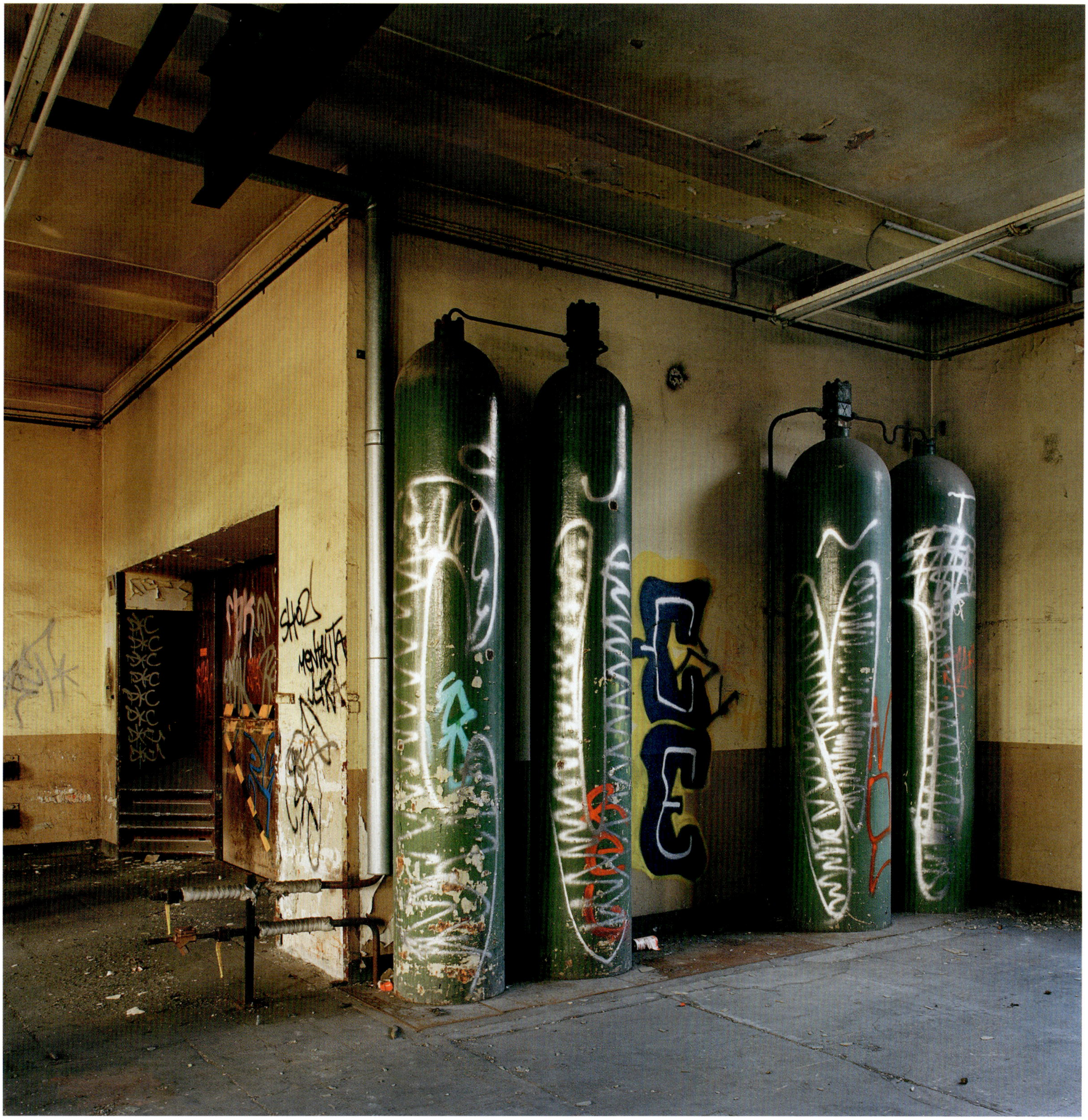

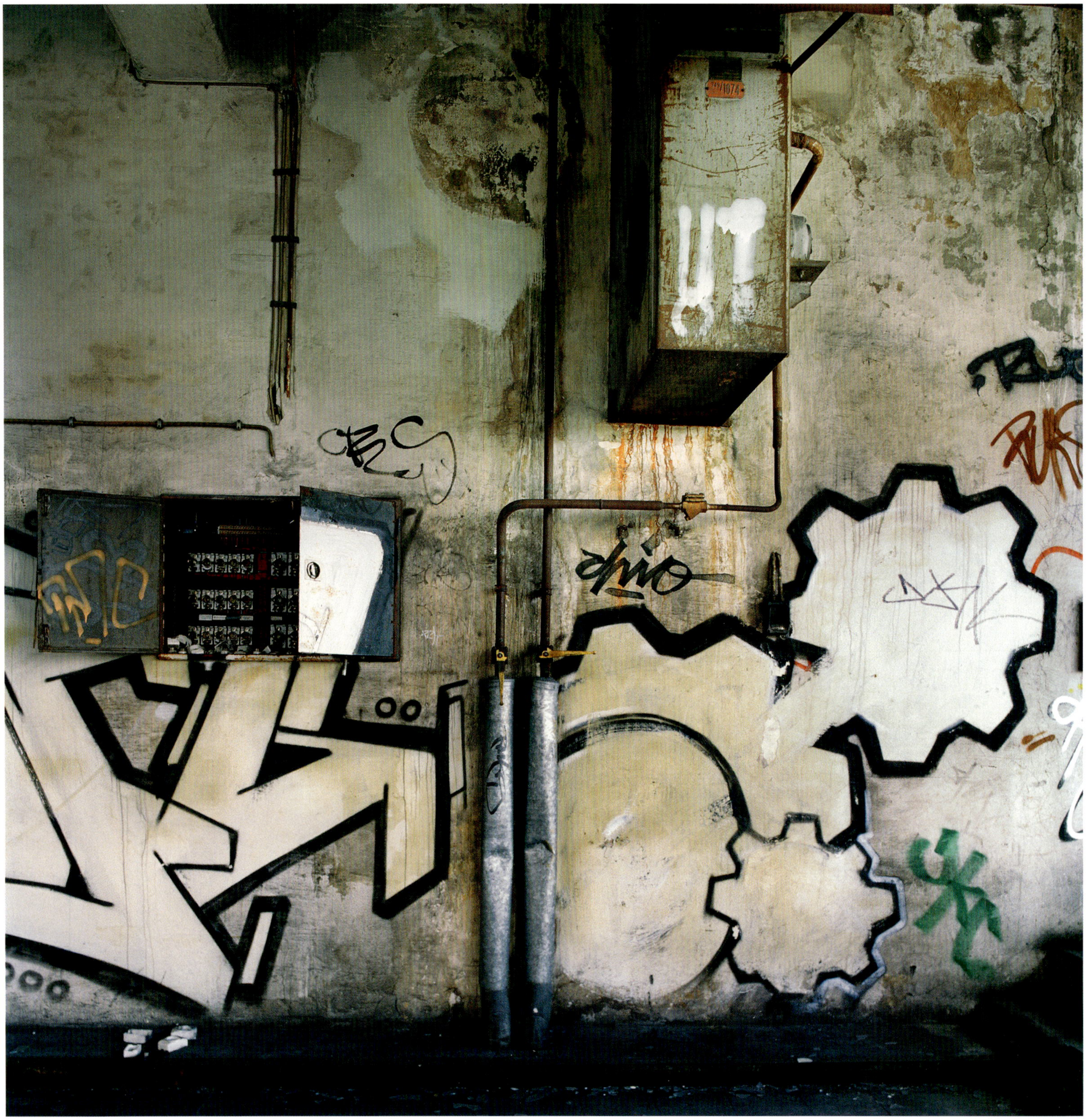

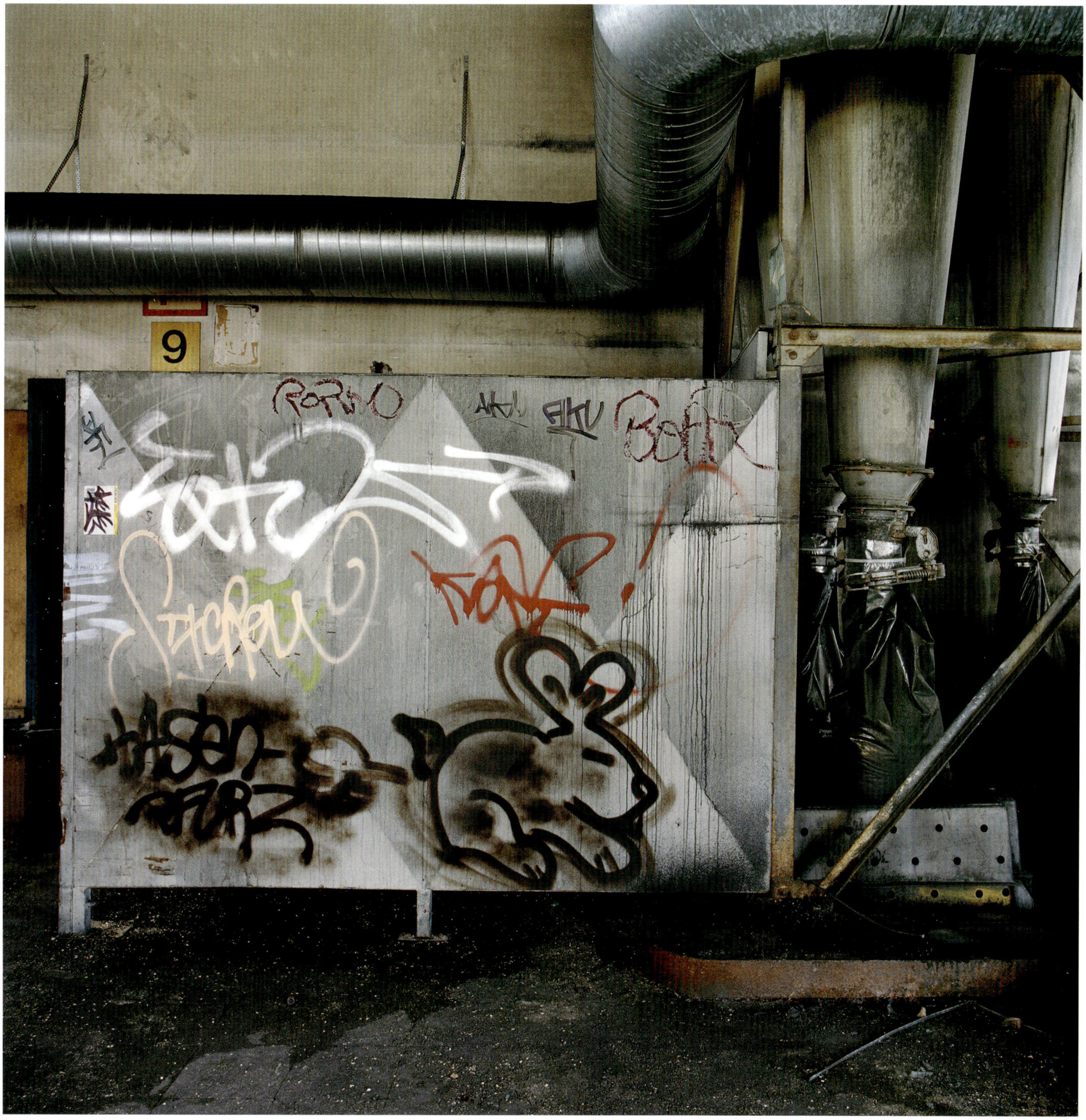
9

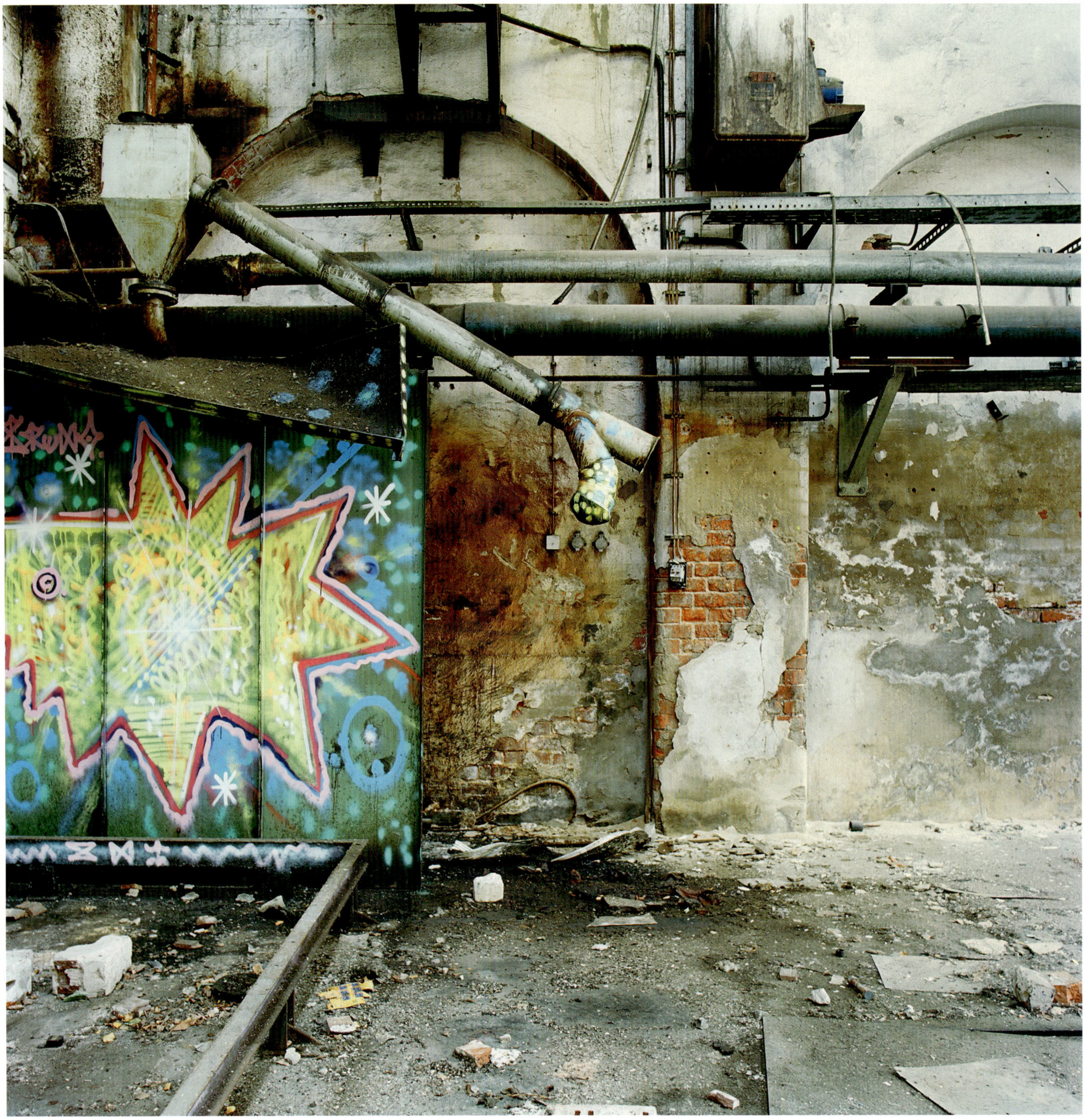

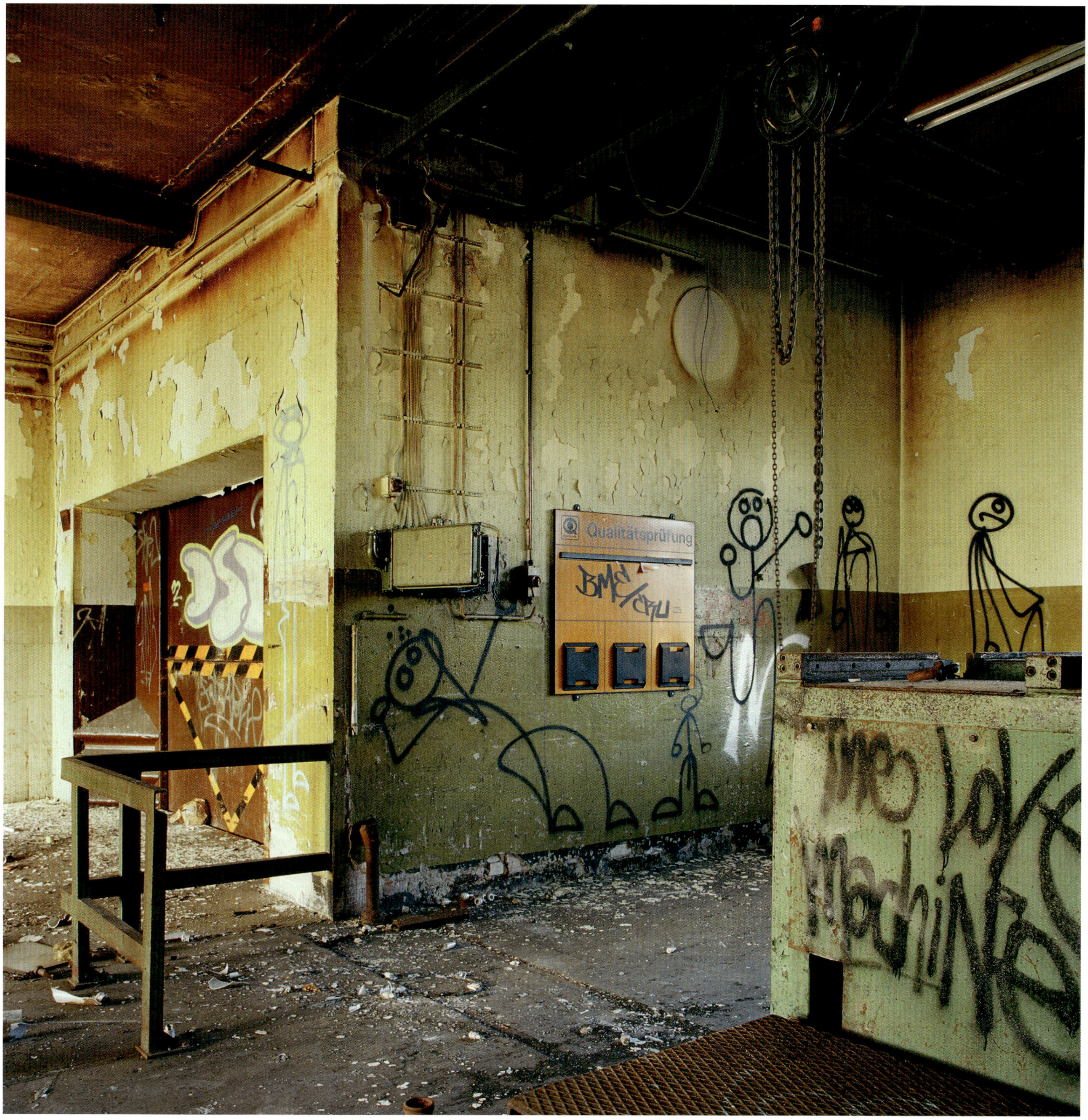
Qualitätsprüfung

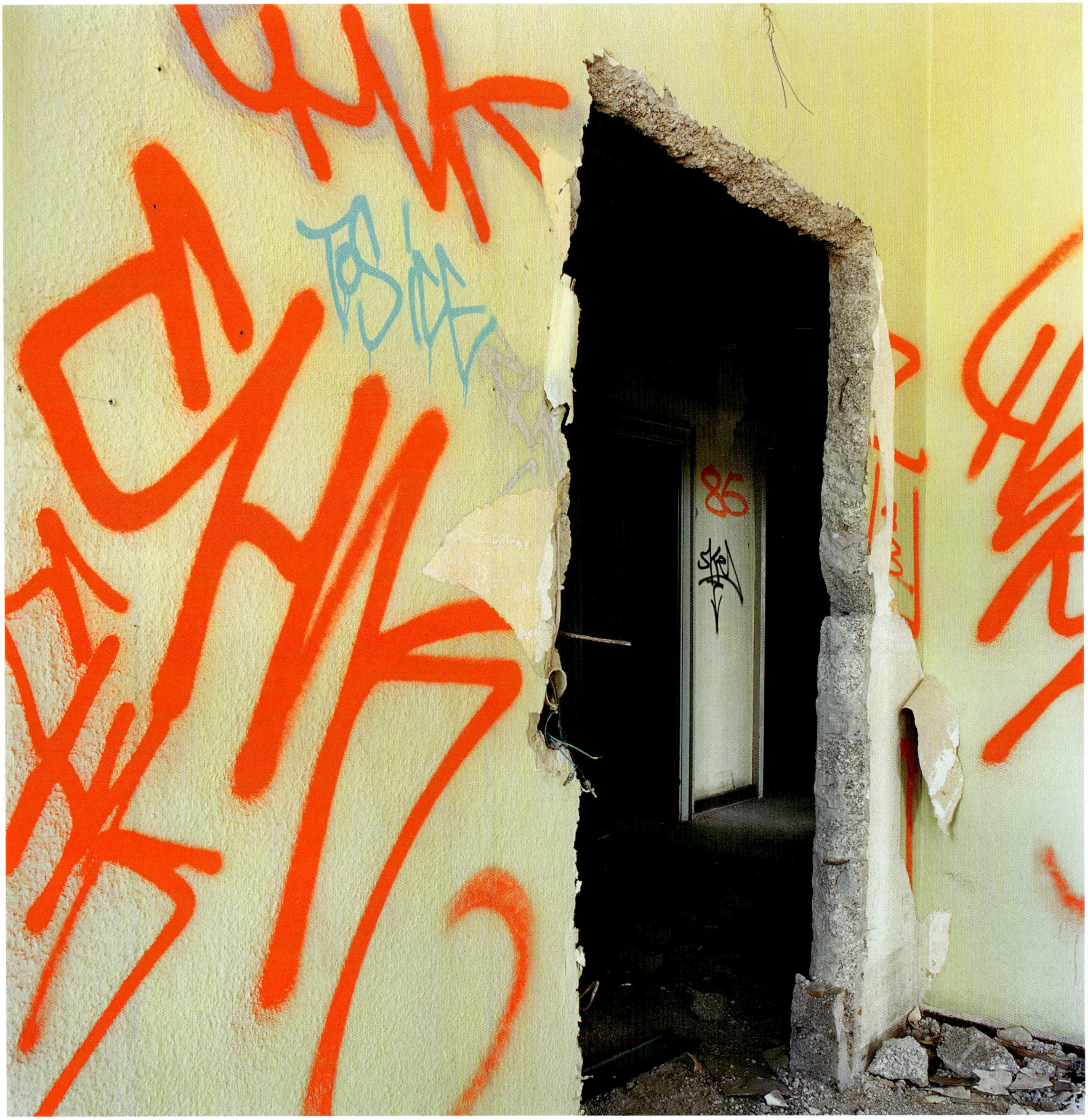
85

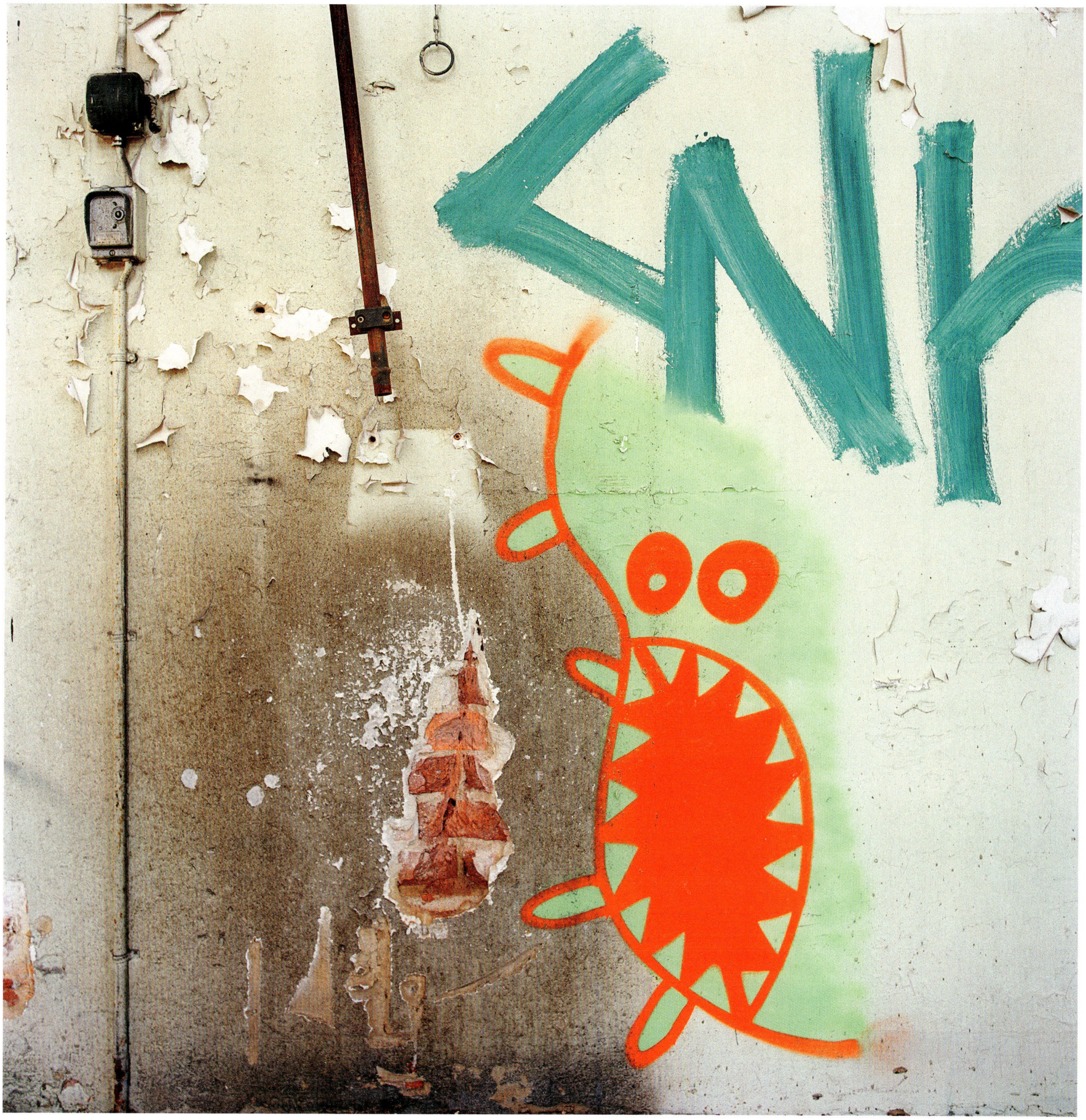

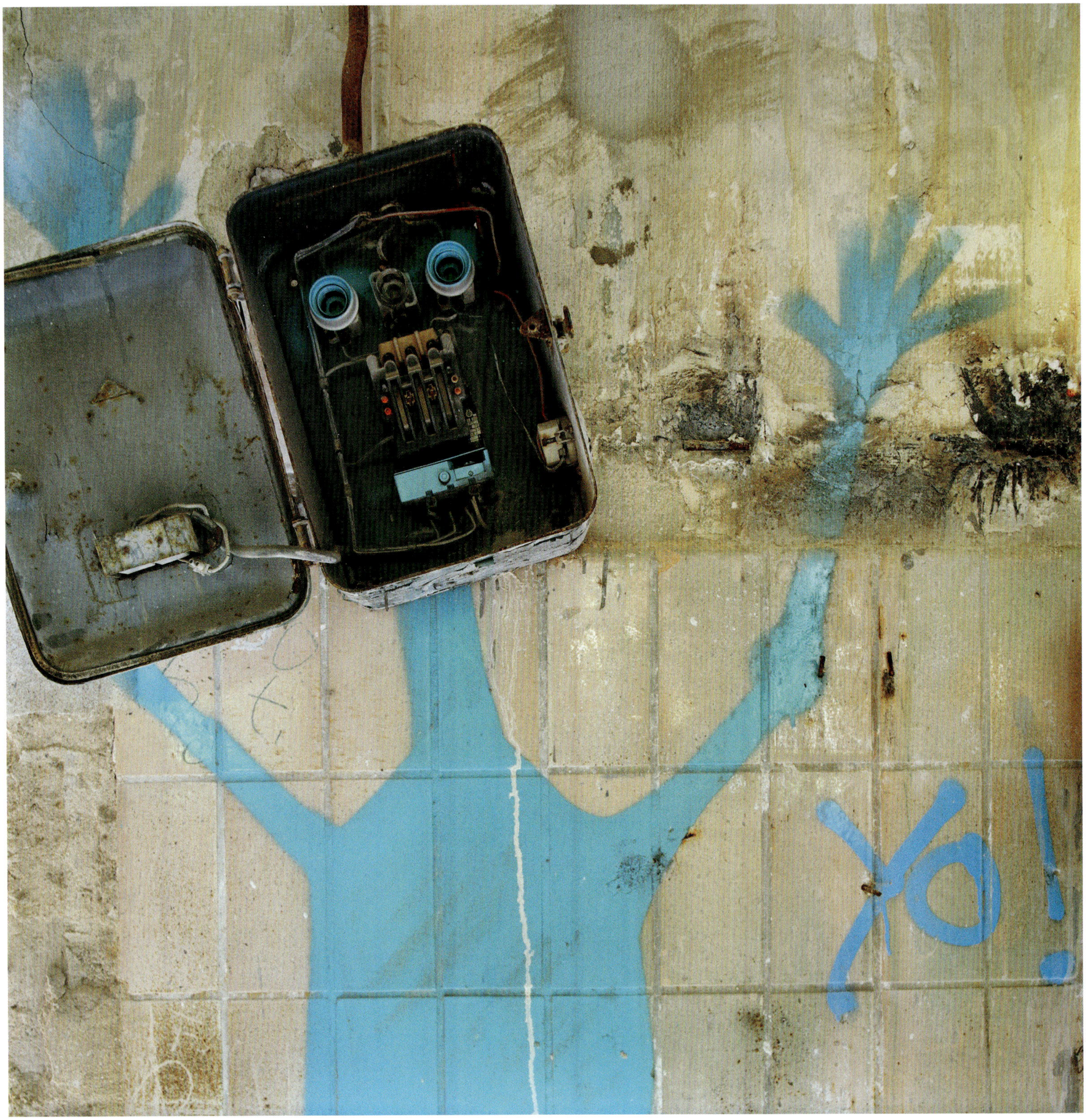

future | no future

Boris von Brauchitsch zur Fotodokumentation ‚Lost In Time'

Das Gelände ist aufgegeben, die mehr als dreißig Hallen der 1871 gegründeten Continental Reifenfabrik haben sich in zweckfreie Installationen verwandelt, selbst dem Licht fehlt die Kraft Schatten zu werfen. Indem wir betrachten und umblättern, folgen wir mit den Seiten dieses Buches dem Fotografen auf seinem Parcours durch Industrieruinen, auf dem sich Totalen eröffnen, dann verharrend Details fokussiert werden, bevor sich wieder neue Fluchten anbieten und uns weiterlocken. Die Leitungen und Hähne, die Rohre und Schaltkästen sind die Insassen dieser Geisteranstalt, die sich hinter unserem Rücken zu immer wieder neuen, grotesken und poetischen Konstellationen zusammenzufinden scheinen. Sie sind die Stellvertreter derer, die sie einst montiert, verlegt und bedient haben. Längst sind diese Arbeiter verschwunden, die Produktion wurde in Niedriglohnländer verlegt, das reizvolle Gelände in der Gabelung von Leine Verbindungskanal und Stichkanal Linden dient jetzt als Projektionsfläche für eine moderne „Wasserstadt". In den Fotografien lässt sich aber noch diese Atempause zwischen Stilllegung und Abriss ausmachen, eine Interimszeit, die keineswegs so unproduktiv war, wie der Verfall der Bauten auf den ersten Blick nahezulegen scheint. Denn diejenigen, die hier tätig wurden, nachdem der Standort aufgegeben war, haben die nun leeren Hallen und sinnlosen Armaturen zu ihren Komplizen gemacht und den Ort, der auf pittoreske Weise seinen Frieden gefunden hat, mit anarchischem Leben gefüllt.

Die Produktionsstätten des weltweit viertgrößten Reifenherstellers, die er 1929 von der Excelsior Gummi-Compagnie übernehmen konnte, waren eine Stadt für sich. Auf siebzehn Hektar wurden hier über siebzig Jahre lang Bälle, Kämme und Gasmasken, vor allem aber Fahrrad- und Autoreifen produziert, gelagert und verpackt, um in alle Welt verschickt zu werden. Als Keimzelle für ein Unternehmen mit heute rund zweihundert Standorten in 46 Ländern auf allen Kontinenten wurde Conti schon als Aktiengesellschaft aus der Taufe gehoben. Tag für Tag die Börsennotierung im Blick herrschten in Limmer die Gesetze der Funktionalität und Profitmaximierung. Doch dort, wo alles seinen Anfang nahm, in Hannover, ist zwar noch das angesiedelt, was man „Firmensitz" nennt, Reifen aber werden hier keine mehr produziert, auch das eine Konsequenz marktwirtschaftlicher Zwangsläufigkeiten. Die leeren Produktionshallen sind eine exemplarische Industrieanlage und zugleich der Traum einer Alternativkultur. Andernorts werden heute – sofern die Lage vielversprechend ist – verwaiste Industriebauten gern umgedeutet und umgenutzt. Ästhetisiert und ausgestellt, verkörpern sie Purismus und eine Moderne, in der die Form noch der Funktion folgte. Lofts sind großzügig, cool, begehrt, sie beheimaten auch dann noch das Flair des Kreativen, wenn sie längst bis zur Einbauküche und Heimsauna verbürgerlicht wurden.

In Hannover ließ sich eine solche Umnutzung – glaubt man den Gutachten – nicht bewerkstelligen, zu verseucht waren Mauern und Erdreich von der Produktion. Die Hallen wurden daher abgebrochen, der Boden entgiftet. Sechshundert maßgeschneiderte Wohnungen sollen entstehen, Tabula rasa, das Terrain bereitet für einen Neuanfang. Stehengeblieben von allem ist als Mahnmal oder Wahrzeichen lediglich der denkmalgeschützte Conti-Turm.

Damit sind auch die Fotografien bereits für die Geschichte relevant, denn sie zeigen, was nicht mehr zu sehen ist. Marc Theis hat dies einkalkuliert. Ohne zum pedantischen Spurensicherer zu werden, hat er im Winter 2004/05, ganz offiziell mit dem Schlüssel zur Anlage in der Tasche, eine Industriearchäologie betrieben, die die Impulse der Massenproduktion, die Folgen der Tertiarisierung und den spielerischen Umgang einer postindustriellen Generation mit den Relikten offenlegt. Und als alles verschwunden war, hat er die Bilder, die in seinen Schubladen zu historischen Dokumenten gereift waren, wieder hervorgezogen.

Industrieruinen verleiten Fotografen, sich in pittoresken Szenarien zu verlieren, Graffiti-Bücher wiederum neigen dazu, rein dokumentarisch die Werke anderer abzuspulen. Sich offensiv auf verlassene Räume und Graffiti zugleich einzulassen und dabei einen Weg einzuschlagen, der distanziert *und* atmosphärisch den Ort in ein neues Medium transferiert, darf durchaus als Verdienst der Serie *Lost in Time* angesehen werden. Sie steht damit als bemerkenswertes Beispiel in einer langen Tradition, die weit ins 19. Jahrhundert zurückreicht. Möglicherweise beruht das symbiotische Verhältnis von Fotografie und Industriearchitektur darauf, dass auch die Fotografie ein Kind der Industriegesellschaft ist. Als um 1850 das Nachdenken über die Industrielle Revolution, über ihre Ursachen und Folgen verstärkt zum Tragen kam, war auch die Fotografie gefragt, die Monumente dieser Epoche zu dokumentieren. Sie war zugegen, als die ersten Stahl-, Glas- und Betongroßbauten entstanden, als die Industrielle Revolution ihre seriellen Produktionen perfektionierte und auch noch, als das Industriezeitalter zu Ende ging. Es ist kein Zufall, dass mit ihm auch die analoge Fotografie verschwunden ist, die mit manuellen Prozessen verbunden war und der computergenerierten Fotografie auf breiter Front weichen musste. Heute ist auch die Fotografie weniger technische Reproduktion als vielmehr dienstleistungsorientiert: handlich, schnell, sofort verfügbar, einfach im Gebrach. Es wirkt fast trotzig, dass Marc Theis bewusst ein Gegenprogramm zelebrierte, mit einer gewichtigen Mittelformatkamera analog zu Werke ging und sich demonstrativ Zeit nahm für seine Bestandsaufnahmen. Bis zu sechs Minuten pro Bild belichtete er sein feinkörniges Filmmaterial, ein geradezu meditativer Akt der Annäherung an seinen Gegenstand.

Der rechte Winkel ist dabei das Maß aller Dinge. Die Senkrechten und Waagerechten konstituieren Räume und Flächen, in denen sich zunächst ein imposantes Verlangen nach Zerstörung Bahn gebrochen hat. Der Ordnung der Linien steht ein Chaos gegenüber, das mit einer Akribie erzeugt wurde, die ihresgleichen sucht. Was sich demontieren ließ, wurde demontiert, der Rest, von der Deckenverkleidung bis zur Klospülung, demoliert. Doch in den Trümmern erwachte neues Leben. Müde schleichen behelmte Arbeiter herbei, während die Uhr über dem Tor drei Minuten nach Zwölf zeigt. Die Zeiten, als es noch fünf vor Zwölf war, sind längst vorbei, aber dennoch haben die gemalten Gestalten ihre Brotzeit parat und lassen sich nicht von ihrem gewohnten Trott abbringen. Ein Hase jongliert mit Ostereiern, pflichtbewusst fegt ein Mann den Schutt weg, der beim Einreißen einer Wand entstanden ist, zwei Strichfiguren tragen eine Resopal-Ablage davon, eine nackte Schwarze steht unter der Dusche. Und auch gemordet wird weiterhin mit Genuss: Der Serienkiller hat den Fön eingestöpselt und verharrt breit grinsend am Rand der Badewanne, um uns zu Zeugen seiner jüngsten Tat zu machen… All diese Figuren interagieren mit vorgefundenen Objekten und belegen den wachen Blick ihrer Schöpfer, die die Graffiti durchaus auch dazu nutzen, sich die Frage nach der Zukunft zu stellen. Hat das alles *no future*, oder ist genau das, was wir hier erleben schon Teil unserer Zukunft?

Zu der Zeit, als Marc Theis seine Aufnahmen machte, erlebte die Graffiti-Bewegung gerade eine neue Blüte, die dazu führte, dass sie einen theoretischen Überbau verpasst bekam. Aktivisten, Fans und Analytiker befassten sich vermehrt mit soziologischen und kunsttheoretischen Hintergründen, wobei die Debatte schnell um die Frage einer verbindlichen Begrifflichkeit kreiste. Das wirft nicht zuletzt ein Licht auf die Selbstwahrnehmung derer, die auf den Fotografien von Marc Theis abwesend sind: die Künstler. Nähert man sich dem Phänomen Graffiti, scheint es hilfreich, sich zunächst zu verdeutlichen, was Graffiti alles *nicht* ist: die Bezeichnung eines Stils, einer Epoche, einer klar umrissenen Technik oder politischen Grundhaltung. Gemeinsam ist dagegen allen Graffiti, dass sie tendenziell illegal und in der Regel im öffentlichen Raum angebracht sind. Das ist allerdings nicht viel an Gemeinsamkeiten. Experten aber leben von Definitionen, die Klarheit verbreiten wollen und zu diesem Zweck – quasi als imaginäre Spür- und Wachhunde der Wissenschaft – ihr Terrain sondieren und markieren. Der Terminus *Graffiti* entzieht sich jedoch in vielfältiger Hinsicht sofort wieder, ganz gleich, von welcher Seite man sich heranpirscht. Das, was landläufig unter Graffiti verstanden wird, sträubt sich massiv gegen eine begriffliche Eingrenzung, obwohl zahllose Versuche unternommen wurden, sich des Phänomens verbal zu bemächtigen. Eine überzeugende Definition hat sich dabei bislang noch nicht durchgesetzt. Stattdessen driften die „Lehrmeinungen" weit auseinander.

Kann man Graffiti womöglich doch als Ausdruck einer Geisteshaltung betrachten, die sich in jedem Fall durch ihre Illegalität auszeichnet? Diese Ansicht ist theoretisch verlockend, weil sie sich von allen Fragen der Technik löst, bleibt jedoch zugleich in der Praxis problematisch, müssten doch bei jeder Betrachtung einer Wandmalerei zunächst Nachforschungen darüber angestellt werden, ob sie wirklich ohne Zustimmung des Wandeigentümers entstanden ist. Erst nach einer solchen Vergewisserung dürfte sie dann als Graffito bezeichnet werden. Es ließe sich folglich bei der Entdeckung eines Werkes kaum zweifelsfrei feststellen, ob es sich wirklich um ein Graffito handelt – und zwei formal identische Zeichnungen könnten damit (einmal legal, einmal illegal angebracht) auch zwei Spezies der Kunst angehören.

Noch schwieriger wird es, versucht man eine Eingrenzung über die Zielgruppe. *Graffiti* richte sich an Eingeweihte, während *Street Art* ein möglichst breites Publikum im Visier habe, heißt es gelegentlich. Graffiti wird dabei im Wesentlichen auf die *Tags* beschränkt, auf jene mehr oder weniger raffiniert verschlungenen Namenszüge, die als an eine Peergroup gerichtete Codes verstanden werden wollen, während Street Art jede darüber hinausgehende gestaltende Manifestation sei. Ob man sich einen Gefallen damit tut, Graffiti in derart enge Grenzen zu verweisen, erscheint fragwürdig, schon weil diese Sicht ahistorisch ist und außer Acht lässt, dass die Geschichte des Graffitos seit der Antike neben Namensritzungen immer auch Sprüche und Zeichnungen einschloss.

Ein weiterer Ansatz versucht sich an einer werkimmanenten Definition mit ähnlichem Ergebnis, indem er eine Hierarchie des künstlerischen Wertes etabliert, die auch von manchen Wandgestaltern geteilt wird. In dieser Hierarchie stehen Tags weit unten. Sie werden als das eigentliche „Kerngeschäft" des Graffitos angesehen und nicht als künstlerische Produktion verstanden. Ein Ausdruck wie *Graffiti-Künstler* wandelt sich damit zu einer Contradictio in adiecto. Graffiti, als Nichtkunst definiert, wird klar von der ästhetisch überlegenen *Street Art* separiert. Doch auch hier haben wir es mit einem launischen Begriff zu tun, denn Street Art umschließt viele Formen einer kreativen Gestaltung des öffentlichen Raums und meint ebenso Pflastermaler wie Straßentheater. *Street Art* klingt aus kunsthistorischer Perspektive zudem wie ein Gegenentwurf zur *Salonmalerei*, die zwar im Salon präsentiert wurde, darüber hinaus aber auch stilistische Übereinstimmungen zeigt, die ihr den Weg in den Salon erst geebnet haben. Was unter Street Art subsumiert wird, besitzt als Gemeinsamkeit lediglich den Ort, an dem sie in Erscheinung tritt. Das aber erscheint als Definition wenig erhellend und als Begriff noch unbestimmter als *Kirchenmusik* oder *Museumskunst*. Deshalb ist die Fülle der Vorschläge, die vor allem aus den Reihen der Aktivisten kommt, vor allem auch Ausdruck einer Unzufriedenheit mit der bestehenden Terminologie. Es ist die Rede von

Urban Aesthetics, von *Urban Take Overs* oder *Poetic Terrorism*, von *Graphic Delinquents* oder *Post Art*, um nur einige der phantasievolleren Begriffe zu nennen, die eine intellektuelle Reflexion des eigenen Selbstverständnisses spiegeln. Das Künstlerische und das Illegale klingen durch, ebenso wie der Anspruch auf Subversion und einen Guerilla-Status.

Gute Chancen einen breiteren Konsens zu finden, hat der Ausdruck *Urban Art*, der sich seit etwa 2004 zu etablieren begann, auch wenn er die Kunstproduktion im öffentlichen Raum vor allem als metropolitanes Phänomen verstanden sehen möchte. Doch im allgemeinen Sprachgebrauch dominiert noch immer *Graffiti* als Oberbegriff, der aus der volkstümlichen Perspektive alles vom Klospruch bis zum Wandgemälde einzuschließen scheint. Vielleicht sollte man es dabei belassen, schon weil er (wie die zentralen Stil-, Medien- und Epochen-Begriffe auch) nur aus einem Wort besteht, weil er eine lange Tradition hat und weil auch das Wort *Grafik* in ihm steckt, das ihn öffnet für neuere Spielarten der Intervention, wie Sticker, Poster oder Adbusting.

Kehren wir zurück nach Hannover, in die Industriearchitektur auf den Fotografien von Marc Theis, dann stellt sich die Frage nach den Künstlern noch einmal anders. Wer sind sie und mit welchen Ambitionen arbeiteten sie? Auch hier gibt es Tagger, die ihr verschlungenes Pseudonym dutzendfach auf die Kacheln eines Sanitärraums schleudern und damit in ihrer Anonymität verweilend zugleich nach Berühmtheit streben. Tags sind Ego-Shows aus der Deckung heraus, motiviert durch den Wunsch nach Ruhm. *Getting fame* ist die Parole, aber ob die verlassenen Hallen der Conti-Werke dafür der passende Ort waren? Sicher, sie dienten als Abenteuerland und Party-Location, aber sie waren eben vor allem Rückzugsgebiet, und als solches eine Parallelwelt, in der man sich ausprobieren konnte.

Waren diese Hallen überhaupt öffentlicher Raum? Das Betreten war illegal, das Bemalen der Wände wohl auch, doch daran dürfte sich keiner gestört haben, da ihr Abriss als beschlossene Sache galt. Aber öffentlicher Raum? – Die Werke, die sich hier fanden, wurden nur von wenigen überhaupt gesehen. Man gewinnt den Eindruck, die Maler haben sie zunächst für sich selbst geschaffen. Es gibt folglich neben dem Bedürfnis nach Provokation und Verwirrung einer möglichst großen Menge an Passanten, wie es Graffiti-Künstler im Sinn haben, die ihre Werke an den Pulsadern der Metropolen anbringen, immer auch eine Gegenbewegung, die ihre eigene Welt im Verborgenen etabliert. Sie schaffen eine Street Art jenseits der Straße, Graffiti unter Ausschluss der Öffentlichkeit.

Die Anonymität des Ortes kam der Anonymität der Graffiti-Aktivisten entgegen und kommunizierte auf eigenwillige Art mit der Anonymität des Maschinen-Zeitalters. Mit Taylorismus dürften sich die mutmaßlich jungen Künstler aber wohl höchstens in der Theorie befasst haben, und auch der Sturm auf die Maschinen, den sie vorfanden und spielerisch interpretierten, hatte nichts mit jener Stürmerei zu tun, mit der Arbeiter einstmals dagegen kämpften, durch Apparate ersetzt zu werden. Die junge Sprayer-Gemeinde der Informations- und Dienstleistungsgesellschaft deutete die Relikte einer untergegangenen Epoche um, von der sie selbst nicht mehr tangiert worden war. Zwei Zeiten trafen aufeinander. Die flüchtigen Zeugnisse dieser Begegnung überdauern ausgerechnet in Fotografien, dem populärsten Medium technischer Reproduzierbarkeit. Auf diesem Weg verbreiten sich die Graffiti Jahre nach ihrem Verschwinden nun doch noch unkontrollierbar im Alltag und überführen das Temporäre in eine relative Ewigkeit.

Was Max Frisch einmal in New York über Kunst – exemplarisch formuliert für die Literatur – sagte, wirkt geradezu, als ob er dabei auch die Graffiti draußen auf den Straßen im Sinn hatte: „Die Funktion der Literatur in der Gesellschaft, meine ich, ist permanente Irritation, dass es sie gibt. Nichts weiter." Und er beendet seine Vorlesung, die er 1981 am City College unter dem Titel *Schwarzes Quadrat* hielt, mit der Bemerkung: „Jede Kollaboration mit der Macht, auch mit einer demokratischen Macht, endet mit einem tödlichen Selbstmissverständnis der Kunst, der *Poesie*. Ihr Ort ist nicht das Foyer der Chase Manhattan Bank. Dort wird sie zur Affirmation. Zur Dekoration der Macht."

Irritation setzt allerdings Wahrnehmung voraus. Der Wunsch, durch Graffiti zu verstören oder anders geartete Aufmerksamkeit zu erregen, wird jedoch heute im öffentlichen Raum immer schwerer erfüllbar. Längst sind sie zu einem visuellen Grundrauschen geworden, das kaum noch ins Bewusstsein der Passanten vordringt. In Städten wie New York, Berlin oder Barcelona stellt sich die Aufmerksamkeit heute oft erst ein, wenn dieses Grundrauschen plötzlich ausbleibt, wenn man an Orte gelangt, die eine frisch renovierte Stille verbreiten. Man vermisst Graffiti in U-Bahnen, wie man Zigarettenrauch in Clubs vermisst hat. Ein vorübergehendes Befremden, der bereinigten Atmosphäre geschuldet.

Das ist bitter für die Graffiti-Kultur, die zugleich eine Macho-Kultur ist. Was nützt das Rebellentum, die bewusste Überschreitung von Gesetzen, wenn sie nicht mehr wahrgenommen wird? Richtig, die Illegalität verspricht noch immer einen Adrenalinstoß, denn staatlichem oder privatem Wachpersonal sollte man auf frischer Tat nicht in die Hände fallen, aber wenn dem Graffito als Beleg für die Missachtung der Regeln so wenig Beachtung geschenkt wird, schmälert das auch den Reiz des Abenteuers. Und doch ist eine Kapitulation nicht in Sicht. Graffiti überleben, sind fester Bestandteil der Öffentlichkeit und Herausforderung an die Künstler, sich im Dschungel der

Großstadt zu behaupten. Neu ist an ihren Ausdrucksformen nicht viel, aber die Vielfalt der lustigen, obszönen, politischen, rassistischen, moralischen, sexuellen, absurden oder gefälligen Botschaften bedient sich der Mittel, die auch die Werbung erfolgreich nutzt: Eine Mischkalkulation aus Überraschung und Wiedererkennen. Graffiti wollen anecken und diversifizieren, sind immer Opposition und in mindestens dreierlei Hinsicht explizit Gegenprogramm. Erstens Gegenprogramm zur Werbung, deren Botschaften sie durch Culture Jamming und Adbusting entlarvt, zweitens zum etablierten Kunstmarkt, der seine Hochkultur in den White Cubes der Galerien pflegt und diese Abgrenzung vom Alltag als Unabhängigkeit und Freiheit begreift, und drittens zum Fernsehen, das ins Haus kommt, den kleinsten gemeinsamen Nenner sucht und tendenziell auf Gleichschaltung zielt.

Graffiti begreift sich als Ausdruck der urbanen Wildnis und als demokratisches Medium zugleich und es verwundert nicht weiter, dass es parallel zum Internet boomt, das seinerseits subversive Kräfte zu entfalten vermag. Doch Graffiti ist immer auch eine Vergewisserung der eigenen Existenz in der realen Welt – und in dieser Hinsicht letztlich auch Gegenentwurf zum Internet. Die Stadt wird als Oberfläche begriffen, die es zu erobern und aufzubrechen gilt. Die Mauern und Wände werden Inspirationsquelle, Material, Bildträger. Umso überraschender ist es, mit welcher Selbstverständlichkeit Architektur und Malerei in den Fotografien zusammenfließen, die Marc Theis auf dem Gelände am Stichkanal gemacht hat. Fotografie, das ist glatte Oberfläche, fast immateriell und ohne haptische Qualitäten. Doch indem sie sich vornehm zurücknimmt, vermag sie etwas von dem Abenteuer zu vermitteln, das zwischen Vorgestern und Gestern, zwischen Raum und Detail, zwischen Stein und Farbe entstanden ist. Ihre Poesie liegt dabei auch in dem, was nicht zu sehen ist. In der Abwesenheit der Aktivisten.

future | no future

Boris von Brauchitsch on the photo-documentation 'Lost In Time'

An abandoned site: the more than thirty production halls, once the premises of the Continental Tyre Factory founded in 1871, have turned into somewhat unorthodox installations. Even the light is too weak to cast shadows. Leafing through the pages of this book, we follow the photographer on his tour of these industrial ruins: vistas open up as long shots, details come into focus, then new alignments appear, luring us on. The occupants of this ghost house – the pipes and taps, ducts and fuse boxes – appear to regroup behind our backs into ever new grotesque and poetic constellations. They have taken over from the people who once assembled, installed and operated them. Those labourers have long since disappeared and the production has been transferred to low-wage countries. The attractive site at the fork of the Leine connecting canal and the Linden branch canal has now been designated as a new modern "Water City". And yet, the photographs enable us to apprehend that pause between closing down and demolition, an interim that was in no way as unproductive as the dereliction of the buildings would seem at first sight to suggest. For those who went to work here after the location had been abandoned turned the vacated halls and senseless fittings into accomplices, filling with anarchic life a place that had settled into a picturesque peace.

The production halls of the world's fourth largest tyre manufacturer, taken over from the Excelsior Gummi Compagnie in 1929, used to be a city in themselves. For more than seventy years, balls, combs and gasmasks, but above all bicycle and car tyres were produced, stored and packed here on a site covering seventeen hectares, for despatch all over the globe. Conti, nucleus of an enterprise with currently about two hundred plants in 46 countries on all the continents, was from its inception a shareholding company. Day in day out, and with an eye on the stock-exchange listing, the laws of functionality and profit maximisation held sway in Limmer. Yet although what is known as the "company headquarters" may still be located in Hanover, where it all began, no tyres are produced there anymore, this too a consequence of market-economy constraints. The empty production halls are both a typical industrial site and the dream of an alternative culture. In other places – assuming the location is promising – orphaned industrial buildings today are converted and rededicated. Refurbished and displayed, they embody purism and that modernism in which form still followed function. The lofts are spacious, cool and sought-after, and are still home to creative flair even when they have long since become bourgeois with their built-in kitchens and private saunas. If one is to believe the experts, such a conversion was not feasible in Hanover, the masonry and the soil having been too contaminated by the tyre production, so the halls were demolished and the soil decontaminated. Six hundred tailor-made apartments are to be built here, tabula rasa, the terrain prepared for a whole new beginning. The only thing that remains, as a monument or landmark, is the listed Conti Tower.

So these photographs are already historically relevant, as they show what is no longer to be seen. Marc Theis took this into account. In winter 2004/5, quite officially and with the key to the site in his pocket, he undertook some industrial archaeology and, without becoming a pedantic trace-seeker, revealed the momentum of mass production, the consequences of tertiarisation and a post-industrial generation's playful handling of the relics. And once everything had disappeared, he took another look at the pictures in his bottom drawer. They had since matured into historical documents.

Industrial ruins entice photographers to immerse themselves in picturesque scenarios, while graffiti books tend to reel off the works of others in a purely documentary fashion. The merit of *Lost in Time* may be that it actively engages with abandoned rooms and graffiti, and in doing so takes a path that proceeds to transpose the site into a new medium in a detached *and* yet atmospheric way. This remarkable series continues a long tradition extending far back into the 19th century. The symbiotic relationship between photography and industrial architecture may well stem from the fact that photography is a child of the industrial society. Around 1850, when people were reflecting more on the causes and consequences of the industrial revolution, they also expected photography to document the monuments of that epoch. Photography was at hand when the first large buildings in steel, glass and concrete were constructed, when the industrial revolution perfected serial production, and again when the industrial era itself came to an end. It is no coincidence that analogue photography, linked as it was to manual processes, disappeared along with it, giving way on a broad front to computer-generated photography. Today too, photography is not so much technical reproduction as service-oriented: easy, fast, immediately available, simple to use. Marc Theis seems almost defiant by deliberately opting to engage in a counter-programme, approaching the task with a weighty medium-format analogue camera and demonstratively taking time for his inventory shots; his fine-grained film was exposed for up to six minutes per image, reflecting an almost meditative approach to his subject.

Here, the right angle is the measure of all things. Verticals and horizontals constitute spaces and planes where, initially, a pronounced desire for destruction had clearly forged its way. The order of these lines is confronted with a chaos that was produced with indisputable meticulousness. Whatever could be dismantled was dismantled, and the rest, from ceiling cladding to toilet flush, demolished. But new life arose among the ruins. Exhausted workers wearing helmets file past, while the clock above the gate says three minutes past twelve. Long gone are the days when it was still five to twelve, yet the painted figures still have their packed lunch at the ready, are not to be deterred from their daily routine. A bunny juggles with Easter eggs, a man dutifully sweeps away the bricks from a demolished wall, two matchstick men carry a Formica shelf away, a naked black woman stands under a shower. Murder is also being committed, with glee: The serial killer has plugged in the hairdryer and waits, broadly grinning, by the bathtub to make us witnesses to his most recent act… All these figures interact with found objects and testify to the keen eye of their creators, who surely also used the graffiti to raise questions about the future. Does all of this have no future, or is precisely what we experience here already part of our future?

When Marc Theis took these photographs, graffiti were experiencing a new boom. A theoretical superstructure was soon furnished. Activists, fans and analysts increasingly engaged with their sociological and art-theoretical backgrounds and in no time at all the debate was revolving around the subject of a strict terminology. This sheds light not least on the self-perception of those who are absent from Marc Theis's photographs: the artists. When approaching the phenomenon of graffiti it seems helpful to clarify at the outset what graffiti are *not*: the designation of a style, an epoch, a clearly defined technique or a political stance. By contrast, what all graffiti have in common is that they tend to be illegal and are found as a rule in the public domain. So they do not really have all that much in common. Yet experts thrive on definitions, in the hope of increasing clarity, and so – a bit like science's imaginary guard or tracker dogs – they sound out and mark their terrain. In many ways however, the term *graffiti* immediately eludes us, irrespective of which side it is approached from. Graffiti, as generally understood, refuse to be terminologically constrained, although countless attempts have been made to verbally capture the phenomenon. So far, no convincing definition has asserted itself, instead, the "expert opinions" differ greatly.

Can graffiti be regarded as necessarily expressing a mental attitude marked by illegality? This view has a theoretical attraction, being distinct from all issues of technique. In practice, however, it is problematic because when viewing a mural one would first have to ask whether it was actually done without permission from the wall's owner. Only when this had been established, could the graffito be designated as such. Consequently, on discovering a work one could scarcely establish beyond doubt whether it was really a graffito – and thus two formally identical drawings could (one done legally, one illegally) also be two species of the art. Any attempt to narrow them down to a specific target group is probably doomed to failure. *Graffiti* are sometimes said to be aimed at the initiated, whereas *street art* strives to reach the broadest possible audience. This essentially limits graffiti to their tags, those more or less proficiently convoluted names in a coded idiom intended to be deciphered by a peer group, while street art would amount to every creative manifestation that goes beyond this. Whether or not one is doing oneself a favour by placing such narrow restrictions on graffiti seems questionable simply because this view is ahistorical and disregards the fact that since Antiquity the history of the graffito has always involved slogans and drawings alongside names.

Another approach uses a work-immanent definition leading to a similar conclusion by establishing a hierarchy of artistic worth, which is also shared by many wall designers. In this hierarchy, the tags rank very low, being seen as the actual "core business" of the graffito and not regarded as artistic production. So an expression like *graffiti artist* becomes a *contradictio in adjecto*. Graffiti, defined as non-art, are clearly distinguished from the aesthetically superior street art. But here too we are dealing with an unpredictable term, for street art embraces many avenues for creatively designing public space and includes pavement painters as well as street theatre. What is more, from an art-historical perspective street art sounds like an alternative to salon art, which may well have been presented at salons but at the same time also exhibits stylistic compliances that smoothed its path into same. Manifestations summarised under street art merely have their location in common. As a definition this is not very enlightening, and as a term is even more vague than church music or museum art. So the wealth of suggestions emanating mainly from the ranks of the activists is above all an expression of their dissatisfaction with the existing terminology. They speak of Urban Aesthetics, Urban Take-Overs or Poetic Terrorism, of Graphic Delinquents or Post Art, to mention just a few of the more imaginative terms, all of which mirror their intellectual involvement with their personal identity. The artistic and the illegal resonate here, as does the aspiration to be subversive and to achieve guerrilla status.

The term Urban Art, which began to establish itself around 2004, has a good chance of gaining a broad consensus, even though it would like to regard the production of art in the public domain chiefly as a metropolitan phenomenon. In common parlance, however, graffiti is still the dominant umbrella term that seems, from the popular perspective, to include everything from the toilet maxim to the wall painting. Perhaps we should leave it at that, because (like the terms for all major styles, media and epochs) it is just a single word, has a long tradition and also comprises the word *graphic*, thus widening its scope to include new variants like stickers, posters and adbusting.

But if we return to Hanover and the industrial architecture in Marc Theis's photographs, the question of the artists arises again in a different way. Who are they, and what were their ambitions? Here too there are taggers who sling their convoluted pseudonyms at the tiles of a toilet dozens of times and, though lingering in their anonymity, strive at the same time for recognition. Tags are undercover ego-shows motivated by the desire for fame. "Getting fame" is the slogan, but was the Conti plant's abandoned production halls the appropriate place? Certainly, they functioned as an adventure playground and party location, but above all they were a haven and, as such, a parallel world in which to experiment.

Were these halls ever public spaces at all? Entering them was illegal, as was painting the walls, but no one cared because their demolition was a foregone conclusion. But public space? The works found there were only seen by very few people. One gets the impression that the artists initially did them purely for themselves. Consequently, in addition to the need to provoke and confuse the largest possible number of passers-by, as is the intent of graffiti artists who do their works on the arteries of the metropolises, there is a counter-movement that establishes its own world in secret. They create street art away from the street, graffiti in camera, closed to the public.

The anonymity of the place corresponded to the anonymity of the graffiti activists and communicated its own particular quality to the anonymity of the machine age. At most, the presumably young artists engaged theoretically with Taylorism, and the storming of the machines which they came upon and playfully interpreted had nothing to do with that other attack by means of which workers once opposed the prospect of being replaced by machines. The young sprayer community of our information and service society reinterpreted the relics of a lost era that no longer affected them. Two eras clashed here, and the fleeting witnesses of that encounter survive in photographs, of all things, the most popular medium of technical reproduction. Thanks to these images, the graffiti are now being disseminated unchecked in everyday life years after their disappearance, converting the transient into a relative eternity.

Something that Max Frisch once said in New York about art – in particular about literature – suggests that he might also have been thinking about the graffiti outside on the streets: "I believe the function of literature in society is to constantly irritate by the mere fact of its existence. Nothing more." And he ended his lecture, held at the City College in 1981 under the heading "Black Square" with the remark: "Every collaboration with power, even with democratic power, ends in a lethal self-misunderstanding on the part of art, of *poetry*. Its place is not the foyer of the Chase Manhattan Bank. There it becomes an affirmation, an adornment of power."

Irritation, however, presupposes perception. The desire to irritate with the help of graffiti or to attract some kind of attention is becoming increasingly more difficult to fulfil today in the public domain. Graffiti have long since become a visual ambient noise scarcely penetrating the consciousness of passers-by. In cities like New York, Berlin or Barcelona, attention is often only caught today when that ambient noise ceases abruptly, when you arrive at a place that emanates a recently restored stillness. You miss graffiti in the underground, like you miss cigarette smoke in clubs. A passing disquiet owing to the purified atmosphere.

This is a bitter state of affairs for the graffiti culture, which is also a macho culture. What use is rebellion, deliberately breaking laws, if it is not even noticed? Certainly illegality may still hold the promise of an adrenalin rush, as one should not get caught in the act and fall into the hands of state or private security guards. But if the graffito, that proof of a disregard for rules, receives so little attention, this also detracts from the whole point of the adventure. Yet capitulation is not in sight. Graffiti are surviving as a fixed component of the public domain and a challenge to the artists to assert themselves in the jungle of the big city. There is not much that is new about their expressive forms, but the diversity of their funny, obscene, political, racist, moral, sexual, absurd or appealing messages employs means that are also successfully exploited by advertising: a mixed calculation of surprise and recognition. Graffiti want to scandalise and diversify, are always oppositional, and are in at least three ways an explicit counter-programme: a counter-programme first to advertising, whose messages they unmask by culture jamming and adbusting; second to the established art market, which maintains its high culture in the white cubes of galleries and understands this dissociation from everyday life as independence and freedom; and third to television, which enters people's homes, seeking the lowest common denominator and tending towards enforced conformity.

Graffiti are seen both as an expression of the urban wilderness and as a democratic medium, and it is hardly a surprise that they are thriving parallel to the Internet, which is also capable of unleashing subversive forces. But graffiti are also about affirming one's own existence in the real world – and so ultimately are a counter-draft to the Internet. The city is seen as an interface to be conquered and transgressed. Masonry and walls become sources of inspiration, material, picture supports. All the more surprising therefore is how architecture and painting converge as a matter of course in the photographs taken by Marc Theis took at the site on the branch canal. Photography, that implies a smooth surface, almost immaterial, with no haptic qualities. But by being politely reserved, photography is capable of conveying something of the adventure that took place between yesterday and the day before yesterday, between the broad picture and detail, between brick and paint. Its poetry also lies in what is not to be seen, in the absence of the activists.

Marc Theis wurde 1953 in Luxemburg geboren. Er verbrachte einen Teil seiner Kindheit im französischen Metz und kehrte nach Luxemburg zurück, um an der Ecole des Arts et Métiers Dekorateur und Schriftenmaler zu lernen.

Nach dem Abschluß 1971 ging Marc Theis nach Stuttgart an die Adolf Lazi Fotoschule, anschließend studierte er an der Staatlichen Akademie der Bildenden Künste Werbegrafik. Im Alter von 23 Jahren ging er nach Hannover, arbeitete zuerst an der Medizinischen Hochschule, schloss 1979 sein Studium zum Diplom Grafik Designer ab und arbeitete anschließend fünf Jahre in der Werbeabteilung des Reiseunternehmens TUI.

Seit 1983 ist Marc Theis selbständiger Fotograf.

Er hat zahlreiche Bildbände und Fotokalender veröffentlicht. Seine Bilder werden in Ausstellungen im In- und Ausland gezeigt und sind in verschiedenen Sammlungen vertreten.

Marc Theis was born in Luxembourg in 1953. He spent part of his childhood in Metz and returned to Luxembourg to study visual merchandising and sign writing at the Ecole des Arts et Métiers.

After graduation in 1971 Marc Theis went to Stuttgart to join the Adolf Lazi photo school, later he studied graphic design at the State Academy of Fine Arts. At the age of 23 he went to Hanover. First he worked at the Hanover Medical School, then in 1979 he completed his studies as a graduate graphic designer and worked subsequently for five years in the advertising department of the travel company TUI.

Since 1983 Marc Theis has been an independent photographer.

He has published several photobooks and calendars. His images are shown in exhibitions at home and abroad and are represented in various collections.

Alle Fotos wurden mit einer Rollei 6008 integral auf dem damals feinkörnigsten Mittelformat- Negativfilm Agfa Ultra 50 aufgenommen.

All images have been taken with a Rollei 6008 integral using the in those days most fine-grained medium format negative film Agfa Ultra 50.

Mein besonderer Dank gilt:
Meinem guten Freund und Berater Bernd Künne, Danielle Igniti vom Centre d´Art in Dudelange / Luxemburg, Hannah Koeppel von der Gesellschaft zur Förderung der Schönen Künste e.V. Schloß und Gut Liebenberg, Frau Dr. Susanne Pfleger von der Städtischen Galerie Wolfsburg, Frau Botschafterin Martine Schommer und Ann Muller von der Botschaft des Großherzogtums Luxemburg in Berlin und Christof Zwiener vom PG Lab Hannover.

Danken möchte ich auch:
Meinem Verleger Hannes Wanderer, Boris von Brauchitsch für seinen großartigen Essay, Jean Back vom CNA Dudelange, Ralf Kleint vom htp, Dr. Michael Zingk, seinerzeit Leiter der Wasserstadt Limmer, Joachim Buck vom DLF Trifolium, Christian Fahlke, Geli und Jochen Nauck, Christiane Heering und natürlich Marie und Kathrin für die Familienunterstützung – ihr seid immer meine ersten und wichtigsten Kritiker.

Impressum | Imprint

Marc Theis
Lost In Time
First Edition 2011

Copyright © 2011 Peperoni Books
www.peperoni-books.de

Copyright © Photographs: Marc Theis
Copyright © Text: Boris von Brauchitsch
Design: Hannes Wanderer
Translation: Pauline Cumbers
Production: Wanderer Werbedruck, Bad Münder

ISBN: 978-3-941825-28-4

www.marctheis.de